I0781038

WORKBOOK PRESS LLC
187 E Warm Springs Rd,
Suite B285 Las Vegas NV 89119 USA

Website: https://workbookpress.com/
Hotline: 1-888-818-4856
Email: admin@workbookpress.com

Ordering Information:

Quantity sales. Special discounts are available on quantity purchases by corporations, associations, and others. For details, contact the publisher at the address above.

Library of Congress Control Number:

ISBN-13:   978-1-963718-48-5   Paperback Version
                  978-1-963718-50-8   Digital Version

REV. DATE: 10/25/2024

Shades of Remorse

A NOVEL

By

Charlie Hudson

ACKNOWLEDGEMENTS

It has been a few years since last being in the fictional town of Verde Key with Police Detective Bev Henderson and in the way of fiction, no one has really aged.

I once again thank Betty Orr of Dan Orr Consultants, LLC for her skilled editing and also the staff of WorkBook Press for all the intricacies involved with taking a book through publication.

My husband, Hugh's, loving support for my years of writing is something I depend on, and he has once more provided a background underwater photograph as part of the cover design.

Lastly, and never last, my thanks to the fans who come along for the adventure.

Charlie Hudson

CHAPTER ONE

Bev Henderson nudged against Kyle's shoulder to move his attention from the school of midnight parrotfish swimming by part of the ship's wreckage. They were her favorite of the many varieties of parrotfish with their dark blue coloring, but the large green moray eel in the open during daylight was an extra treat. It was of course moving rapidly to find another tucked-in spot to stay in until nighttime when the reef's nocturnal inhabitants would emerge. Kyle nodded his appreciation as the eel disappeared through a hole. Bev checked her dive computer to see they had time for one more pass along what had been a steam cargo ship until colliding with another vessel during World War II. The two ships running under blackout conditions were among many that made the same destructive error. The only good news was when crews managed to survive the sinking. Decades of submersion in salt water and the impact of repeated storms meant it wasn't recognizable from its original structure. It did serve as a thriving artificial reef though with growth of coral and sponges, fish of all sizes, turtles, rays, and the occasional hammerhead sharks that would cruise through the area.

Kyle tapped his dive computer to indicate it was time to return to the boat. They swam leisurely toward the mooring line, angling up, keeping watch for any last-minute sights. A large barracuda was under the bow, using the boat as cover. This was another behavior they'd become familiar with on their dives. Kyle motioned Bev forward when they surfaced, and he positioned behind her on the tag line tied to the orange float ball. There was little current and she quickly removed her fins, passed them to the mate, and climbed the ladder.

Danny Garza steadied her onto the bench to slide her tank into the holder. "Good dive?" She removed the regulator from her mouth. "Oh yeah. Sixty feet of visibility and the turtle was exactly where you thought it might be." He slid her fins on top of her dive bag beneath the bench and pivoted to go back and assist Kyle. "The couple from Ohio saw a reef shark. Did y'all?"

"Just barely," she said and unfastened her dive vest. "It wasn't hanging around."

"We saw - well Bev saw it first - a green moray going from one spot to another," Kyle said taking his place next to Bev.

Danny grinned. "That's always fun."

Kyle stood, not yet unzipping his wetsuit. "Ready for towel and Diet Coke?"

She leaned down to remove her dive booties. "Thanks, yes."

Captain Moira stepped in with Danny to assist the final three divers aboard, each chattering about what they'd seen. This was the second dive of the morning and time to head for the dock to turn the boat for the afternoon trip.

Kyle held onto the cans of Diet Coke while she unzipped and peeled out of her wetsuit. "Scarlet Macaw for lunch or you want somewhere else?"

She took the towel draped over his forearm, rubbed her face briskly, then wrapped it around her waist and reached for the can. "I'm good with the Macaw. All those yellowtail snappers on the wreck have me thinking fish sandwich depending on what Steve has for specials."

"Works for me," Kyle said with a grin. "I'm thinking calamari even if we didn't see squid."

"Hey everybody, good dives and glad you're with us," Captain Moira said. "Quick roll call and we'll be off." She was the newest captain with Adventures Below and this was their third trip with her. She was an inch taller than Bev, maybe in her early thirties, her naturally curly black hair cut short for easy care. She was lean and muscled, reminding Bev of competitors when she ran track. Comparatively speaking, she had few tattoos - a mermaid on the outside of her right leg and the Celtic band on her upper left arm was covered by her tee shirt.

She'd come to Verde Key from Jacksonville and Walt, owner of Adventures Below, hired her immediately based on a recommendation from one of his former captains. Good captains were never unemployed for long and even though early April wasn't peak dive season yet, he didn't want to give another dive shop a chance at her. From what Bev heard, she must be good with equipment repair because Walt had turned some of the regular maintenance over to her when they didn't have both boats on the water.

The *World Below* was the fourteen passenger Island Hopper and re-equipped with a new Cummins engine, and they were idling into the channel in just under thirty minutes. The trip back was the usual friendly exchanges among divers as they broke their gear down and hydrated, Danny circulating to ensure they were happy with the day, giving instructions to the trio who would be with them again for the afternoon. He was one of the first people Bev had met at Adventures Below years before during an investigation, before she'd really thought personally about diving. Now she couldn't imagine why it had taken her so long to try and was glad it was one more sport Kyle enjoyed. They were able to go out once a month, more often if they were lucky with their schedules. They hadn't made it beyond the Florida Keys for diving yet as vacation time was more theoretical than practical.

"I'll take the wet stuff and start rinsing if you'll get the dry bags," Kyle said, pulling both sets of BCDs and regulators from the tanks.

Bev nodded and side-stepped the couple from Ohio on her way to the dry box to the left of the captain's chair. She lifted the new waterproof drawstring backpacks Kyle had surprised her with at Christmas - his in black, hers in blue. She pulled on her extra-large, green short-sleeve Adventures Below tee shirt and slung the damp towel over her shoulder. She held back a minute while Danny and Captain Moira hauled tanks off the boat. One of the advantages of

Adventures Below as a dive shop was their location on the ocean side canal with dock space for two boats.

The concrete pad in front of the storage building was set up with two dark gray rinse tubs and an open outdoor shower was to the right of the building. The dockside tiki hut to the left covered two wooden picnic tables. A second, larger tiki hut was in a fenced in, graveled yard to the left of the dive shop. Three picnic tables and several scattered chairs, a grill and round fire pit had seen plenty of planned or impromptu parties.

Bev settled the dry bags on the bench of the closest picnic table when her cell phone in the outside pocket rang. Shit, it was the ringtone for Les Martin. He was on call today and wouldn't be calling her if it wasn't important.

She put the phone to her ear and walked away from the hut. "Hey Les, what's up?"

"Sorry to bother you," he said with no preamble. "Kevin and Beau are at Palmetto Paradise. Got a body, well, I guess a skeleton. I'm at the emergency room with Pam. It's her wrist and might be a hairline fracture. It'll probably be another hour or so before they can finish with her and I can…"

"It's okay," Bev said quickly. "Kyle and I were heading to lunch. I've got a set of clothes at the office I can change into. Tell Kevin I should be there in about forty-five minutes."

"Thanks, they've given her something for pain and she's starting to get a bit loopy."

"You take care of Pam. I'll call you later after I know what's going on."

This wasn't the first time a leisurely lunch with a couple of cold beers had to be put on hold and was why she kept a stash of protein bars and packages of trail mix in her desk. She turned and saw Kyle moving in her direction.

"I know that look," he said with a lopsided grin. "Something Les can't handle?"

"He's at ER with Pam. She busted up her wrist and there's an old body – or more like a skeleton he said – out at Palmetto Paradise." She spread her hands in apology. "Sorry about the afternoon. If you run me by the office, I'll take one of the cars."

Kyle shrugged. "Part of the job. We can go to the Macaw for dinner if you feel up for it later. No telling how long you'll be on this."

"Just another reason why I love you," she said and was glad again of marrying a man who understood her career. Although his move from the District Attorney's office into private practice meant his schedule was more predictable, he knew finding a dead body would take time to process.

Less than an hour later, she slowly drove the final segment of graveled road into the still vacant former high-end fishing camp. The legal tangle of the property involved in a nasty estate settlement had apparently kept potential buyers away, but someone was maintaining the place well enough to be able to show it as a credible investment. The dark green metal gate was swung fully open, an ambulance and two patrol cars parked on either side of a pier sized for half a dozen boats. The once blue paint of the stucco marina office and store to the left and hexagon-shaped clubhouse to the right was faded and peeling, accordion hurricane shutters closed over the windows. The ones on the front doors were partially open, no doubt to give access when needed. Bev suspected the dozen square cabins arrayed along a winding path behind the clubhouse were in similar shape.

She exited the car and raised her hand to Kevin Blackwell, senior sergeant in the Department. He stood at the back of the ambulance with two first responders Bev didn't recognize. Beau Wilson was taking notes from two men in shorts and tee shirts next to his patrol car. What was no doubt their Contender 28 T center console was the only boat tied up.

Someone had already cordoned off the mound between the boat ramp and pier.

"Hi Detective," Kevin said, stopping outside the yellow tape. "Sorry to screw up your Saturday. The new assistant medical examiner is on her way. Maybe another ten minutes untill she gets here." He pointed to the men with Beau. "Randy Tindell and Carlos Rivera. They were right outside the cove when Rivera snagged the body. Got it far enough up to see what it was. Both grew up near here and been fishing the area for years. Had a little current and weren't sure it was safe to leave it in the water. Brought it in and called us."

Bev ducked under the tape and stared at the mound lying in water puddled on the concrete. Much of the debris covered sail cloth was torn, revealing part of a skull and other bones. Heavy duty rope was wound the entire length of the bundle, overlapping in multiple spots. That was probably why the skeleton was mostly intact. "Somebody knew how to tie knots," she said, crouching down, not touching it. She hadn't met the new assistant ME and presumed she would want to see the remains as they were.

Kevin crouched next to her and pointed to the jagged end of the rope snaked across the concrete. "Guess whatever they used as weight finally gave way. We had that storm Thursday. Long as it looks like this has been down, that might have been enough to take it past the breaking point."

"Makes sense," Bev agreed and heard a car approaching. She and Kevin stood, waiting.

A dark blue Ford Explorer pulled in and the woman who emerged was dressed in khaki-colored slacks, a royal blue polo shirt, and tan boots. A short lanyard was around her neck, the plastic badge holder no doubt identifying her. Luis Gonzalez, one of the Forensics photographers, was coming around from the passenger's side.

Bev lifted the tape. "Donna Sweeny," the woman said, thrusting her hand to Bev first. She was a couple of inches shorter, maybe mid-thirties, slender with a firm grip of lightly callused hands, toned forearms, skin the color of coffee with a dash of cream. Bev immediately thought of kayaker or canoeing. Her black hair was cut in a mini-Afro. The gaze from her brown eyes beneath sculpted brows were direct as she shifted to greet Kevin. Her voice was a bit husky, no discernible accent. "Detective Henderson and Sergeant Blackwell? And you know Mr. Gonzalez?"

"Yes, pleased to meet you." Bev said and stepped to the side. "Sergeant Blackwell and Officer Wilson were first on the scene."

"Luis, go ahead and get the initial shots," Dr. Sweeny directed and motioned them to follow her to give him unobstructed access for the photographs.

Bev noticed the woman positioned herself at an angle to be able to respond to the photographer if needed. "What do we know so far?"

Kevin gestured toward Beau. "Rivera, the one in the yellow shirt, called it into the station. They're familiar with the place like most local people who are on the water a lot. It would have taken them nearly an hour to get back to their dock, which is why they brought the body in here. They gave us the exact coordinates of where Rivera snagged it. Tindell is an EMT and Rivera is a firefighter. They're more used to dead bodies than skeletons though."

"Okay, give me a few minutes to do my first visual. It appears most of the bones have been contained. We'll get the kit, cut the rope and covering for those photographs, then do the transport."

Bev and Kevin nodded and went to join Beau. He introduced Bev to the two men. He had their contact details in case there were questions later. "No surprise there's nobody else in the area," Beau said after they left. "The company that takes care of the place only sends a crew out about every six to eight weeks depending on the season. I was waiting to ask you before we call Thornton for the dive team."

Bev thought for a moment. They were obviously dealing with a cold case. They had the coordinates of where the body was found and if Kevin was correct about the rope breaking loose, if whatever had been used to originally weight it was heavy enough, it might not have moved much. "Kevin, call and see how soon they can get here. Explain the situation. As far as I know, the weather is normal the next few days and I don't think it will make much difference if we wait until morning. I'll go with whatever Thornton thinks it best."

Donna's voice carried to them. "I'm ready for you, Detective."

Bev doubted much could be determined on site. Then again, the oldest body she'd ever seen was one unmarried man in his seventies who had a heart attack alone at home and lain undiscovered for a week before a neighbor became concerned and called the station. She wondered how old this victim was and if they would get lucky with something to identify him or her.

CHAPTER TWO

Bev refilled their mugs with coffee, waiting for Les to finish his call. She stirred in the one packet of sweetener she preferred. He always took his black. It was fairly quiet for a Monday morning, traffic violations and a couple of domestic calls over the weekend, nothing she and Les were involved with. Luck had been with the dive team. Bev had met them Sunday morning at Palmetto Paradise and they'd soon found three concrete blocks half-buried in the murky bottom close to where the bundled skeleton had been pulled to the surface. The blocks were still lashed together with the same heavy ropes as had been wound around the body. The end of one rope was frayed, an understandable result of decades submerged and subject to years of rubbing against the concrete. Their luck in a quick find did not extend to anything out of the ordinary about the blocks or rope. She'd returned to the office where Les had the list of all white males reported as missing in the 1970s and threw in the 1960s for good measure. That, and Dr. Sweeny's report of probable cause of death as blunt force trauma to the left side of the skull was as much as she could provide until she competed other tests. And, as with the rope and blocks, the sailcloth used to conceal the body was common in an area filled with marinas. They collectively determined disrupting the rest of everyone's Sunday wasn't necessary with no more to go on.

Les hung the phone up and ran a hand across his white hair, cut in the same short military style he'd worn since he'd transferred to Verde Key. "You took the afternoon off instead of puzzling over this, didn't you?"

She passed him his mug and rocked her left hand back and forth. "It is my first cold case. Kyle and I talked about it of course, but I'm not losing sleep over it yet." She inclined her head to the telephone. "That was Dr. Powell?"

"Yes, and the Chief was correct. Back during the timeframe our John Doe disappeared, there were only two dentists in town. Both are retired now and did sell their practices. Dr. Powell is sending me the names of both the new practices. So, assuming he was from here *and* had dental work done, *and* the new guys decided to hang on to the old records, we should be able to get a match." He held up one finger as he took a sip of coffee. "When does Dr. Sweeny – or does it pass to Dr. Cooke – expect to have something for us?"

"Cooke is actually taking a vacation. Sweeny told me to come by early afternoon and she would have a little more. Oh, how's Pam?"

"Hairline fracture, pain is gone, soft cast. Could have been worse, thanks for asking."

Bev moved to the white board mounted on the wall next to the table that held the coffeemaker. The office in the new building was a little more spacious than before, but the institutional look was similar with dark green linoleum flooring, lighter green paint for the walls. Their desks were standard office type each with a center drawer and two drawers to the left. The black leather-like chairs were higher quality than the previous, although the three five-drawer gray metal filing cabinets against the far wall had been moved from the old building.

She picked up a blue marker. Under "John Doe" was what they knew. Time and place found, male, white, estimated age of thirties when killed, estimated dumping of mid-1970s to early 1980s. Names of four missing persons still in the files. Ernie Dalton, reported 1976. Henry Staples, 1978. Roger Neely, 1979. Andy Brown, 1982. She added, "Probable COD blunt force trauma to skull."

She turned to Les. "How many cold cases have you had?"

"None, if you mean that I solved. Had two over the years that bothered me to the point of checking up on them periodically. A guy was killed in what was most likely drug related. The only reason I cared about that one was we narrowed down the suspect to a real son-of-a-bitch and could never prove anything. He was killed later in a separate incident. The one that pissed me off the most was this one guy - had a wife, two daughters. Worked late one night, which happened sometimes. Found him the next morning by the dumpster behind the building. Shot twice, seemed to be robbery and his Cadillac was gone. Nothing to go on; that was in the days before surveillance cameras were as common as they are now. There were two more, but those got solved when the slimeballs were arrested for something else and there was evidence to tie them to the cold cases."

Bev raised her eyebrows. "Damn, you weren't kidding when you said you came here because you needed a break from big city crime."

He gave a half smile. "Much less crime except we have had bodies pile up more than once."

"True. So far the good guys have won every time though."

"Point well taken."

Kevin knocked on their partially open door and stood in the doorway. "Owner of the storage facility on Pelican was checking video from last night and saw a guy acting suspiciously. Alvarez is on site and looks like an attempted break-in of one of the units. Thing is, the owner says the guy who rented the unit hasn't been around for almost a year and the telephone number he has for him is no longer in service."

Bev looked at Les. "I'll go unless you want to."

Les shook his head. "Not particularly. I'll try to track down the second retired dentist to see who he sold his practice to and how far back they keep records."

K&L Storage was one of the older facilities in town, on a side street between two neighborhoods off the water. Most of the modest houses had carports instead of garages. The sign at the entrance advertised the units as ten-by-ten and humidity controlled. There were three rows of buildings forming a U-shape. They were standard stucco covered concrete block construction, with roll-up doors, dark red paint somewhat faded. The area was clean, if non-descript, two dumpsters on the far end of the lot. The single vehicle at a storage unit was all the way at the end where a white Ford van was backed in with the door to the unit rolled up. The office was on the right-hand side, a blue Ford F-150 with a black cover over the bed, parked next to the empty handicap spot, a patrol car on the other side. Officer Magda Alvarez came out, notepad in her left hand.

"Mr. Dixon, the owner is inside, Detective. I have his statement and the unit in question does have marks indicative of attempts at being pried open." Alvarez, still junior in the Department, had graduated in the top three from the Basic Law Enforcement Academy. At five feet four inches with a face that no doubt got her carded in bars, a few of the veterans had wondered about her. That was until they saw the photograph of her being awarded her black belt in karate and went to the pistol range where she outshot all but one.

Alvarez opened the door for Bev and she stepped into a rectangular room that, other than the computer on the desk and monitor mounted on the wall behind the desk, didn't seem to have been updated since the 1980s. A window air conditioner was fairly quiet and little furniture included two viny padded, straight-back chairs in front of the desk. A worn-looking credenza against the front wall was wedged between two gray metal filing cabinets and a compact, once white refrigerator. Closed doors on the right-hand wall probably led to a bathroom and storeroom. There was a single window on the left wall, a yellowed white shade pulled two-thirds of the way down. Bev had seen the security camera at the entrance and based on what was on the screen, there were two other cameras.

The man who stood from the chair was average height, pudgy without being fat, skin dark brown and as much gray as black in his hair cropped close to his scalp. "Ken Dixon; the L is for Leon, my son. He's only here parttime since I'm still a ways from retiring." His handshake was firm, palms callused to where he obviously didn't spend all his time behind the desk. "You're Detective Henderson if what this young lady told me is right. Get you a cup of coffee?"

"No thank you," Bev said. "You had an attempted break-in?"

"Looks like it," he said and gestured to the screen. "We don't generally lock the gates so clients can have access whenever they want it. Not that I know everyone by sight, but I do most of them. Security cameras only set up at the end of each row. My routine is I get in about 7:00 and check the video with my morning coffee. Just from about midnight to dawn, fast forward, 'cause except for some kids hanging out a few years back partying and leaving trash around, we don't get trouble." He hit the button on the recording to a time of 1:03 a.m. Even though lighting in the yard was minimal, the Florida tag number to the old black Honda Civic was easy to read, but the angle the camera was set to did not clearly capture the driver. He, if a *he* drove slowly to the row of units on the left, wasn't picked up by the next camera for a few seconds, turned right at the row in back, left again along the row to the right and disappeared from camera view again. At 1:21 a.m., it exited.

Dixon stopped the recording and nodded to Alvarez. "Like I told her, two things made this funny. Most people come straight in, to their unit and it was like this fella – assuming a fella – didn't know which one it was. Since he drove past first two sets and was out of range of the cameras for a while, I took a stroll to the middle and far units. Number 36 had a couple of cigarette butts by the door. I do a walk-thru every evening before I lock up and they weren't there yesterday. Looks like somebody took a crowbar or something to the door to try and pry it. This place isn't brand new by any stretch, but we're harder to break into than that." He tapped a thin manila file folder on his desk and motioned for them to take a seat. "Easy to remember Michael O'Hara. Nice guy and we shot the sh---, talked for a while," he quickly corrected. "He been around for a few months, staying with a friend. Had a thirty-three-foot Sunray he was planning to take to the islands. Paid cash for eighteen months on the unit. Figured he'd be back by then. That was September last year. Haven't heard from him since. Phone number on the form isn't in service now. Address he gave is out at Miller's Point, the contact listed is R Jaworski, no number for him. I called their management office asking and was told he was no longer a resident. That's when I called the station." He spread his hands. "Maybe it's nothing. It just don't figure. If Mike lost his key, he would call, wouldn't he? I mean, we've had some punk kid trouble like I said, never anything else. With all the units we have, how is it someone goes after this one?"

Not that they'd had a case, but use of storage units for illegal purposes was not uncommon. Bev could understand Dixon's concern. "Do you have any idea what's in the unit?"

"No. I either wasn't here when he brought his stuff in, or he didn't stop in to talk. We don't track people coming and going."

Bev shifted to Alvarez who had her phone in hand. "I sent a text requesting to run the tag number," she said. "Would you like to see the unit while we wait?"

Bev was impressed with her initiative. "Ask for a check on a Michael O'Hara, too, with last known address."

Dixon stood and removed a key from the bottom desk drawer. "I don't feel right going into the unit."

"That may not be necessary," Bev said. "Let's walk over."

Alvarez went to her patrol car and Bev saw what Dixon meant when they paused outside the unit. There was enough dirt on the concrete for faint tire tracks and footprints to show and marks in a line approximately six inches in length could have been made by something like a crowbar.

Alvarez drove up parallel to them and got out leaving the door ajar. "Uh Detective, registration on the Civic is to a Samuel Frost, address is an apartment in Tavernier. A Michael O'Hara, age fifty-six, drowned at Richmond Marina, Plantation Key last week. Ruled an accident." She held her phone out for Dixon to see the image on the screen.

"Well, I'll be damned," he said. "Guess you never know, do you?" He dangled the key. "Might as well check then, you think?"

Bev nodded, quickly processing the unexpected news. "Officer Alvarez, call the station for either Sergeant Blackwell or Wilson. Tell them we'll need to get prints."

Dixon pushed the door up, stepped inside to the left and flipped on the switch. Light flickered on from the rectangular florescent fixture in the center of the ceiling. Despite the dehumidifier, the slightly musty smell was to be expected if it hadn't been opened in almost a year. There were several standard brown packing boxes against the left wall and a small wooden rolltop desk with a matching chair to the right next to a pair of dark green leather wing back chairs. A car under a gray cover took most of the space.

"I must not have been here when he brought this," Dixon repeated. "Okay we should see what it is?"

"Yes, and I suggest you make an inventory with photos with Officer Alvarez as a witness," Bev said. "The boxes seem to be all taped and labelled. If so, there won't be a need to open them."

Dixon began a low whistle the moment he lifted the back corner of the cover. He carefully peeled the rest of it away to reveal a red Shelby GT500 Convertible with a white top. "Jesus, look at that; must be a 1968 or so. It sure as hell is something worth trying to steal if that's what the guy was up to. I think these run around a hundred grand."

Despite driving her own classic Spitfire, Bev wasn't an expert at values, but she wasn't surprised at the estimate. It wouldn't take much effort to get the car cleaned and polished to be ready for a car show.

"Okay," Bev said briskly. "Officer Alvarez, let's go ahead and treat this as a crime scene. No need to disrupt the whole place. Just tape off this and the adjoining two units. As soon as they finish with the prints, you can observe Mr. Dixon and the inventory. Mr. Dixon, we'll need your prints for elimination."

"Sure," he said, waiting to replace the cover as Alvarez was already snapping pictures, one from each angle. "We can close this back up and go to the office. I'll make a fresh pot of coffee."

Bev moved next to Alvarez who seemed to be trying to suppress a smile. No doubt she was excited about what had the potential to be a real case. Bev pitched her voice low. "You good with staying until one of the sergeants arrive?"

"Oh yes, ma'am," the young woman said, the right amount of confidence in her tone. "I've been told you never know how a call will turn out. This might be like that?"

"Could be. There are several questions to be answered. You can finish getting Mr. Dixon's statement, too." She threw a quick wave to Dixon and punched in Les's number while walking to her car. He answered on the second ring. "We have an interesting wrinkle here. If you don't have anything hot on the John Doe yet, we may be taking a ride to Tavernier and Plantation Key."

"I'm in waiting mode," he said. "What's up?"

"Not sure. I'll explain when I get there. Hey, I'm going blank on the detective's name that covers that area. Do you remember?"

"I've got a card somewhere, I think. If not, I'll call and get it."

Rather than spend time at the station, Les swapped into the driver's seat and gave Bev the number for Detective Derrick Osborne. They were in luck that he was in his office and knew both about the death of O'Hara and Frost. "Straight up accident with O'Hara. It was early morning, and he was drunk on his ass based on blood alcohol levels. He was apparently trying to get onto his boat, slipped, whacked his head hard enough to knock him out, fell in the water and drowned. No one else around and his body got caught under the pier where he was found a little after sunrise. No one knew next of kin for notification.

Had to go through his stuff to find an old address for his son. Took a couple of days to contact him up in Colombia, South Carolina."

There was a pause as he probably pulled up another report. "Frost is kind of a jerk. Couple of traffic violations with driving with an expired license as one of them. I had him in several months ago for questioning about some marine equipment thefts. His name came up. Turns out he wasn't involved. Just tight with the two guys that were. Might have known more than he was saying, but we caught a break in the case and didn't need to go back to him. He fills in at times as a mechanic at the marina and hangs out in the bar. That's the likely connection between the two, if you're looking for one. What have you got?"

"Not sure at this point. Possible attempted break-in of a storage unit belonging to O'Hara. Owner hadn't seen O'Hara for a while, thought he was cruising the islands."

There was another short pause. "Tell you what. I'll get patrol to run by Frost's place to see if he's around. The book is closed on O'Hara, and I don't know the situation with the son. Zeke Richmond owns the marina. I can call and tell him you're on the way."

"Thanks, appreciate it," Bev said. "I know where it is."

Les kept his eyes on the road, traffic slowed with an RV towing a small car three vehicles ahead. "What are you thinking?"

Bev was mentally fitting pieces into place. "If no one knew where O'Hara's next of kin was, maybe he doesn't know anything about his dad's life here. Maybe O'Hara had gone to the islands, came back, and just hadn't gotten up to see Dixon yet to check on the Shelby. Maybe Frost found out somehow and thought he could boost it before anyone discovered it."

Les nodded. "That's a workable scenario. Let's see what we find out about O'Hara's son, and we can deal with Frost after?"

"Yeah. Richmond's is ocean side, about two more miles." If she was correct, this should be straightforward as most of their cases weren't complicated. Based on what Osborne said about Frost, he would be like a lot of criminals, or would-be criminals, who weren't nearly as smart as they thought.

CHAPTER THREE

Richmond's Marina was another family business passed from father to son. It was at the head of a canal that led directly to the ocean. Metal buildings for the office, workshop, and warehouse were to the right, with a fuel station in the yard. A white Ford Transit Van and a black F-150 with Richmond Marine Mobile Service vehicle wraps were next to the warehouse. The door to the workshop was rolled up, men moving around inside, whatever they were working on too deep in to see clearly.

There were eight slips on either side of the canal with none designated with fishing or dive charter signs. Approximately half the slips were filled and The Pelican's Nest, the restaurant, was at the head of the canal between the two. A small store with an ice machine outside was to the left of it. Those buildings were standard stucco, painted in coral. A mural of three brown pelicans flying low over water was vibrant enough to be either new or freshly touched up. The five vehicles parked in front all had Florida plates.

Les drove slowly to the office where a burly man in khakis and a dark green polo lifted his hand. When they exited the car, the aroma of grilled meat reminded Bev they were well into lunch hour.

"Zeke Richmond," he said, thrusting his hand to Bev first. Richmond Marine in gold thread was embroidered on the shirt. "You the detectives John called about?" His short hair was white, green eyes set under bushy white eyebrows, a pair of polarized sunglasses dangling from a black Croakie. Everything about him marked him as a man who'd spent years on the water, probably a linebacker in high school and college. He was surprisingly devoid of visible tattoos. A three-inch scar on his left forearm was well-faded and probably came with an interesting story.

"Come on in," he said after introductions. "Mike's son, Joel, is staying in town, not on the boat. He's taking care of some things and can be here in about an hour. Figured I could answer whatever questions you have and you could grab lunch."

"Uh thanks," Bev said, appreciating the down-to-business attitude.

The desk in the front office was empty, as Richmond led them through a door to the right motioning them into the two straight back green padded chairs in front of a large wooden desk strewn with papers and folders. A ceramic pirate's head mug was jammed with pen and pencils. Bev noticed there was no computer although there had been one in the front office. He didn't seem to be quite of an age where he would view computers with disdain. "Can I get y'all a water or anything?"

"No thanks," Bev said to Les's head shake. His notebook was out, pen poised, and Bev leaned forward in the chair. "How well did you Mr. O'Hara?"

"Hell of a thing. Been thinking a lot about him," he began. "Anyway, he was through here about three years ago for right at a month and is an easy to remember kind of guy. Been around boats for years, the kind of client you want. Social, swaps stories without having to be the center of attention. First time he was here he was down from Philadelphia. He was in project management and wanted a break from winter. We have a few rentals and he went with a thirty-two-foot Sunray. Did some fishing, took it easy, closed down the bar more than once. Nice tipper so he was popular." He paused, reflecting. "Fourteen months ago, I think it was, he came in. The company he worked for got acquired. He was pretty vocal about – what's the term – being made redundant? He got some kind of a settlement and did the time-for-a-big-change people can go through. Sold up stuff, came down and was staying for a while with a friend up your way. Not sure who, but he – the friend, I mean – had the Sunray that needed some work. Once it was finished, he - Mike, I mean – brought it here, stayed a few days getting provisioned and took off for the islands. He'd check in occasionally, not sure when he would get back. It was Tuesday a week ago. Being honest since I imagine that's what's important, he looked like he'd spent a lot of time in a bottle. He's a happy drunk though – know the type?"

Bev nodded and saw regret flash across Richmond's face. "Anyway, this is a hell of a thing," he repeated. "We've have had a few accidents over the years. Nothing like this. Trish Conner was the bartender that night and said he was putting the Johnnie Walker away more than usual and closed the place down. She didn't think he was that bad though."

"We haven't seen the report," Bev said. "Who found him?"

"Caleb Cooper. He runs the store. Has it open 6:00 a.m., usually gets here about 5:00 o'clock. If he gets everything ready, he takes a mug of coffee out to the end of the dock. Mike is – was – the only one living full time on his boat right now. The others are mostly weekenders. Caleb knows him of course. He was looking down in the water and saw a leg sticking out from under the dock. Hell of a shock. He jumped in, but there was nothing could be done. Responders got here pretty fast and then there was everything that goes with something like this." Richmond's forehead puckered. "He didn't have an emergency contact listed in the file. Most of us knew he was divorced. Didn't know where the ex was. John – Detective Osborne – went through his papers on the boat and found a telephone number with a Pennsylvania area code. Turned out to be an old friend who knew Joel's name. Told him Mike and Joel were estranged, too, and he didn't know where he was either. Took some searching to track him down. He's only been here a couple of days trying to straighten everything out. He's a high school math teacher in Colombia, South Carolina. Polite, not very talkative." His forehead smoothed. "What else do you need to know?"

Bev knew the Shelby would have been a matter of note if anyone had seen it. "Did Mr. O'Hara have a car?"

"I don't remember from first time he was here. He probably had a rental. When he was here before leaving for the islands, he'd brought the boat down and didn't mention a car or truck. We have services in town that deliver whatever people need." Richmond idly scratched the back of his hand. "Is that important?"

Bev saw no reason to be evasive. "We're here because Mr. O'Hara's storage rental unit in Verde Key had what seems to be an attempted break-in and a Samuel Frost was recorded on video being at the storage facility at an odd hour. The owner of the facility had not heard from Mr. O'Hara since he rented the unit. The officer who ran the tag did a check on Mr. O'Hara, too."

Richmond didn't look surprised. "Sammy, huh? John told you he works here part-time? He's an okay mechanic when I need extra help and he was with me last week. He was here the day after Mike's accident. The reason I remember is because I was out on a run for most of the morning and I thought my head guy, Rico, might have called him in. He said he hadn't, and I figured Sammy was hanging at the bar. He's kind of a regular." He shook his head sharply. "Sammy's not the brightest bulb in the lamp and he doesn't have a steady job because he's another one of these guys who can't stick to a schedule. He doesn't have the best judgement in the world either. I hope he hasn't crossed the line on something like this." He pulled a notepad toward him, consulted his phone, scribbled a number, and held it out for Bev. "Like I said, Joel O'Hara should be back in a while. You can text him and let him know you're here. The Nest has the best fish sandwich around if you want to grab a bite."

Bev knew Les would have spoken up if he had anything to add and her stomach gave a not quite audible signal lunch was a good idea. Les waited until they were outside and gestured to the restaurant where the scent of grilling meat reinforced the plan for lunch. "You good with taking Richmond's advice and having lunch?"

"Works for me," she said, and they covered the short distance, coming to the covered terrace side. It was about ten feet from the end of the canal with the open ocean visible beyond the canal. None of the dozen tables were occupied, and when they stepped into the main room, only a third of the tables inside were taken. The L-shaped bar to the left was mostly empty. Bev had the sense this was a locals' place which meant breakfast and after work were the busy times.

The young woman who greeted them, plastic-coated two-sided menus in hand, wore khaki shorts and a burgundy Pelican's Nest tee shirt. A burgundy streak highlighted her short, cropped ash-blonde hair and her smile was quick. "Just the two of you?"

"We might have a third," Bev said, holding her phone. "Outside, okay?"

"Sure, pick your spot," she said, waving them forward. Les was in front and took the table to the left, closest to the water. Bev suspected it had more to do with the fact the only Sunray in a slip was on that side than wanting a water view. The boat no doubt belonged to the late Mr. O'Hara.

The menu was basic, "breakfast served all day" on one side, appetizers, soup, sandwiches, and limited entrees on the other. "Everything is fresh, and Gabby will be with you in a minute. Can I start you with something to drink?"

Bev ordered Diet Coke, Les coffee and ice water and he studied the menu while she sent a text to the young Mr. O'Hara. Gabby, as promised, appeared in a few minutes with beverages and took their orders. If she and the hostess weren't sisters, they were remarkably similar. An incoming text pinged as Gabby stepped away. *Yes, Zeke mentioned you. 30 minutes if you can wait? Joel O.*

Bev sent the short reply. *Yes, we're outside at the Nest.*

"Okay, O'Hara and Frost are drinking buddies," Les said, muted sounds from the marina yard drifting across. "They have some kind of conversation about the Shelby. Frost hears about O'Hara. You figure O'Hara has at least mentioned he and the son are on the outs and Frost suspects the son isn't likely to show up any time soon. Maybe all he's doing at first is trying to find out if the car is there or is it just drunk talk. Remember, Osborne said Frost wasn't part of the marine thefts they investigated but might have known who was."

Bev left her phone out on the edge of the table. "Could be. Unless Dixon had been specifically looking at the unit, he wouldn't have noticed the signs of the attempted break-in. On the other hand, Frost is a mechanic. Boosting a car doesn't require much skill. Plus, Richmond said Frost was hanging around the day after O'Hara died. O'Hara must have a set of keys. Maybe Frost rummaged around the boat and no one realized it. Let's say he couldn't find the keys, but maybe he did find a paper with the storage unit information."

"That's plausible, too," Les said and paused for Gabby to deliver their meals, a grilled mahi sandwich and coleslaw for Bev and fried shrimp basket for Les. "Enjoy, and I'll check back with you in a few minutes," she said cheerfully.

Bev was surprised at the soft brioche bun and wondered if it came from a local bakery. The fish was perfectly cooked, lettuce crisp and tomato nicely ripe. She appreciated the coleslaw was the non-sweet type and Les passed her some seasoned fries. They were delicious with the crunch that came from double frying. Combined with having noticed there were eight beer taps at the bar, Bev could see this as a locals' hangout. They finished their food with little more conversation, Gabby coming with drink refills once. She was clearing the dishes when the text came in. *Have parked. Am on the way in. Joel O.*

She rose from her seat and faced looking inside. A man stopped briefly to talk to the woman who pointed to outside. Les stood, and the man approached, glancing at the table. "Joel O'Hara and I asked Gillian to bring me coffee if that's okay with you."

"Of course," Bev said formally showing their badges. "We're sorry for your loss." She would put him at five-nine since she didn't have to look up much to meet his green eyes directly. Thick light brown hair, parted on the side, cut just above his ears. An average build and she guessed late thirties. No calluses on his palm, a plain gold band on his left hand.

"It's all very unexpected," he said in a baritone voice. They sat and he gestured toward the Sunray. "I don't know if you're aware my father and I hadn't spoken in almost twelve years. We, I mean my mother and I, had no idea about any of this." He waited while Gabby brought coffee, no cream, and Bev and Les declined another refill. "I thought everything was clear with the police. You're from Verde Key though?"

"A different matter," Bev said. "Video footage of a vehicle entering a storage facility area in Verde Key a little after 1:00 a.m., is what caused the facility owner to be suspicious. He discovered what appears to have been an attempted break-in at a storage unit rented by your father last year. He paid for the unit for eighteen months and told the owner he would be cruising in the islands. The owner hadn't been in contact since and the telephone number in the file was no longer in service." She paused, but Joel sipped his coffee and motioned for her to continue. "He did have the name of the individual your father had apparently been staying with in Verde Key, but that individual was no longer a resident, and they had no contact information for him. The license plate for the individual driving the car caught on tape is a Mr. Frost and checking your father's name as the individual renting the storage space is how we found out about the accident. It was Detective Osborne who told us Mr. Frost worked sometimes in the marina."

Joel set his mug down. "It stands to reason my father would put things into storage. You're saying this individual tried – or probably tried to – break into the unit? There's something valuable in it?"

Les spoke for the first time. "In light of what happened, the owner opened the unit with us present. A red 1968 Shelby GT500 Convertible was the main thing."

Joel's eyes grew wide. "Say what? It has a white top? He had a model that my mother gave to him one Christmas when I was a kid.

That was when things were still good for us." A flicker of sadness crossed his face. "One of his dreams was to buy one and the two of us would do the Route 66 trip." He exhaled deeply. "I haven't gone through the boat in detail. In fact, I just picked up his effects. The items he had on him when he…, when they found him." He gave his head a slight shake. "Uh, I'm not sure what happens next. Is there something I need to do?"

No one else had come to sit outside, and they weren't talking loud enough for their voices to carry. "We are operating off the idea Frost knew about the car and he also knew you weren't likely to arrive soon. He was seen here the day after your father's accident and he may have gone into the boat and found the information about the storage unit, but obviously not the key. Detective Osborne is having someone look for him and we will follow up with that. Since he didn't actually break into the unit, nothing has been stolen."

Joel reached for his coffee again. "I asked them to throw away the clothes. His wallet, keys, phone, and watch were what was recovered. Zeke, Mr. Richmond, has been a big help. He recommended an attorney who is walking me through the legal issues. I'll check my father's boat in detail now, then call the attorney about this. I'm hoping to be able to wrap things up – well, the main things, I mean, by the end of the week. If you give me the name of the storage facility owner, I'll call him after I talk to the attorney." There was no mistaking the tinge of sadness although his expression was calm. He gave a half smile. "My parents divorced when I was fifteen. His drinking and cheating became too obvious. The split with me was him showing up at my college graduation dinner with a giggling eighteen-year-old on his arm, knowing my mother would be there. The more he drank, the louder he got until I finally told him they should leave. At least we were in a private room so the scene was somewhat contained. That's the last time we spoke. The irony is his birthday is next month and my wife, who is a wonderful woman, suggested I might want to try and find him and…, well, I guess it doesn't matter now." He straightened in the chair.

"You have my number if you need anything else from me."

Bev saw Les signal to Gabby for the check. "We'll take care of the coffee if you want to go ahead," Bev said, pushing back from the table.

He looked down as if surprised at the sight of the cup in front of him. "Thanks, yes, I, uh, I'll go to the boat and get started on it." Bev passed him Dixon's telephone number while Les took Gabby aside and gave her a credit card. Les's phone rang as she shook Joel's hand. He flipped a wave to Les and walked toward the boat.

"That was Osborne. They have Frost at the station. He's claiming he doesn't know what they're talking about."

"Then we can help jog his memory," Bev said wondering how much of an asshole Frost would be.

Three hours later, Bev and Les said good-bye to Detective Osborne. Getting a confession from Frost did not require intense interrogation. Blustering turned to mumbling from the man who reminded Bev of the guy who played Skinny Pete on the series *Breaking Bad*. Les had slipped away to talk to Dixon as Frost sullenly insisted he didn't really do anything wrong. O'Hara had been clear about his son not wanting to have anything to do with him and didn't even know about the Shelby. He'd been on O'Hara's boat several times and yeah, he'd looked for the keys when he rummaged through where O'Hara kept his papers and found the receipt for the storage unit. For all he knew, it might take months to find Joel. He couldn't miss what he didn't know about, could he? Dixon told Les he didn't want to mess with pressing charges and Joel O'Hara independently voiced his preference to not deal with any more complications that he was already facing.

Bev and Les left Osborne to decide what to do with Frost and a promise to get together for a beer someday. Five miles out of Verde Key, Dr. Cooke's assistant called to let them know the report on the John Doe was completed and the dental records were available. "Drop me at the office before you go. If Dr. Powell has sent the names of the two dentists who bought the old practices, I can call and see if they kept the old records that far back," Les offered. "If so, I'll take them over later."

"We should be so lucky," Bev said. The situation with Frost had been so easy it would be laughable if not for the tragedy of Michael O'Hara. She didn't know if his son would feel guilty for not having tried to reach out before. Then again, his father could have made the first attempt at reconciliation. If it was one thing she'd learned on the force, family estrangements were messy and often went unresolved.

CHAPTER FOUR

Bev didn't know if Donna Sweeny was a minimalist by preference or hadn't had time to personalize her office yet. The rectangular room was not much smaller than Dr. Cooke's and the freshly painted creamy white walls were devoid of art, posters, or the kind of framed certificates many professionals displayed. The desk centered in front of the back wall was the same as Dr. Cooke's except the single in-box and out-box were empty. Donna had the folder with the report and an envelope in front of her. Bev had passed on the offer of a beverage.

"Your copies are in the envelope," Donna said, with a tiny crease in the middle of her forehead. "Nothing in the system for fingerprints or DNA. No previous broken bones. He did have limited dental work, so you might get lucky there. Nothing distinctive in the remaining shreds of clothing." She held up a small evidence bag, a gold chain inside. "Thought there were no personal effects, but we did find this chain tangled in what was probably a pocket. It's broken; basic eighteen inch, no pendant. And no, even with advances in forensics, this is really thin and was too long in the water for fingerprints."

Bev held the bag up to the light. Nothing distinctive about the chain. A lot of men wore medallions or pendants. Maybe he'd stuffed it in his pocket after it broke. If something had been attached, it must have washed away as the clothing disintegrated. On closer look, men usually had heavier chains than this seemed to be. On the other hand, she'd never picked out a chain for a man.

Donna slipped the bag into the envelope. "I had my share of John and Jane Doe in my last job - nothing this old though. As I thought, cause of death was massive head trauma, blunt force. There were two blows. First one might have been enough to kill him. Not sure how much that tells you."

Bev was trying to picture a scene. "If he was attacked from behind, wouldn't the blows have been to the back of the skull?"

Donna shook her head. "Yes, and no. Say the killer was initially behind him. He heard or sensed something, turned and the blows caught him on the side instead. There was no foreign material trace around the wounds. Baseball bats are good for this kind of blow or another heavy round object. Think a full bottle of booze. You might be surprised what kind of force can be delivered."

"It takes someone strong to kill with a first blow?"

"Again, yes and no. Don't underestimate strength that can come with adrenaline pumping. And I put his height around five foot eight, not big bone structure. He wasn't a huge guy. Given the right circumstances, the killer easily could have been smaller." Donna leaned across the desk to give Bev the envelope. "I admit I wasn't expecting to have a case this interesting so soon. You'll let me know when you find out?"

Bev gave a slight smile. "Nice to be optimistic."

Mischief shaded Donna's grin. "I like to get to know the people I work with. Your rep is you won't give up on this just because there's no quick answer."

Bev matched her grin, stood, and took the envelope. "Says the woman who graduated Summa Cum Laude undergraduate, third from medical school, and was the second youngest on record to be certified by the American Board of Pathology (ABP) in forensic pathology."

Donna stood, too. "Sounds like stories probably better discussed while consuming alcohol."

"If you haven't discovered it yet, the Scarlet Macaw is a great place unless you insist on a water view."

"I'm in a condo for now at Miller's Point and have a nice water view whenever I'm there," she said. "Do we set it up or go with a one-of-these-days things?"

Bev laughed. "Since it looks like we won't be discovering our John Doe today, come join my husband and me this afternoon. We should be there about five-thirty, not later than six."

"That's a fit for me."

The telephone on the desk rang and Bev left her to the call. She was glad she'd thought of inviting Donna to the Macaw. Bev had been in Dr. Cooke's office not long after they'd selected Donna and she'd been intrigued with the idea of someone of her apparent upward mobility potential choosing to come to Verde Key for what appeared to be a step back professionally. Dr. Cooke had conducted the final interview via teleconference and been impressed with everything he'd asked about. Her responses matched the descriptions of her as a workaholic who nonetheless got along with colleagues. He saved the question of why the move to the last. She told him she was ready to make a major change and the opportunity with him provided ideal timing. She'd never left the state of Ohio, growing up there, attending every level of school and completing residency at the Cleveland Clinic. In an aside to Bev, he'd confirmed he was looking at another two to three years until taking retirement. If the new assistant worked out, she could be the perfect replacement. If she decided the area was not for her, he would at least have a younger, obviously energetic assistant for a while who could allow him to take long overdue time off. On a personal level, Bev wasn't the type to have many female friends and if Donna was as professional as she seemed, it would be a nice addition to her small social circle.

She called Kyle to tell him about the invitation and spent almost two hours at the office completing the easy report on the K&L Storage case and catching up on some articles she'd set aside earlier in the month. Les left as soon as she returned to take Pam to the doctor for a follow-up. Bev made it home a few minutes before Kyle and when they entered the Scarlet Macaw, Donna was getting acquainted with Desmonda, the bar's namesake. The black wrought-iron cage occupied a large space between the door and the end of the bar.

"She's a beauty," Donna said, turned and shook Kyle's hand. "Donna Sweeney."

"Kyle Stewart, otherwise known as Bev's husband, if you're local." He gestured toward the back left. "With three of us, let's get a table." Steve Dillworth, the owner, was behind the bar talking to George, the bartender on duty. He looked over at them as they neared, and smiled, pointing to the row of taps. Kyle nodded and led them to a round table close to the bar. The bowl of pretzel mix was filled, napkin wrapped place settings on the table. Most of the rattan bar stools were occupied, as were half the tables. Rattan-tipped ceiling fans revolved quietly, Jimmy Buffet's, "Down at the Lah De Dah," came through the speakers, a low volume in keeping with being able to actually carry on a conversation.

Donna was taking in the décor that couldn't have been picked by anyone other than a diver. Old equipment from the pioneering days of Jacques Cousteau, photographs of dozens of divers that veterans would recognize and framed breathtaking underwater shots dominated rough wood walls. The wooden floors were wide planked. Stain glass rectangular pieces hung in the two windows on the right-hand wall looking onto the parking lot. One was of a scarlet macaw, the other three an octopus, a pair of seahorses facing each other, and a green sea turtle. The artist owned a studio where she taught classes, created her designs, and did sales.

Natalie, the senior waitress, was carrying a pitcher of Shark Tooth amber ale and three frosted mugs, menus tucked under her arm. Bev didn't know if her jet-black hair was helped by a bottle. Although Bev knew she was in her fifties, her dark skin showed only the faintest of crow's feet around her brown eyes and she didn't seem to slow down even when the place was filled to capacity. She had basically come with the restaurant when Steve bought it. He claimed there wasn't a job in the place she couldn't handle, including occasionally substituting as a cook in an emergency. "Didn't know if you were a beer drinker," she said placing a mug in front of Donna and the pitcher in front of Kyle. "We've got plenty other choices. I'm Natalie and welcome. I don't think I've seen you in here before."

"Beer is a good start and it is my first time," Donna said, taking a menu.

Natalie half-turned to Bev as Kyle filled Donna's mug. "We haven't changed the menu yet, but Steve has a guy delivering lionfish now. If he can keep it up, we'll add it as a regular choice. Got mahi and yellowtail as usual and if your noses haven't identified it yet, Bart got in the mood to do his prime rib. Y'all want appetizers?"

Kyle passed the second full mug to Bev and looked at Donna. "I mostly skipped lunch. Are you a calamari person? Perfectly fried, but the nachos are great, too. Actually, everything is good."

Donna lifted her mug partway. "I'm not a picky eater, so whatever the two of you prefer is fine."

"Let's go with the Ocean Bounty Sampler," Bev said to Natalie. "Any chance Bart will swap lionfish for the mahi bites?"

Natalie winked. "He will if I tell him to, sweetheart. I'll bring water in a minute."

Donna held up one finger while she took a sip. "Nice flavor. I like amber, most red ales and have to sample browns first because I find some to be on the bitter side. It's local? And since I'm asking questions, what's the deal with lionfish? Don't they have poisonous spines?"

Bev waggled her free hand. "Yes, the beer is local. The short answer about lionfish is they're invasive and different groups are trying to get them under control. Carefully cutting off the spines takes care of the venom, and they are delicious – similar to hogfish, if you've tried that."

"We've got a great marine education and conservation organization that runs a couple of Lionfish Derbies where teams go out to catch as many as they can," Kyle added. "There's always a big party at the end and they do demonstrations about safely catching, cleaning, and cooking. Then they give out pieces of grilled lionfish. That's how we learned about it."

"I'm game," Donna said and glanced around the room. "Speaking of locals, does this get much tourist trade not being on the Overseas Highway? I like it by the way, thanks for inviting me."

Bev poured some pretzel mix into her hand. "Steve doesn't do much in the way of advertising. He's well-known in the diving and fishing communities and has been here long enough to have a following. Most of the tourists come off the diving or fishing charters because like I said to you, if you're okay with no water view, it's a great place. That's what we always tell people who ask for recommendations."

"Did I hear my name?" Steve had approached the table carrying three glasses of ice water while they were talking. "You've brought someone new?" He set the glasses down and leaned across the table to shake Donna's hand. "Steve Dillworth." He'd been an avid diver until an injury during Desert Storm left him with a collapsed lung and a series of scars on the side of his neck that extended below the collar of his shirt. He was forced to restrict his diving to occasional and shallow, but he stayed current with the industry and constantly encouraged non-divers like Bev and Kyle to give it a try.

"This is Dr. Sweeney, recently hired Assistant Medical Examiner," Bev said and motioned to the fourth chair.

The other woman gave a tiny shake of her head. "It's Donna, please. Love Desmonda and the way the place looks."

"I took a little grief when I renamed the place, but it didn't take long for her to become everyone's favorite." He gave a half smile to Bev. "Heard about the skeleton. Something like that, word gets around pretty quick. Any idea yet as to who?"

Donna nodded when Kyle held the pitcher toward her. "No

television style forensics magic on this one, I'm afraid. An ID will have to come from something else."

"Bev is usually up for a challenge," he said and stood as Natalie arrived balancing a tray with loaded platter, small plates, and a basket of sauces and packages of crackers. "Nice to meet you, Donna. Always good to see two of my favorite customers. Enjoy the food, one of the sales reps is due in a few minutes."

Donna's eyes widened a bit. "This is an appetizer?"

"Nobody leaves here hungry and it is meant for sharing," Natalie said cheerfully and deposited extra napkins. "Holler when you're ready for another pitcher or to swap."

The mound of calamari was next to half a dozen coconut shrimp, completed with a pile of fried fish pieces and a bowl of smoked fish dip in the center. Orange and chili flake sauce, traditional cocktail and tartar came with the platter. Before Donna declined to stay for dinner, they learned in-state tuition for schooling and the reputation of Mayo Clinic had been her primary reasons to stay in Ohio. Her father, an accountant for a two-man firm in their small town, and her mother, day manager at a local motel, had no other family remaining in the area and were considering a move to warmer climate. Probably not all the way to Florida, but Alabama and Georgia were on the list. She thanked them again and reluctantly accepted Kyle's refusal to let her pick up the check.

"Great idea to invite her," he said when they decided to stay with the seafood theme and split a shrimp with Cajun Cream Sauce pasta dish. "Bet she's good at her job."

"That's my impression," Bev said, snagging the last piece of lionfish and pushing the platter to the side. "We'll see how she likes the weather when it hits mid-summer."

Kyle grinned, no doubt recalling his first sweltering summer after moving from Chicago. "Remember, many of us do adapt and enjoy our little paradise."

Bev, whose family was four generations in Verde Key, reached for his hand and gave it a squeeze. "And I am certainly happy you did."

The next morning brought an overcast sky and light rain. The morning fishing report on the radio assured listeners it would clear before noon. Les was looking at his computer when she came into the office. "Good news, not great," he said by way of greeting. "I'll let you get coffee first."

She deposited her purse in the bottom drawer of her desk, readied her caffeine hit and perched on the edge of her desk. "Our John Doe?"

Les pointed to his screen and hit the print button. "Thank God for packrats, extra storage space, and the human inclination to procrastinate. Turns out Dr. Powell's assistant did keep records going back to when they opened. The boxes were neatly organized by year, sitting in a storeroom where doing anything with them was not high on the to-do list of the current staff. Edward James Newton, date of birth 02/10/1948, had two fillings done in 1975."

"Huh, not one of our missing persons."

Les took the page from the printer tray. "Nope, and the address given at the time was rezoned and there's an apartment building now, put up twelve years ago."

Any chance an emergency contact was listed in the dentist's file?"

"That's the not great part - none listed," Les said. "I was getting ready to search property and voter rolls."

"He might have moved. I'll do property and you do voter?"

"Sure."

Bev extended the search into adjoining Miami-Dade County after a blank in Monroe County and turned when Les sat up straighter. "You got a hit?"

"Not directly. Mr. Newton may not have been civic-minded. I do have a Rosalind Marie Newton, Verde Key address who is age seventy-two. That's the right range for wife, or other relative. You want to switch to marriage records or refill my coffee?"

Bev laughed. "Not that I mind getting you coffee, but my fingers are on the keyboard." A few strokes later, she spun her chair to face his desk. "We can once again thank whoever actually invented the internet. One Edward James Newton married Rosalind Marie Mosley February 23, 1968, in Bristol, Florida. While two people can have the exact same name, it is probably our lady."

"No phone number listed and nothing on social media," Les said looking at his screen. "Considering I did get it from the voter rolls and I don't know how often they clean them up, I'll check death certificates."

Bev drained the last of her coffee. "You said she has a Verde Key address. I don't mind going over to check it out if she's still with us. No reason us both going, and I was on-site with the body."

Les turned his head as the search processed. "While I am curious to know why a missing person report wasn't filed, the simple answer might be it was and somehow the report disappeared. In which case, the lady will probably be seriously pissed. If she didn't report it this is likely to come as a shock anyway and no telling how she will react. I've done plenty of these in my years and don't mind avoiding one." He shifted back to the computer screen. "No death certificate on file."

"Okay, I'm off then," Bev said, realizing Les could have a point. Assuming this was not some improbable coincidence and Rosalinde Newton was the wife – well, widow – and had reported him missing, explaining there was no report on file would add to the shock. Another logical outcome was desertion by husbands and wives did happen. If that was the case, she might have resolved years before he wasn't returning. The fact he was murdered would still probably be a shock. Hell, maybe she shouldn't have volunteered to do this alone.

CHAPTER FIVE

Ruth Branden took her third mug of coffee with her for the usual morning stroll around the property. She checked that nothing odd had washed onto the short beach or none of the feral cats had given birth in the shed where they stored tools, three generators, folding beach umbrellas and the lightweight chairs and tables they tucked away each evening. It was one of the mornings that none of the others had appeared outside yet. Bayside was calm, no sound of jet skis or boats from neighboring houses shielded from view by massive red and white bougainvillea planted decades ago. Streaks of white clouds against blue sky indicated rain was gone, the sun not yet high enough to require a hat.

She walked to the entry from the street, always taking a moment of pleasure in the artistry of the black wrought iron gate's custom design of flowering vines, butterflies, and birds. She rarely set the gate for automated operation, preferring to manually roll it open each morning and closed at night.

She was a few steps away from her front door when she glanced to her left and saw a car driving slowly across the oyster shell lot. She didn't recognize the green sedan and lifted her hand in greeting. The woman driving turned slightly, stopped, and got out.

"Uh good morning. May I help you with something?"

The woman, who looked to be in her thirties, was the same height as Ruth and was dressed in a burgundy pants suit, a cream-colored blouse and wore plain black flats, a black purse hung from her left shoulder. Her auburn hair was pulled into a loose braid, hazel eyes friendly, although she wasn't smiling.

Ruth was startled when she held open a small leather case to show a badge. "I hope so," she said. "I'm Detective Beverly Henderson,

Verde Key Police Department. We have this address, Apartment 104 for a Mrs. Rosalinde Newton. We couldn't find a telephone number. Do you know if she is here?"

Ruth felt a tiny flutter in her stomach. "Uh yes, well, I mean her car is here. I'm Ruth Branden. I own the property. Is everything all right?"

"Do you happen to know if she is up yet?'

This was odd. "We all tend to be morning people. She's in the building across from here, apartment on the left. Would you like me to walk you over?"

The detective's tone was even, not exactly business-like. "You're friends as well as landlady?"

"Goodness yes, all four of us," Ruth said immediately. "Rosalinde has lived here the longest, I mean longer than Renata and Rochelle. Is something wrong, Detective?"

"I need to speak with Mrs. Newton, ma'am. If you are friends though, having you with me might be best," Detective Henderson said and gestured to the car. "Shall I leave this here?"

"That's fine," Ruth said and stepped forward. "Rosalinde has no family in the area and she doesn't have much of a social circle beyond us," she added as they crossed the yard. She saw the blinds on Rosalinde's front windows were raised partway. She, like Ruth, was normally up around six o'clock, rarely later than seven. She should be dressed by now and when they stopped in front of the door, it was already opening.

Rosalinde, in navy blue pull-on slacks and a blue polka dot round neck short sleeve top, swung the door wider and stepped onto the stoop. Square terra cotta planters filled with anthurium flanked the stoop. She understandably looked puzzled. "Hello. What's going on, Ruth?"

"I'm Detective Beverly Henderson Verde Key Police Department, ma'am. I have a matter I need to explain to you. May I come in? We can speak in private if you prefer."

Rosalinde looked at Ruth, then back to the detective. "Ruth and I are close friends - I think I prefer to have her with me. Come on inside."

They followed her in, and Rosalinde indicated the woman should sit in the matching upholstered armchair to the left of the dark green sofa while she patted the cushion next to her for Ruth. The apartments were identical in layout with an open floor plan of living room, dining nook in front of the back window overlooking a terrace and kitchen with an island. Nine-foot-tall ceilings, sand-toned tile floors and white walls gave a sense of more space. "I can't imagine what this is about," she said, sitting on the edge of the sofa, her gray eyes intent on the detective. The thinnest of the four of them, her shoulders were straight, her hands clasped loosely in her lap.

"I'm afraid I'm here with bad news about your husband, Edward James Newton." Detective Henderson said quietly.

Rosalinde's voice quavered. "My husband? Ed? What do you mean?"

Ruth tried not to show her surprise and she instinctively reached for Rosalinde's hand.

The detective quickly and calmly explained what had been found. Rosalinde's thin face tightened, and she gripped Ruth's hand. "Are you certain it's him? Ed? You see, Ed left me in 1977. At least I had no reason to believe otherwise."

The detective drew in a deep breath and exhaled. "If you filed a missing person report on him, we didn't find it in our records."

Rosalinde shook her head rapidly. "I didn't. You see, we had our share of troubles and more than once he said he never should have married me. That one day he would have enough and be gone. I got home from work that evening. He wasn't here, which had become common. I assumed he was out with his so-called friends. I didn't think to look in his closet until the next morning when he still wasn't back. I didn't really see anything missing, but then he didn't wear much except jeans." She paused and rubbed her other hand across her forehead. "What little cash we had in the house was gone. I called the only two guys whose names I knew, and they hadn't seen him. I couldn't see any reason to call the police. I mean, you hear about men deserting their wives all the time." She rubbed her forehead again and dropped her hand. "You're certain it's him?"

"Yes, ma'am."

The statement hung in the air, the room silent. Ruth struggled to know what to say. Jesus, what must Rosalinde be feeling?

Rosalinde gave a slight shudder, and her voice was barely above a whisper. "When you say dead, you don't mean some kind of accident do you? I mean how could an accident go unnoticed this long?"

"No ma'am, it was not an accident," Detective Henderson said gently.

"What you're telling me is he was murdered? Murdered and…," Rosalinde trailed off.

"Yes ma'am, I'm afraid so," Detective Henderson said. "Would you like a glass of water or something? If you feel up to it, I need to ask some questions."

Rosalinde squeezed Ruth's hand once more and let go. "Quite honestly, I'm not sure how I'm doing. This is a shock as you can imagine." She turned her head. "Ruth, dear, there's coffee in the pot. A cup, please and for yourself of course." She looked back at Detective Henderson. "For you? I have juice, ice tea, and water, too. I don't keep soft drinks."

"No thank you, I'm fine," the woman said and took a notebook from her purse. "Do you recall the date?"

Rosalinde's laugh was harsh this time. "Oh yes, it was February 23, 1977, what would have been our ninth anniversary. He hadn't bothered to celebrate it since our first. That's part of why I thought he'd simply gone. It made a bit of a statement, don't you think?"

Ruth was in the kitchen and couldn't hear the detective's response. She carried Rosalinde's coffee in, deciding to wait for herself. She didn't want to miss any more of the conversation.

"Was there anyone who might have wanted to harm your husband?"

"He, he could be quite obnoxious when he had too much to drink. The two bars where he usually went were quite rough, frankly. Neither are here now. To say someone planned to harm him, I doubt it."

The detective waited until Rosalinde had taken a sip of coffee. Her voice was soft again. "You said there were problems in your marriage. Was your husband abusive?"

"Ed's pattern was to criticize and belittle, control the money, leave barely enough for bills. Part of why I worked at the grocery store was because of the employee discount. The other reason was we were renting a house within walking distance of the store. We only had Ed's truck and he would take it every day."

"You mentioned two friends you called about him. Do you know where they are now?"

Rosalinde shook her head. "One I know was killed in a wreck a few years later. I saw it in the paper. The other, Nick Black, I have no idea. My husband had no real family. We were from Bristol, both anxious to leave. My only brother, Reggie, left as soon as he finished high school. He lived near here, and that's why we eventually came. Ed was sort of in construction. There weren't any jobs when we first arrived, and Reggie helped him get work at the marina where he was. He didn't have a special skill, but Ed was handy and strong enough.

He was like a day laborer. The marina wasn't a good fit for him, and he found something else later. Not always steady work with any kind of benefits, but we got by. When he left me…" She blinked rapidly. "When I *assumed* he left me, I imagined whoever he was with had money or some kind of connection he wanted."

Ruth knew bits of Rosalinde's past but not much about her husband other than he'd left her. Well, obviously not.

"And your brother? Would he know of anyone with a grudge? An argument before he disappeared?"

"Reggie, God rest his soul, passed almost ten years ago." Rosalinde lifted her cup, then set in on the coaster without drinking it. "Detective Henderson, I don't know what more I can tell you. But what happens now? Not whatever you will be investigating. I mean with Ed. What am I supposed to do?"

The detective laid two business cards on the coffee table. "I realize this has come as a shock and our condolences for your loss. Your husband's remains are in the morgue. The card on top is for me, please call if you think of anything and I will of course let you know of any developments. The second card is for the medical examiner's office. Dr. Cooke is away, but Dr. Sweeny has the case and can be reached at the same number. Once you decide who will be handling the arrangements for him, they will contact the office." She held her notebook up. "I don't have a telephone number for you, ma'am. And do you have email?"

Rosalinde looked to Ruth quickly, then lowered her eyes briefly to her hands. Ruth stood. "Detective, Rosalinde has a pay as you go phone for emergencies and no computer. I have a landline, my cell, and email. I'll send you her number and my contact information as I might be easier to get in touch with. We'll help her with everything of course."

Rosalinde was up now, her shoulders straight, her face calm. "Yes, thank you, Detective. I… I just have a great deal to think about.

I'll try to remember if there is anyone who might have information. It was a such a long time ago, and as you can imagine, I was finally able to put it behind me. Or I…I'm not sure how this changes things. I mean, this simply isn't the kind of news I was ever expecting."

The detective slid the notebook into her purse. "That's understandable and yes, Mrs. Branden, please email me the information. I can let myself out."

Ruth didn't correct her to "Miss" as she had never been married. It was hardly important, and she was already considering what steps did need to be taken. As soon as the door closed, Rosalinde sank back onto the sofa, inhaling and exhaling deeply. Ruth realized she was trying to center herself, not going into some kind of hyperventilation. She sat beside her again. "What can I get for you?"

Another three breaths passed, then Rosalinde turned, her voice normal. "God, I never really thought this day would come, certainly not like this. We have to tell Renata and Rochelle, but let's make a fresh pot of coffee because I want to tell you a few things first."

Ruth moved with her to the kitchen. They didn't speak while Rosalinde dumped the remaining coffee and silently set the new pot to brew. Ruth took another cup from the cabinet, the blue ceramic sugar bowl, and a square blue wire container with packets of sweetener and non-dairy creamer from the counter and carried them to the round pine dining table. She went back to get napkins and spoons as Rosalinde opened the cabinet next to the refrigerator.

"If ever a moment called for chocolate, this would be it," she said and removed a bag of chocolate chip cookies. By the time she filled a plate, the coffeemaker gave a final gurgle. Ruth picked up the cookies, laid napkins for the coffee cups and waited at the table for Rosalinde to sit.

"Okay, I can do this now," she said passing one cup to Ruth and placing hers on a napkin. Her eyes were clear. "The real reason I didn't report Ed missing? I was relieved he was gone. I didn't want to know where he was. It was more than a year before I began to believe it was over, that I could stop worrying."

"You said he was controlling and emotionally abusive."

Rosalinde gave a sad half smile. "We were so young, went to school together. I don't want to get into our lousy home situations of alcoholic fathers, enabler mothers. Ed didn't have brothers or sisters. Reggie was my only sibling. I wasn't much better in school than Ed. Like I told the detective, we just wanted out. I suppose there might have been signs of what a lousy husband he would be, but that wasn't what I was thinking about. It was easy to think we were in love." She held up a hand to wait while she took a swallow of coffee. "I didn't mind I had to work, and for a while, it wasn't bad. We lived in a couple of places before coming here. Ed couldn't keep a steady job. Always saying it would be better in the next place."

Ruth nodded rather than interrupt, wondering if Rosalinde had ever been able to confide in anyone. She noticed Rosalinde was idly fingering the gold crucifix she always wore. It was a nervous habit she didn't seem to be aware of.

"I did think when we made it here what with Reggie close by – he worked at Richmond Marina down south a bit – this would be the right place. It was better for a few months. Then it started all over, Ed going from job to job, gaps in between. It wasn't just that – he never helped around the house, he was a slob, too. I would work all day, then…, well you get the idea."

Ruth spoke carefully. "Your brother knew?"

"He worked a lot and didn't come up too often. He guessed after a while. He didn't say anything for a long time and finally said he would take care of me and him if I would leave Ed. I told it wasn't as bad as he thought and everything would be okay." She dropped her eyes for a moment before looking up. "Back then, self-esteem and being an introvert weren't things we understood. All my life, I'd been trying to please other people and I kept thinking that if I just waited a little longer, it *would* be okay. It wasn't up to Reggie to take care of me." She stretched her left hand out and Ruth clasped it lightly. "With Ed gone it seemed odd to be on my own and I did let Reggie help some with finding a new place, the rent for a while and he bought and fixed up a little Honda for me. I never expected to have a career and being a cashier suited me. I got along well with everyone." She smiled fondly this time. "You remember how we met?"

"Oh sure," Ruth said, the image of a bird-like woman rushing out of the store, waving something in her hand. She'd been distracted for some reason and instead of putting her credit card back into the usual holder in her wallet, she'd dropped into her purse. Or thought she had. It had fallen to the floor and Rosalinde, the cashier one over from where she'd checked out had noticed and dashed to catch her. Coincidentally, or perhaps not, Rosalinde was her cashier the next few times she was in the store. They chatted pleasantly and one day Ruth saw her at the library. They started talking about favorite authors and extended the conversation into the nearby coffee shop. Their friendship grew and not long after Ruth converted the old motel into apartments, Rosalinde's landlord sold the house she was renting. Finding a place she could afford was proving difficult. Ruth explained what she'd recently done with the old motel, ready to take in a few, select tenants.

"I know I've told you before, but moving in here truly was one of the best days of my life," Rosalinde said, slowly withdrawing her hand. "And I'm so glad you were with me this morning. I'm pretty sure I would have fallen apart if I'd been alone with the detective."

"I didn't know what she wanted with you and couldn't think it was anything good."

Rosalinde pushed back from the table. "There's no way we could have imagined it would be this. Look, we have to tell Renata and Rochelle. I'm sure they both noticed the visitor and are probably wondering what's going on. I love them both, too, but you and I have been together longer, and I don't want to go into all the details. If you'll get Renata, I'll call Rochelle."

Ruth nodded and left the apartment at a brisk walk. Who would have thought this was going to happen today?

CHAPTER SIX

Ruth settled onto the green Adirondack chair made of recycled plastic, a glass of pinot noir in hand. She often came out at night like this at times and after the intensity of the day, she needed the fresh air. She'd eaten the small portion of leftover pork tenderloin and roasted asparagus for dinner, not particularly hungry. Had Rosalinde accepted her invitation to come over, she would have cooked something special. The other woman was understandably exhausted, and Ruth hoped she would be able to sleep. There were no clouds to obscure the three-quarter moon and stars and front lights from their three buildings were behind her, providing almost no illumination. Other than a few insect sounds it was quiet as it had been that morning in the peace before the detective arrived. The water in the bay was calm, enough breeze to be comfortable in the caftan she'd changed into.

Renata and Rochelle had been considerate in asking what they could do to help, not probing for details. Ruth wasn't surprised. They had formed a basic sisterhood in what was now three years since Rochelle, the youngest at sixty-nine, had moved in two years after Renata. It was more than their similar ages as they each understood loss. Not only loss but also the regrets they struggled with in their own ways.

Ruth's thoughts drifted back forty-plus years into her own arrival in a place she had never imagined in her youth. When Rosalinde had spoken that morning about her terrible home life, Ruth could sympathize. Not empathize as she couldn't claim abuse, at least not in the common term. Deborah did call it abuse when she was old enough to use the term. Ruth shook her head sharply as the image flashed unbidden. The ghost no doubt was summoned because of today's drama.

She sipped her wine, willing to allow the unbidden memory a few minutes. The first one of Deborah as an infant, six years between them because of her mother's two miscarriages. Had the complications with Deborah's delivery been a sign of what was to come? Of the difficult child she would be? Or perhaps she was born into the wrong family. Modest, father working in a hardware store, stay-at-home mother. Church every week, affection never shown, rigid routines for every day, no wasting of money on frivolity. Unlike what Ruth had apparently been as a baby, Deborah was fussy, wearing on their mother who turned to the older sister to take on more chores. Also, unlike Ruth, she was a pretty child, not average as to easily blend into a crowd. Always asking for treats and toys, tantrums when denied. Ruth tried to explain, to reason away the tears. By the time Ruth had dutifully gone to secretarial school, was working in the hardware store, and still living at home, Deborah's behavior was beyond reason and patience. Total disgrace in the small town was only avoided because she managed to not get arrested for underage drinking and no doubt worse. The fight that sent her into the night was when the week's grocery money disappeared. Her father's bellowing, "You're no daughter of ours." Her mother's weeping of, "We've done everything we can." Deborah's scream of, "What do you know about me? You've never cared." The glare directed at Ruth. "You, the perfect daughter is what they want. Not me, not who I am. Damn you, damn all of you."

Was it irony her parents were killed in a head-on collision not quite two years later? Despite a life of frugality, there was no life insurance and meager savings, the house of marginal value in a stagnant town. In what was an automatic act of duty, she'd taken half of what was left after funeral costs and opened a certificate of deposit she could give to Deborah someday. She had no way to find her sister short of spending money for a private detective, an expense beyond her means.

One of the few women she could call a friend came to her quietly, an offer Ruth initially refused. Drive all the way to Florida to help move her to where an elderly aunt was living away from the Pennsylvania winters? The woman had the promise of a job and others might be available, too. Leave to maybe look for a new beginning? Away from the only town she'd known? In truth, leave what? No family, a job she'd never really cared for, no wide circle of friends, no romance for a rather plain, shy girl who'd unthinkingly accepted always fulfilling others' needs, meeting those expectations, her adventures bound within books. It was an absurd idea. Surprisingly, her boss somehow heard – then again, not much was private in their small town – and gently suggested she take a few weeks and go. Don't rush with the drive, take time to think.

Where had it been? Not over dinner in the four days they caravanned, the trustworthy AAA Trip Ticket guiding them south away from a dreary March of lingering dirt-flecked snow piles, trees still bare branched. Not even the first two days in the comfortable bungalow in Vero Beach, a short walk to the water. Warm air and sunshine, abundant fragrances, and so much green in the neighborhood where people enjoyed front porches, exchanging pleasantries. Her friend's aunt was welcoming, and yes, she knew of people hiring in several places. Actually, it was the third night of the five Ruth allotted for the stay. Rather than the porch, they were on the terrace in back, sipping tea in late afternoon, sunset colors beginning to tinge the few clouds.

"If you want a genuine change to your life, you want to continue on to the Florida Keys," the aunt said, offering another freshly baked oatmeal cookie. "It's a different lifestyle."

Ruth had laughed at first. "I doubt I am a different lifestyle person."

"You might be surprised. I came here when several friends basically paved the way for me, but there is something special about the Keys. A lovely couple own the Retreat Motel and I can call to see if they have a vacancy. It's a full day due south, but not a bad drive down."

A stirring in her flickered, something she couldn't define and, with her friend starting her first day of work in the morning, she decided to make the trip. Arnold and Rebecca Schoopman were indeed lovely, and not quite three months later, her life had changed – or was poised for change. Her concern about what to do if Deborah did finally try to reach her or return home was met with assurances by the man who bought the house, he would forward mail and keep her new telephone number to pass on. Once again, she took half the money from the sale of the house and added it to what she would give to Deborah. Surely one day she would reach out.

The first letter did arrive six years later. An address in New Orleans, no telephone number. No sorrow expressed as to how she'd heard about their parents. A demand for money, a child to support, no mention of a husband, the assumption Ruth's life was unchanged. Ruth's letter in return was long, thinking she could bridge the divide with not only the check, but also an offer for Deborah and the unnamed niece to join her, to give them a chance to embrace a place she'd grown to love. She tentatively allowed herself to think it could happen, a real family without the strain of the past. She'd tucked the short response away in her desk, wanting to believe the anger would someday soften. *Still need to feel superior, don't you? Like you know better what I should do. I only want what was mine by right. If you're doing so well, send more money.* Not one to give up, she'd thought maybe, just maybe over the next few years, her offer would break through the wall between them. By the fourth check sent to yet a different address with the same demand as always, she made it clear she would pay for their move, let them live with her while she helped Deborah find a job. There would be no more checks and that was the last she heard from her.

Ruth's glass was empty and a cup of chamomile tea was more likely to help with sleep than another wine. The hope for Deborah and the niece whose name she barely knew had faded to what was only a glimmer. In the moments of accepting hard truths. She knew what was gone for her was gone and right now Rosalinde needed her.

CHAPTER SEVEN

"Your daddy plans to grill chicken and corn when he gets in. Potato salad and coleslaw are in the refrigerator and there are leftover scalloped potatoes if you'd rather microwave those." Emma Henderson pointed to a foil covered package on the section of counter between the stove and refrigerator. "There are rolls for him to warm up on the grill."

Bev grinned at the predictable amount of food and wiped a drop of condensation from her glass of tea. "That's your cream cheese frosting behind you, isn't it?"

Her mother moved the second layer of red velvet cake and the bowl of frosting to the middle of the peninsula. The bottom layer was on the same milk glass cake plate Granny Henderson had received as a wedding present. "Take this before you get that hand in my way," Emma said affectionately and passed Bev a spoon with a large dollop of frosting. "I have half-a-dozen cupcakes for here after I get this ready. Your Daddy and I don't need a whole cake for the two of us." She loaded the plastic spatula with frosting, put it in the middle of the bottom layer and began to spread it evenly around. She glanced at Bev. "So, I hear there's been quite the stir with the Four R's."

Bev almost didn't make the connection. "The Four R's? Oh, Mrs. Newton and the others at Miss Branden's? You know them?"

Emma added more frosting. "Not very well, but Rebecca Schoopman – she and her husband Arnold owned the Retreat Motel originally – had her regular hair appointment with Agatha the same day I did. Lovely couple, not that I saw Arnold much. I remember back when they hired Ruth. She only came into the beauty parlor occasionally."

Bev's mother was not the type to gossip, but she did pay attention when people talked and could generally sort fact from rumor. "Then you know how the whole arrangement came about?"

Emma placed the spatula in the bowl and gently moved the second layer on top of the first, aligning the two. She nodded without looking up. "I don't recall exactly where Ruth came from, up north somewhere. It was oh, must have been in mid-1970s. Not sure I ever heard exactly why she moved and doesn't really matter. She didn't have family and never married. Anyway, point is Rebecca said she fit right in from the beginning." She moved the bowl of frosting next to the cake, adding the rest of it while still talking. "Rebecca and Arnold ran the place and Ruth was willing to learn just about anything. She was trained in secretary and maybe some accounting work. She cleaned too, helped with outdoor work, reception, whatever was needed. Then when Arnold had his stroke – oh that was maybe twelve years later, he never did recover full strength. Rebecca had him to take care of and the motel – they never had kids – and Ruth was even more help. I remember one day Rebecca said she didn't know what she would do without her." Satisfied with the top of the cake, Emma started on the sides, slowly rotating the plate rather than trying to reach around with the spatula.

"That's why Ruth has the motel? She converted it into apartments though."

Emma nodded again. "Arnold passed away a few years after the stroke and Rebecca and Ruth ran the place together officially. Developers came in buying up as many of the old-fashioned motels as they could. The name brand ones were being built, or they were cramming rental condos in. Rebecca and Arnold were like us, three generations living here. She hated the way the Keys were changing."

Bev, fourth generation of born and raised in the Keys, knew older residents were concerned about the rise in population. Aside from increased traffic, housing prices had skyrocketed as a major impact and many people working in the service sector were forced into longer commutes because they could no longer afford to rent or buy in town.

Emma, satisfied with the cake's appearance, set it on the back counter, and moved a foil covered plate to the island. "Now mind you, people from here understood why Rebecca, God rest her soul, did the will the way she did. Well, not like it was public knowledge, but Rebecca herself told us – that is Agatha and the two of us who had appointments. She'd finished at the lawyer's right before. Anyway, she and Arnold didn't have a huge amount of savings, but what with the motel, they hardly ever traveled and with no children or, really any other family, they were okay for money. The real asset of course was the motel." She removed the foil and reached for the spoon Bev had licked clean. She laid it on top of the foil and picked up the spatula to begin frosting the six cupcakes.

"Where was I? Oh right. Now they did have a little house not far from the motel. Rebecca left everything to Ruth – who she hadn't told by the way – except she could only inherit the motel if she agreed not sell it for a period of fifteen years. If she didn't agree to the provision – is that what it's called? – the motel was to be given to that Wild Bird Sanctuary Rebecca always contributed to."

"That's different," Bev said, wondering what Miss Branden's reaction must have been when she learned about the unusual inheritance. She edged her finger toward the frosting bowl.

Her mother smiled. "Stop that, young lady. You and your daddy want to have dessert before dinner, at least wait until I'm out of the house."

Bev laughed and picked up her tea. "Fair enough. Did Miss Branden convert the motel right away?"

Emma paused in concentration. "Let me see, it was maybe five years later Rebecca passed. God love her she was like ninety something and worked at least somewhat until not long before. Ruth was mostly running the place for a couple of years before."

No reason for her mother to get straight to the point. That wasn't the way she told stories.

"Like I said, I never became what you would call friends with Ruth – not to where you have detailed conversations. She did decide to convert the motel and stayed in the house until it was all done. See, she had this idea – now I didn't hear this part direct – but I trust what Agatha says. There are five apartments in all and the only tenants she wanted was other older women who weren't married. I'm not talking about one of those we-hate-men situations, but remember, the name was the Retreat Motel. Now, Ruth is the only one who's never been married. That Renata Lopez and Rochelle Sancerre are both widows and well, I guess Rosalinde is too, since her husband didn't run off and leave her after all."

"Ah, got it," Bev said. "A retreat for women. Odd, their names all start with an *R*."

"That probably is a coincidence. Any idea what happened to him? Rosalinde's husband, I mean. Your daddy had a case kind of like that one time. Well, not nearly as old as this one. Just a guy went missing for a couple of years and finally turned up dead, truck in a canal somewhere."

Bev would have to ask her dad about that. "We're working on it. Where is it you're going tonight?"

Emma finished frosting the last cupcake and picked up the bowl. "Quilting circle at the community center. Well, I'm working on embroidering some squares for now." She looked toward the front door. "Your daddy should be home shortly. I need to get going."

Bev smiled and slid off the cane bottom bar stool. "Here, I'll clean this up while you change."

"Thanks, sweetheart, I won't be long."

Neither Bev nor her brother protested at their parents selling the home they'd grown up in to be able to afford a still modest three-bedroom, two-bath house, the added value of being on a canal with direct access to the ocean. The common open floor plan of entryway, den, dining area, included a galley kitchen deliberately designed for one cook. Emma had scoffed at the trend for stainless steel appliances and, even though they were white, cabinets were milk paint pale blue, counters and the island topped with off-white quartz, scattered blue and green chips adding highlights. Repainting of the house had been to freshen the tones of sand-colored walls, and the major change to replace the tile floors throughout with engineered wood in a light-colored oak. Emma's intent had been simple. "No grout to get stained. These are easier to deal with." Practicality, comfort, and on the water where the Pursuit DC 246 dual console design bowrider was kept made it the dream house her parents deserved.

Later with dinner over and the kitchen cleaned up, Bev and her dad were relaxing on the deck overlooking the canal. Lights were coming on as twilight faded, lingering aromas from other grills, faint music two houses up as people moved in and out. They hadn't turned the deck lights on, enough illumination came from inside.

"It's been a while since we've done this," Frank Henderson said as he clinked the neck of his Budweiser against Bev's bottle of Shark Tooth red ale. "Kyle gets back tomorrow?"

"Uh, huh. Three days in Tallahassee for meetings. Said it was going well. Mom was giving me the background on what she called *the four R's*. Interesting story."

"We do have plenty of those around here. You having any breaks with the case?"

She filled him in on what they had. "More than forty years and the two places Newton frequented are long gone. So far, we can't find anyone other than his wife who knew him." She gave him a synopsis of her conversation with the widow. "I don't get the not filing a missing person report. I mean, okay, she thought he'd run off, but that would be grounds for a divorce if that's what she wanted."

Frank angled his chair slightly toward her. "Things were pretty wild in those days. The Keys have always been a place where a lot of people come to start a new life, to not be bound by some of the regular rules. If the wife never remarried and there were no children involved, and she wasn't trying to collect on insurance or some other asset, him just being gone wouldn't have been that uncommon." He gestured to the canal that led to open water. "Sure, there's still smuggling, poaching, and what have you going on. It was a lot more open back then, miles of coast, inlets to tuck into, places back country where you could be for weeks and never see another person. You have an accident out there, capsize a boat, disappear, become fish food. Depending on the time of year, storm comes along and scatters the bones, breaks up what's left of the boat. Or instead, guy takes off, heads deeper into the Keys, leaves for the islands, takes on a new name, nobody cares."

Bev tapped her fingers against the cold bottle. "This was sure no accident."

He nodded his head. "I was referring to the wife's reaction not being unusual. The flip side was plenty of bodies were found back then, too. You mostly hear about the cocaine wars in Miami in the 80's. It started before then and wasn't exclusive to there. Double crosses, wannabees in over their heads. We didn't have the same level of open violence, but you add some of that with other ordinary motives and no telling how many skeletons wrapped in tarps are still out there." He tilted his almost empty bottle at her. "Let's accept the guy was an asshole. What were the two hangouts?"

"Fat Jack and Half-Mast Henry," Bev said immediately. Chief Taylor was out of town and no one else had been on the force long enough to remember them.

Her father nodded. "Fat Jack's burned down in the 80's. Most likely insurance fraud. Half-Mast didn't survive Hurricane Georges. Those were places that took care of their own problems. Think about Gill's and imagine it on steroids. My point is, Newton's regular hangouts were because other guys like him went there. He gets crossways with one or two other tough guys or he's trying to work some kind of shady deal. One night after closing, they get into it in a deserted parking lot or it's a deliberate attack. Instead of a gun or a knife, let's say it's a tire iron upside the head. Sounds like the stuff he was found in was standard to be found in any marina. The kind of stuff lots of guys carried around in their trucks. Even if you only have one guy, he hauls the body away in Newton's truck, car, whatever he's driving. Has his own boat or access to one. Disposes of the body, takes the vehicle somewhere else, sinks it and makes his way back to his own truck. If he doesn't get it that night – no big deal. One more drunk left his truck in a bar's parking lot and got it the next morning. Late at night back then, it wouldn't be hard to be alone long enough to make all that work. If there were two of them, just makes it easier."

They'd brought the small cooler out onto the deck and Bev wordlessly pulled fresh bottles out while listening to him. She exchanged his beer and set the empties by the cooler. "That's a possible scenario, or if it's a deal went bad, maybe it happened at a meeting out at Palmetto Paradise. What was it like back then?"

"Even more isolated than it is now. Good place to meet and not be seen."

"You thinking we'll probably not solve it?"

He chuckled softly. "I know if anyone can, it will be you. The only cold case we had when I was on the job was a missing person. Turned out to be natural causes though."

"Is that the one mom mentioned earlier? Man in his truck?"

Frank nodded. "Yep, divorced, two sons lived in Georgia. A neighbor contacted the one he had a number for when four days of newspapers piled up in his yard. If he was going away, he usually asked the neighbor to pick up the mail for him."

Bev wasn't surprised her father remembered the details. It was a trait they shared and part of why he'd been genuinely missed when he decided to retire from the force after her second year on the job. He agreed his wife shouldn't have to worry about both of them.

"He didn't have a boat and liked to fish different canals from the bank. We checked every place we could, no trace, no witnesses. In fact, the youngest son was between jobs. He was single, so stayed on in the house and took a job in town. The missing guy was finally found when they had to do some dredging. Medical examiner figured he had a heart attack while he was driving, lost control and went into the water. Tough break, but at least they had answers and it wasn't a homicide."

"That's the other thing bothering me," Bev said, holding the beer on the arm of the chair. "Mrs. Newton didn't seem to really react to the idea her husband had been murdered. I can't say exactly what was off about it."

"Forty-plus years thinking one thing and finding out you had it all wrong had to be a hell of a shock. It can take a while to sink in."

"True." She lifted the bottle. "Kyle should be getting back to his hotel soon. Thanks for dinner and the talk."

"Always enjoy having you over and don't let this case get under your skin. It did happen before you were born."

"I guess you do have a point." They finished their beers and her dad walked her to the door for a goodbye hug.

Her phone buzzed an incoming text while she was opening the car door. *Still at your folks?* She added a heart emoji to her response. *Be home in about ten. Call you then.* One more night alone. If she had time the next day, she would pick up fresh fish for dinner. She knew the guys he'd been meeting with were into steakhouses and there were a couple of excellent ones in Tallahassee. Or so she'd been told. Her one venture into the state capital when she was a new criminal justice graduate had not included a budget for high end restaurants.

CHAPTER EIGHT

Lauren Smith gently walked Old Manny to the door, locked it behind him, and shut off the front signs. When he and two other regulars were the only ones left, she'd told Boomer and Polly, the single waitress for the night, they could take off. It had been as quiet as G's Place ever was. Boomer had broken up one fight around ten and stopped another because they all knew the signs of Georgie getting increasingly obnoxious and started looking around to pick a fight over whatever struck him as annoying. Being the owner's nephew and godson was why he wouldn't be kicked out. The standing practice was to slip him a little something in a drink and call a cab to get him home once he was feeling the effect enough to be manageable.

Lauren turned the main lights off, having already finished wiping down the scarred wooden tables of the rectangular room with the requisite two pool tables and juke box close to the back wall. She appreciated George having a reliable cleaning team to limit her close-up duties. They would be in during morning hours to take care of the dark plank floors that weren't as sticky as at times and at least no one had been sick in the toilets for a few days. Smoke was soaked into the equally dark wooden walls although the cook did change oil in the cramped kitchen's fryers often enough to keep the odor from being overpowering. A single bulb behind the bar was enough illumination even though the bulb over the back door hadn't been replaced yet. The dumpster was not quite three feet from it and the streetlight at the head of the alley was working.

The earlier rain had stopped, most of the water drained although the smell of damp mingled with that of the dumpster's interior when she tossed the bag of trash in and fastened the door. None of the wandering cats were hanging about and she was turned facing the alley as she heard the first shouts and saw the shapes. Shit, the man running in front wasn't far ahead of the other two and they had guns drawn.

He tripped behind the back of the pawn shop across the alley and they were on him before he could recover.

Shit! She couldn't get back into the bar without risking noise. She pressed against the side of the dumpster, trying to keep her breath shallow. The sounds of the man being beaten were punctuated with curses and moans for what couldn't have been longer than about a minute.

"Hold it, man. It's Tyrone coming. He said he wanted to deal with this motherfucker hisself."

"Better be saying your prayers, asshole."

Oh, God, she knew that voice. It was Tommy Blue, one of the regulars. Among those who were said to be within Tyrone Baxter's circle, he didn't carry himself with the arrogance of others. He was always nice to Lauren and she wanted to believe his reputation for violence was exaggerated.

The Cadillac's lights were off as the black car drew close, the nose clear of the dumpster. The dome light came on though as Tyrone Baxter threw the back door open, gun in hand. "Think I wouldn't find out…"

The rest was lost in the first shot's echo. Lauren's legs felt as weak as her heartbeat seemed to be in overdrive. But with everyone in front of the car, she had a few precious seconds she might be able to slip inside. The second shot was clear and the third faint when she closed the heavy door, her hands shaking so badly she could barely slide the bolt into place. Surely the sound of the click hadn't carried, and she had only the one light on behind the bar. She hurried in and hit the switch, sending the place into darkness other than what filtered in from the streetlight in front across the street and the glow from the jukebox in the far corner. She slumped behind the bar, hearing the back door rattle, muffled voices. Then she heard them at the front door. She couldn't breathe, didn't move, knees hugged to her chest, arms wrapped around them. Then it was quiet. She exhaled silently, hands moved to press against her mouth in case she accidentally whimpered. She didn't know how long she sat on the floor thinking. They must be gone. They wouldn't have hesitated to break the door in if they thought someone was inside. If the guy was dead, and she didn't see how he wouldn't be, they would have to do something with the body. Even though no one lived on the street and the bar was the only place open that late, the cops did patrol occasionally.

She finally slowly unfolded her knees and pushed to her feet. She thanked God again she knew the layout of the building well enough to not need light. She crept quietly into the small office where her purse was in a locker behind George's desk. She would wait another hour and if she didn't see anyone, she would walk two streets over and take an alternate bus. What the hell was she going to do? What could she do?

Two hours later, Lauren exhaustedly entered her second-floor apartment. The former mansion, converted as so many had been, was dark. There wasn't even a light on in either old Mr. Devereaux's ground floor unit, or in the two-bedroom apartment shared by the musicians, whom often didn't make it in until dawn. She knew she wasn't likely to sleep. The kitchenette was as much as she needed considering how little she cooked. Like everything else she owned, the French Press had come at a bargain price from the Saint Agnes thrift store. She added an extra scoop of dark roast coffee and filled the battered tea kettle with water. There were a couple of slices of raisin bread in the scratched-up refrigerator and maybe a chunk of cheese. Her throat tightened at the thought of trying to swallow food.

Two competing ideas continued to swirl in her brain. She didn't know who the guy was last night. Maybe the body wouldn't be found. If it was, maybe they wouldn't associate it with Tyrone or there wouldn't be a reason to suspect the alley was where he was killed. If not, all she had to do was keep her mouth shut and no one would ever know. It had seemed obvious the guy was either part of Tyrone's operation or maybe a rival. G's Place wasn't a drug scene although in that neighborhood, it was always best not to look too closely at whatever quiet dealings might be taking place. Tommy Blue and sometimes a couple of other guys would come by two or three nights a week for a few drinks, never causing trouble. Not long after she started working there, Boomer told her Tommy Blue kept an eye on things for Deshaun, Tyrone's older brother, and he'd stayed on after Deshaun was killed. She hadn't wanted to know more. With what she'd seen and heard tonight, there couldn't be much doubt of his role. The kettle began to rattle. She lifted it from the burner and poured steaming water carefully into the carafe. She paced the narrow distance between the short counter and the two-person square-topped kitchen table for the three minutes she would let the coffee brew.

RUN! That was the option slicing through her reasoning. Get the hell away as soon as the bank opened. She'd stuffed the meager tips from the night into her jeans' pocket before she'd taken the trash out. She had maybe fifty dollars in her dresser drawer and almost three hundred in the bank. How far did she need to go? One state away in any direction? Two? Where the hell would she go anyway? She poured coffee into a plain brown mug and sat heavily onto the yellow vinyl padded straight back chair at the table. She breathed in the strong aroma and curled her hands around the mug. She'd lived in New Orleans all her life. A life laced with pain and sorrow, learning to survive in ways she shouldn't have had to. A harsh reality punctuated by infrequent kindnesses that had perhaps been what saved her from the self-destruction of her mother. Despite it all, she'd felt pangs when the police tracked her down to tell her about the body found in a motel in a part of the city Lauren had left almost two years before. She'd finally accepted no matter what she sacrificed for her mother, the drugs, booze, and men wouldn't or couldn't be given up. She'd just begun work at George's Place, offering to do double shifts, wanting to make sure she could pay the rent for what might be considered a crappy apartment for anyone who'd never seen some of the places where she'd lived. In the string of dive bars she waitressed, watching and learning how to be a bartender, she'd come to George's after Midnight Lounge had been torched. The owner wasn't smart enough to hire a professional and he was arrested for attempted insurance fraud the next day. George, after years on the offshore rigs, had bought the bar and understood the neighborhood he'd grown up in. No working girls hustling, no open drugs sales, an unspoken neutral territory for whoever came in. The 12-gauge under the bar was seldom needed – never actually fired. He was a good boss, treating his few employees decently. Jesus, she didn't want to have to leave.

Tyrone though, he was different from his brother. He'd come in right after Deshaun's murder – word already spread about the gruesome deaths of the men he held responsible. Even though he'd barely nodded to her and Tommy Blue was the one who ordered the drinks and carried them to the table in the back, she could sense danger in him. Not tough guy type. More of a cruelness he exuded. He hadn't stayed long, a short conversation with George, who retreated to the office for more than an hour.

Boomer had waited several minutes after Tyrone, Johnny Blue, and the other guy with them left. "Too bad the wrong brother is dead," he said in a voice so low she could barely hear. "You didn't mess with Deshaun, but he was a businessman. Tyrone is a crazy son-of-a-bitch."

That scene and those words flashed like one of the neon signs in the bar. The fact was if the guy in the alley was found, would the cops bother with a real investigation? Whoever enraged Tyrone wasn't the kind of person of concern to police. She finished the coffee, eyes gritty from a lack of sleep, her back aching. Aspirin and a hot shower might help. She stripped out of her clothes and was glad for a change the shower wasn't large. She leaned forward slightly, braced her hands against the sides and let the hot water hit directly on her upper back, easing her muscles, steam filling the fiberglass enclosure. She stood for a moment, wondering if perhaps she could burrow under the covers and sleep. She pulled the shower curtain back and grabbed the towel draped across the sink. She stopped suddenly and looked at it. Faded yellow, a palm tree and *Visit Florida* in equally faded green print. No doubt someone's souvenir. She'd bought a box of mixed towels from the thrift store for a few dollars. She dried off and wrapped the towel around her, a memory surfacing. Fragments of words slurred in drunken anger. *Bible thumper. Bitch. Sister. Florida.*

She closed her eyes, trying to remember. It was so long ago. A letter? Yes, a letter clutched in her mother's fist, a beer bottle in her other hand. She was jolted back to when? Eight years old? Maybe nine? There was no man – only the two of them. A semi-dark room, the smell of smoke soaked into thin walls, a full ashtray and an empty beer bottle knocked to the floor.

"Move to Florida, the bitch says." Ripping the letter into pieces, showering to the floor. "Always the righteous one. Always thinks she knows best."

"Is Florida not nice?"

She hadn't been prepared for the slap this time – stronger than usual. Her mother's eyes dark, then widened as she drew back. "I'm sorry, baby, I'm sorry. I didn't mean to do that. It won't happen again."

The clutch came next, as always, the weeping hug pressing her into her mother's stomach. "Your aunt, she won't send us more money." A pause, swaying, release. Stumbling toward the kitchenette, to the refrigerator. Another beer, then passing out.

Lauren shook her head rapidly, the memory too vivid to ignore. She'd crept forward, taken the discarded envelope from underneath the couch and crammed it into the pocket of her shorts. Why? An instinct she hadn't understood? Later, still moving quietly, her mother asleep, she read the return address. *Ruth Branden, 402 Seagull Lane, Verde Key, FL.* An aunt who wanted them to move to Florida? What made her mother mad? Was she a terrible person? She couldn't ask any more questions. Maybe another time. She had torn the address part away from the envelope and placed it inside the only book she owned, *The Tale of Peter Rabbit*. Her mother said she'd outgrown it, but she didn't care.

Lauren left her clothes on the floor, moved into the bedroom, changed the towel for the worn short terrycloth robe she kept on the end of the unmade bed. Florida. An aunt she'd never met. Was she even still alive? The book? The box in the closet. She crossed and slowly opened the folding doors that would come off track if she wasn't careful. The shoebox containing the few things she kept from place to place was in the corner. She hadn't looked at it since moving into the apartment. She carried it to the bed and exhaled a deep breath when she lifted the lid. A set of Mardi Gras beads, a folding fan from a kind old lady who'd briefly been a neighbor, a slightly crumpled program from yet another failed promise of rehab and her mother had taken her to a free performance of *The Nutcracker*. The book was at the bottom and the slip of paper fell out as she fanned the pages. The barely legible ink was still readable. Lauren sank onto the bed, holding the paper, fatigue making it feel as if she was weighted down. Maybe if she laid there for a little while, things would seem clearer. She pushed the box to the side of the bed, the paper under the second pillow and pulled the sheet and thin bedspread over her shoulders.

She awakened groggily after some sleep to morning sounds from tenants coming and going. Everything seemed normal. She made her way in for another coffee and managed to toast and eat the raisin bread. She kept coming around to the odds of, if the guy was found, no one was likely to care. She could go to the bank though and take out all but twenty dollars and if things stayed quiet for a few days, she would put the money back. She couldn't help looking around extra when she went out to the bank and on the walk to the bus stop. She took deep breaths before she entered George's, the place almost empty. Nora was her usual self, tired from being on her feet, swearing she was too old for this shit and would fucking quit if her fucking worthless husband would ever hold down a job. Oh, and Polly called in sick, so Lauren was going to have to handle the whole place by herself which might be okay since it was a Tuesday. George was at his brother's birthday dinner. Call if there was a problem, otherwise he wasn't coming in. Lauren was glad of the routine complaining, agreed she was fine without Polly, and Boomer was whistling softly while hauling in a keg of Miller Lite to swap out.

Tommy Blue strolled in not long after eleven o'clock – alone for a change. Other than Old Manny at his regular seat on the far end, the bar was empty. She'd refilled the pitcher for the three guys shooting pool and Zac Brown's, "Same Boat," was playing. Tommy Blue sat on the second stool from the end, easy to watch the front door. Boomer was gone to pick up his cousin to give him a ride, promising to be back in an hour. Lauren tried to think Tommy Blue's appearance was a coincidence.

She smiled, hoping her voice was steady. "Your regular?"

"Sure," he said, gesturing toward the few customers. "Pretty quiet, huh?" His face was expressionless, his light blue eyes the origin of his street name. Boomer once told her he'd toughed out the beatings as a kid and shooting up to six foot in his teens put a stop to those. In days when the term was still used, he would have been called a mulatto. He took the drink in his large hands, his eyes still.

She shrugged and picked up a damp rag to wipe the already clean bar. "Uh, yeah – you know it's a Tuesday. Haven't seen you for a few days."

"Got some business later– thought I'd have a drink first. Been quiet like this all night?"

She wanted to think there was nothing unusual about his question. "Yeah, slow after the weekend."

He tilted his head. "You know I grew up couple of streets over? Neighborhood hasn't changed a lot."

"Uh, no – I mean I figured you were from around here."

He sipped his drink. "You've always reminded me of one of the ladies lived on the same street as us. We didn't have many white folks left. Most moved out in the 70's from what I was told."

"Oh?"

His voice was pitched low. "Nice lady. She'd left the neighborhood after school, came back when her husband ran off and her mamma took sick. She stayed on after her mamma passed. Worked at the store on the corner and did baking. Sold some at the store and always had extra to give to us kids. Damn, she made great cookies. Had flowers boxes in the front windows, too. Not many people did that."

Lauren concentrated on keeping her breathing even. What was this about?

"See, we all made sure nobody messed with her, know what I mean? One day though, couple of stupid motherfuckers got into it. Things got out of control, shot up the fucking street." He slowly blinked his eyes. "She was on the porch, watering those damn flowers."

"Oh?"

"Fucking shame, bullets flying all over the place. Shit like that happens though, don't it? People minding their own business and in the wrong fucking place at the wrong fucking time."

Lauren willed her hand not to shake and lifted the bottle of Crown Royal. "Yeah, that's a real shame. Ready for another?"

He drained the glass and shook his head. "Naw. Gotta' get to business. You take care of yourself, okay?" He put money under his glass, slid it to her and left without saying anything else.

Her stomach gripped and she stared at three one-hundred-dollar bills underneath the ten on top. Shit, shit, shit!

Old Manny's voice cut through her rising fear. "Hey, Lauren, let me have my last one for the night, please." She poured his double rye, no more ice needed, and smiled as expected. "Are you all right, my dear? You seem a bit pale."

She tapped a finger to her temple. "Headache starting up is all. I'll take some aspirin in a minute."

Boomer came in, drops glistening on the top of his shaved head and grabbed a towel to wipe dry. "Almost made it in without getting wet. Looks like rain off and on for a while. Still quiet?"

"Yeah, yeah," she said, not meeting his eyes. "Give me a second, okay? I'm going to get a couple of aspirin."

"Sure." He walked behind the bar to pour the nightly, neat bourbon he allowed himself in the closing hour. "Look, hey, I'll give you a ride home tonight, okay?"

"Yeah, thanks," she answered with more gratitude than he could imagine. She closed the door to the office behind her and sat in George's chair, working out time. She didn't need to take much with her. She booted up his computer and checked the Greyhound schedule to see a 7:12 a.m., bus to Mobile. She ought to be able to make it and then figure the best route. If she couldn't find her aunt, there ought to be bars in the Florida Keys where she could work and that ought to be far enough away.

CHAPTER NINE

Bev was alone in the office. Les had called in from an appointment to say he was running later than expected and wouldn't come back to the office if there was nothing new. She frowned at the still-thin folder on the corner of her desk with the file on the Newton case. After official notification of next of kin, they released a short paragraph to the local paper with identification and requesting information. She'd spoken with the few leads she'd tracked down, nothing useful from any sources. The one man who was a bartender at the Half-Mast recalled Edward Newton and couldn't add much to what they knew. He verified what her father told her about the bar. It was strictly for regulars, fights were common. Anything bad, though, was to be taken outside. Newton was quick to throw a punch although no worse than most of the others. He did remember him seeming pretty tight with Fred Teller who was part owner of Sid's Cycles, a motorcycle repair shop close by. He also remembered notice of Newton no longer coming in was briefly speculated at because he probably ran off with some woman, and no, he hadn't paid attention if a name was mentioned. The idea of a jealous husband or lover taking retribution was logical as a motive. *Where was* still in question at this point. If the guy Teller was a drinking buddy and could be located, he might have an idea of a likely woman on the side. A cursory search drew a blank. Sid's Cycles had been closed for more than ten years and a telephone call to the primary owner hadn't been helpful. He had no idea what happened to Teller, nor in his words, "did he care where the son-of-a-bitch had gone." Coming in drunk on the job was bad enough. And screwing up customers' repairs led to a buy-out of the small percentage of the shop he owned. There was nothing on social media which wasn't a surprise considering his age. No Florida death certificate or driver's license which might not mean anything if he was no longer a state resident.

Kevin Blackwell stepped into the office through the open door.

"Hey Bev, you got a minute? My cousin Martha wants to come talk to you about something."

Bev looked up at him holding his cell. "Uh, sure. Is she here or on the way?"

"Called a minute ago. Is now all right? She's at her office."

"Now is fine. Tell her I'll make fresh coffee."

He grinned as he withdrew. "She said she's been baking again." Bev hadn't seen Martha for a while. She was glad from a professional view, because Martha Sears was a social worker and work-related encounters usually involved abuse and domestic violence cases. Personally, she liked the woman and respected the fact she sought genuine solutions for individuals. She had a well-deserved reputation for getting families to seek help for their problems, or more often, convincing women there was a support network to allow them to leave abusive situations. Bev hoped this was a case where Martha simply wanted her to come speak at a gathering of some kind.

The coffeepot signaled the brew cycle was complete a few minutes before Martha came in carrying her brown purse over her left forearm and balancing a square plastic container on the palm of her right hand. Bev stood and Martha shook her head when she reached for it. "I'm balanced," the plump woman said and deftly slid it onto a spot on Bev's desk and set her purse on the floor next to the empty chair. "Blonde brownies with butterscotch chips and yes, I brought a batch for the break room, too. Kevin took them."

Bev stood, noting Martha was wearing a pair of dark green slacks with a matching lightweight buttonless jacket, and cream-colored top. No jewelry other than a pair of small jade ball earrings. Sensible brown flats. "You're at work and sharing brownies around? Still take your coffee with cream, no sugar?"

"Good memory," she said and took the chair Bev had positioned at the corner of her desk. "Did the baking last night. Had a birthday celebration for one of the women in the office and I got on a roll after I made the batch of cupcakes. There's always someone can use a good brownie. Oh, is Les around?"

Bev brought the two mugs and napkins. "Not this afternoon. I promise I'll save a couple for him."

Neither woman was inclined to idle small talk. "Not that I don't appreciate good baking, but you have one of your workshops you want me to speak at?"

Martha exchanged a brownie on a napkin for the coffee. "I wish. At the moment, this is what I suppose is an initial inquiry and not directly for me." The maternal air of comfort and calm she often projected in tense scenes Bev had witnessed wasn't her mood today. She paused for a sip and a bite. "You don't have anyone in the department for forensic accounting, do you? That's a county asset?"

"Correct," Bev said, a little surprised at the question. "That's not your usual area."

"Not directly, no. Are you familiar with the non-profit, Start From Here?"

Bev shook her head and gave a thumbs up pointing to the rest of the brownie on the napkin.

Martha returned the gesture. "The group has been around for maybe six years and a friend recently joined the board. I've worked with them some because they focus on helping girls and women either get on track for education or job training. I'm talking those who maybe dropped out of school, are recently divorced with no job skills and held back by issues like low self-esteem, generational poverty, you know. The name *Start From Here* is based on the idea of where you start in life doesn't dictate your future."

"Got it. Sounds worthy and the problem is what?"

Martha's brown eyes clouded briefly. "Okay, I'm having lunch with my friend the other day. She agreed to go onto the board after another woman moved unexpectedly and the absence left them without the required number according to their charter. My friend sits on a couple of other boards and didn't really want to add an extra, but she agreed to do so until they could maybe find someone else. Even though they aren't a large organization, they are pretty well funded and, in fact, had a fundraising gala a few months ago. Apparently, the woman who is and has been the treasurer has her own idea of how to report their financials that isn't overly detailed. The way my friend explained it, she gives a verbal report of here's how much money we have, here's what we spent last month." Martha quirked her mouth upward. "According to my friend, when she asked for the backup details, she was told they don't get into all that at the meetings."

"Don't they have a regular audit?"

"All their funding is from private sources and again, apparently, an actual audit has never been conducted." Martha grimaced. "And yes, they submit a tax form each year which is done through the treasurer's cousin's tax business. At no cost, of course, as a favor to the organization."

Bev pinched a small piece from the little left of her brownie, determined not to have a second one. "Other than this seems sloppy, does your friend have a reason to think there may be something wrong?"

"As I mentioned, she sits on other boards and is familiar with how most of the fundraising events work. The amount they took in from their fundraiser seems small compared to attendance, revenue from the tickets, and I guess they did a raffle. The kicker is the day after she raised questions, the President of the Board dropped by her office for a chat. After polite preliminaries, the message was, while they really appreciate her willing to be on the board, the treasurer has been with them a long time. They don't want to upset her since no one else wants the job. Plus, no one can imagine she would be doing anything wrong."

Bev saw the flicker of something she would have called cynicism in Martha's eyes. Not an emotion she associated with the woman. "Your friend is considering doing what?"

"She called the individual on the board who asked her to help out and who, by the way, wasn't at the meeting when my friend started asking questions. They met and she eventually indicated she, too, had some concerns because there has been a pattern of expenses that seem high for what they were getting, there were never details about credit card expenses, and she didn't know what to do."

Bev raised her eyebrows. "Sounds like someone looking for a second pair of eyes, maybe? Your question about forensics accounting. You know we would need a formal complaint?"

Martha nodded. "Yes, and right now, there isn't anything specific to go on. What I told my friend was she pretty much has three choices. She rolls over like everyone else, she insists the board takes a closer look and if the treasurer doesn't like to be questioned, tough – or she walks away from the whole thing." She paused, put another brownie on her napkin, broke it in half and nudged the napkin to Bev. "The fact is, you and I deal with this too often. People who are corrupt or abusive behind their public selves. Allegations start and no one wants to believe it could be true. The flip side to the coin is someone has a grudge and starts rumors that aren't true."

Half a brownie wasn't the same as a whole one. The sad image of Rachel and Herb Mecklenberg when they discovered their youngest son was stealing from the family business immediately came to mind. The case had been yet another lesson in how treacherous people could be. "Yeah, that's for sure. You've given her good advice and I can talk to her, hypothetically, if she has questions about process."

Martha lifted her coffee mug in a sort of salute. "I'll let her know. Different subject if you have time?"

Bev stood. "A refill?"

Martha passed her mug and waited until Bev returned. "I heard about recovering Edward Newton's body. Talk about a cold case."

Bev was startled. Not about the story raising curiosity but more by why Martha brought it up. "You knew him?"

"No. Rosalinde, is a longtime volunteer at the library. The way I sort of met her is one of those odd things you tend to remember. Aside from my personal use of the library, a support group I occasionally work with meets there twice a month."

Bev sensed something in Martha's tone. "The group is for abuse survivors? Rosalinde is in it?"

"Not in it. I was there because Sharon McCauley, the organizer, wanted me to explain a new state program. One middle-aged woman came for what I think was her first meeting. She didn't seem comfortable and left fairly quickly. I finished my pitch, answered a few questions and when I went out, I saw Rosalinde in the parking lot with this woman. They were next to a car close to the library entrance and from their body language it looked like Rosalinde was maybe encouraging her." She ran a finger around the top of the mug. "I wasn't close enough to hear them – nor would I have wanted to. In a minute, Rosalinde put her arm around the woman's shoulders, and they went back inside. I had to do a quick follow-up with Sharon the next day and asked if the one woman had returned to the meeting. She said yes, kind of laughed and referred to her as another of Rosalinde's recruits." Martha paused for a sip of coffee. "I asked what she meant, and she said at least three other women started with the group after Rosalinde recommended it."

Bev thought to Rosalinde's explanation for why she thought her husband had deserted her. How strained had their marriage actually been?

"Sarah said after the first time, she thanked Rosalinde and asked if she would like to join. She was very clear she wasn't interested – she just thought it was a good group for women who needed support. We're both familiar with people who manage to come through difficulty and are supportive of others even if they don't want to openly share their own experience." Martha gave a half smile. "Anyway, I would casually chat with Rosalinde after that. She's a really nice lady. The impression I had was she was divorced, and I thought finding her ex-husband's body the way y'all did might have been a shock. You get anything from the initial news story?"

"Nothing so far."

"I moved here not quite twenty years ago. My contacts don't usually go beyond current generation, but I will keep my ears open. You never know when someone will pop up." Martha tapped the top of the container with the rest of the brownies, pushed her chair back, and grinned. "You saving these for Les or shall I remove temptation and take them to the break room?"

Bev stood and reached for the empty coffee mug. "He would hear about it and never forgive me if he missed out. Always good to see you." She waited until Martha was through the door to take the mugs to the small sink. She walked to the whiteboard, not surprised by the idea Edward Newton might have been an abusive husband. Rosalinde's assertion he'd simply deserted her was believable, except in adding what little they'd learned about him, if he was prone to bar fights, physically lashing out at a wife he obviously didn't respect was likely. She added the question, realizing it wasn't particularly helpful. The places he frequented could have involved any number of potentially volatile situations and running around with other women held its own risks. Rosalinde had an older brother at the time who, again, in all likelihood might have known if Newton was abusive and decided to do something about it. Right, the brother who was dead. Considering the age of anyone involved, it was equally possible the person or persons unknown were also dead. In remembering the rule of always suspect the spouse, especially if Newton was abusive, Rosalinde couldn't be discounted. The only certainty was it was highly improbable for her to murder her husband, haul his body away, and dump it in the water with no help.

CHAPTER TEN

Lauren sat on the bed, both pillows propped against the headboard. She tuned the television to some talk show, the sound too low to hear what they were saying. She only wanted the distraction as she thought about her next step. The past days had been draining, most of the time on different buses. She hadn't wanted to come directly to Florida. She'd gone north from Mobile, catching a bus to Chattanooga, Tennessee barely half hour after she arrived. Late night passage to Macon, Georgia was next, and she'd checked into the cheapest motel she could find, exhaustion allowing her to sleep more than she expected. A quick turn barely stopping in Tampa, Florida to go a short distance this time to Sebring – a town she'd heard of from one of the truckers who was a regular at George's Place. Another cheap motel for one night, a box of hair dye, and a pair of beauty scissors. She still wasn't accustomed to the look of a chestnut-colored sort-of pixie cut instead of a strawberry blonde braid. If nothing else, short hair might be more practical if she was still around for the heat of summer. She purchased an inexpensive prepaid cell phone, transferring only two numbers before depositing her old one into a trashcan outside the store.

She'd eaten little other than peanut butter crackers and coffee during the travel. Her lack of appetite saved money too and the hundred-dollar bills from Tommy Blue stretched her limited funds. Having spent most of her life with little money, she knew the value of a public library and was glad to find one in Verde Key. Based on nothing more than her mother's long-ago derision of her aunt as a "righteous one," she thought being a property owner or for certain a registered voter would fit that characterization. With a quick prayer she was alive and in town, the property tax records did list an address different from the one on the old envelope she'd carried with fragile hope. It was surprisingly close to the library. She slowly made the walk, stopping on the sidewalk at the edge of a parking lot. Having also spent much of her life constantly moving, she felt a surge of momentary despair in recognizing a converted motel. The comparison was starkly different to those from her memory. The three buildings laid out in a standard "U-shape" were nicely painted coral with cream accents. Landscaping bordered on minimal but was well maintained. What looked to be planters with blooms were at each door. Three cars present were older models and the depth of the parking lot prevented her from seeing beyond the back building. She didn't want to risk stepping closer and turned to walk away, not wanting to draw attention if someone came out. Interestingly, there was a single decorative mailbox rather than separate. She'd noticed others like it – an upright dolphin sculpture holding the mailbox between its flippers.

She paid attention to her surroundings in the half-hour it took to make it back to the motel that was on a side street off what she'd been told was the Overseas Highway. She had also paid attention as the bus rolled into town, noticing franchise-named motels, restaurants, strip shopping centers with a mix of businesses, gas stations, and at least three places for scuba diving and snorkeling. Tourist areas often had high turnover and her willingness to take unpopular shifts might work in her favor. Even if her aunt was willing to take her in and it was a bearable situation, she would need a job.

She practiced her mostly true story continuously. Omitting portions of the truth flowed more smoothly than constructing a lie. The difficult life with her mother and why they hadn't been in touch was sadly easy to be truthful about. In reality, her reason for suddenly appearing was what required polishing. She had no more family. Her few relationships had been disastrous, her lack of formal education did limit the type of jobs she qualified for. No matter how strong her work ethic was, with those jobs, it wasn't possible to accumulate much beyond paying for essentials. Her thirty-sixth birthday had passed and wasn't that a common age to assess one's life? To think maybe a major change was needed?

She knew Aunt Ruth – a term she rehearsed – was older than her mother. Was she the kind who mellowed with age – or enhanced and clung to bitterness accumulated over the years? Lauren was familiar with both types. She did locate a telephone number and that was central to her internal debate. To call or not? Which would be the greatest shock to the woman? She wished she could have received her last week's pay from George, but that couldn't be helped. She had left only twenty dollars in her bank account and she could last for one more week in the motel. If her aunt immediately rejected her, she could look for work and assuming she could get hired, she could inquire if there was some kind of homeless shelter where she could stay temporarily to allow her time to find a place. Even as low as they'd been in the years with her mother, they had managed to stay off the streets and only turned to a shelter on a few occasions. She batted away memories of times when being in a shelter might have been preferable to some of the so-called boyfriends of her mother.

She swung her legs off the bed, realizing she hadn't eaten since a pack of peanut butter crackers for breakfast. The nearby Wendy's was advertising a five-dollar deal and unless her appetite increased to normal, she might get two meals out of it. As much as she'd really like to head to one of several bars she'd seen for a cold beer, that pleasure would have to wait. Christ, how many dinners of stale, dry cereal and tap water were there growing up when booze or drugs were her mother's priorities over groceries? She shook the memory away, turned the television off, put her sneakers on again, and grabbed the Miami Dolphins hat she'd been given at the bus station in Sebring. The attendant was gathering a scattering of items left on chairs. There were no ugly sweat stains inside what looked to be a fairly new hat and Lauren assumed she would be on foot for at least a few days. It had come in handy since not many stretches of sidewalk were shaded.

She stepped outside the room, the sound of a vacuum cleaner coming from the room two down, the linen cart next to the door. Most of the parking spots were empty and the *No Vacancy* sign was not lit.

The place was clean though and the palm tree close to the office seemed healthy. An hour later, she fixed on a plan and the man on the desk at the motel was different from the one who'd checked her in. The dour woman the day before had been more bored than rude, but Lauren hadn't wanted to engage in idle conversation anyway.

The rectangular room reception area was as basic as the rest of the place. The floor was beige tile, one window next to the entry doors. The counter was wood-look Formica, a door behind leading to what was no doubt the office. The computer at the end of the counter was definitely not new, although they did have Wi-Fi in the lobby. A window unit air conditioner to the left wasn't too noisy and a basic overhead fan turned on a low setting. Two mis-matched upholstered armchairs against the far wall with an end table between provided the only seating. Stacks of brochures for attractions and businesses were in a two-shelf bookcase under the air-conditioner.

"Help you with something?" Gray-flecked brown hair was close cut, with a receding hairline. His brown eyes were friendly, a wide mouth in a lined face. He was average height and shoulders slightly rounded. A fishing magazine was open on the counter and a green ceramic coffee mug to his left. He was wearing a pair of faded blue chinos and a pale blue polo shirt stretched a bit snug across his middle.

Lauren gave a smile. "I was wondering if I could get a piece of paper and maybe buy an envelope?"

"Don't see why not," he said cheerfully and hooked his thumb over his shoulder to the open door. "You need a stamp, too?"

Lauren shook her head. "No, just doing a note for someone."

"I don't remember seeing you around," he said, not turning toward the office.

"I came in yesterday. Room 18."

"Staying with us for long?"

Okay, he was the chatty type – or maybe he didn't have a second magazine to read.

"I'm not sure yet. I have the room for three nights and the woman yesterday said I could extend if I need to."

His laugh was pleasant as he looked around. "Yeah, we're not expecting a big rush. You here for anything special?"

She hadn't planned a discussion, then realized she hadn't actually spoken with another person for days. "Not exactly. I mean, I may be just passing through. It depends on a couple of things."

"Well, we've got all the usual things to enjoy in the Keys depending on what you like. Most folks come for the water – fishing, scuba, kayaking, and what-have-you. Got a real nice wild bird sanctuary not far away, too. Great sunsets on the bay side if you didn't catch it yesterday."

"No, I've been on the road for a few days."

"Well, you want to do sunset, Skipper's is a few minutes' drive and about ten minutes walking to the south. Down a side street and the sign to it isn't big, but if you're paying attention, you'll see it. Not fancy, neither are the prices. Real good Happy Hour, too. Doesn't go after the tourists. You decide to go, tell them I sent you."

Lauren understood his unsaid part of if she was staying with them, she was on a budget. "Thanks, I'll keep that in mind."

He paused and when she didn't say more, he half-turned. "Okay, then, I'll get you a couple of pieces of paper and an envelope. Got the ones with the motel name printed if you don't mind that. Hey, I made some fresh coffee. Want to take a cup with you? Don't have anything to put in it though. I always drink it black."

"I take mine the same," she said instead of the refusal she intended. "That's nice of you."

He brought back a to-go cup with a lid on it, three pieces of paper and an envelope paperclipped together. She took her wallet from her purse and he waved his hand. "Shoot, I don't need that. I'm Clyde Hopkins, by the way."

"Lauren Smith," she said. "Thanks a lot, I really appreciate it."

"No problem. I'm on 'til seven, so let me know if you need anything else."

Her smile was brighter this time. "I will." God, he reminded her of her favorite regulars. She went back to her room, suddenly glad he'd given her the extra paper. What sounded good inside her head might not be the same in trying to write it.

With no desk in the room, she pulled the one straight-back chair to the corner of the dresser, maneuvered to a less awkward position and sipped the coffee. It was fresh, strong, and better than expected. She had struggled with the opening to the note. *Dear Ms. Branden* didn't sound right. *Dear Aunt Ruth* was something she hoped she would be saying from now on. She crumpled the first attempt in trying to say too much. How to close though? She could hardly say *love. Fondly? Hopefully* seemed too needy even if it was the truth. *Truth?* Oh, *truly* should be okay.

Dear Aunt Ruth.

I know this might be a shock. I am sorry for whatever happened between my mom and you. I was a kid then. She was never able to get well and passed away two years ago. I spent my life in New Orleans. Not long ago, I found the envelope from your last letter. I decided maybe the City wasn't a good place for me anymore. I am not looking for charity, but I don't have any other family. If you are willing to meet, I am at the Gull's Nesr Motel and my cell is 555-492-6378. I hope you don't mind me finding your address by looking at the library.

Yours truly,

Lauren Smith

The library opened at nine in the morning. She would walk to her aunt's place, leave the note in the mailbox, and go back to the library from there. She would talk with the librarian about what she had to do if she did stay in the area. In a town this small, a single question might bring out a lot of information about potential jobs and places to live. One of the reasons she loved libraries was when she was old enough to understand what they did, the research librarians had always been nice. School was miserable in every way, but it was important to at least graduate high school. The library became a refuge for study in quiet safety and no sneers at her shabby clothes and willingness to take food from the plates of students who could be picky about what they ate.

She abruptly straightened in the chair, not wanting to revisit the younger version of herself. She folded the note, slid it into the envelope and printed the address. She stood and did a quick inventory of the room. Despite all the walking she'd done, she wasn't tired. In looking at the envelope, she felt a surge of regret at having left everyone with no explanation. No telling what they would think or the inconvenience for the landlord in clearing out the apartment, although the rent was paid in full, and she didn't have a lot to remove. She didn't really have a choice, did she? If questions were asked, they could all genuinely say they had no idea what the hell happened, and until two days before, even she didn't know she had a connection to Florida. She should be safe and so should they. She recognized that running was the same as admitting she'd seen something, but she understood Tommy Blue's warning. With someone like Tyrone, he might not know she had, and simply decided not to take the chance. One more dead gangster or wannabee or whoever the guy was wouldn't be important for long. New Orleans was the only place she'd ever lived and maybe she wouldn't like the Keys. In taking the bus the way she had, she'd seen enough other places to try if she needed to.

She thought about Clyde's suggestion of Skipper's. If he was right about the prices, she could think of ten or fifteen dollars as an important expense in scouting out the town and the neighborhood. As she well knew, bartenders were a great source of local information.

CHAPTER ELEVEN

Ruth opened the door to Renata's familiar knock. Each woman had a distinct approach just like specialized ring tones on cell phones. Renata sharply rapped twice with her knuckles rather than use the bronze dolphin-shaped knocker. Rosalinde preferred the knocker and Rochelle simply opened the door slightly and called out.

"Good morning. Coffee is fresh and I have bagels if you want a nibble."

Renata, almost as tall as Ruth, held up an envelope. She was the only one of the four whose hair showed no gray and they knew her straight black hair was her natural color. She kept it short, easier to deal with as she swam every morning, weather permitting. As usual, she was wearing capris, a short sleeve tee in pale yellow today. Her favorite leather sandals had stripes in yellow, green, and blue, selected to coordinate with most of her wardrobe. She stepped inside and passed the envelope to Ruth. "Coffee is fine. I went to put a letter in the box and saw this for you. Someone must have dropped it off either last night or maybe today."

Ruth didn't recognize the handwriting and no name was included with the imprint of the Gulls Nest Motel. "That's odd. Maybe they have some promotion or something going on. Not sure why I would be getting it. Inside or on the patio?"

"I'm good either way. I've already had my swim. Lovely sunrise this morning."

Although none of the women tended to sleep in, Renata's pre-dawn habit usually made her the earliest riser. She claimed it came from being the oldest of five children in the migrant farmworker family where tasks began with the 4:00 a.m., awakening of her father six days a week.

"I'm at the table then," Ruth said and pointed to the neat pile of paperwork where she had been finishing writing checks for the few bills she didn't have on automatic pay. She laid the new envelope next to the stack and waved Renata into a chair. The round teak table with four ladderback straight chairs were the only antiques in the apartment, pieces she'd kept from Rebecca Schoopman. The story, whether true or not, was they had been handcrafted by Rebecca's great-grandfather after he gave up life as a fisherman.

Ruth carried the second mug of coffee and a bottle of creamer to the table and knew the expression on Renata's face. "What's on your mind?"

Her deep brown eyes were framed by stubby lashes and always looked directly at whomever she was talking to. "I understand what a shock it was for Rosalinde about her husband. She seems to be having problems sleeping and it looks like she's lost some weight. Has she said anything to you?" Renata's apartment was next door to Rosalinde; easy for her to notice a change in routine patterns.

"Not exactly," Ruth said. "There have been several things to deal with and when I invited her for lunch yesterday, she didn't have much to eat. Not that she's ever been a hearty eater, but I took her to Bojangles and all she wanted was a cup of gumbo, plus she didn't have more than a couple of bites of bread pudding. You know how we love that."

"The best in town," Renata agreed. "Any news from the detective?"

"No, and quite frankly, with all this time passed, I would be surprised if they find anything."

"Will Rosalinde be okay with that? Does she need an answer, or does she maybe feel guilty now thinking he'd deserted her?" Renata gave a bittersweet smile. "I only ask because as the primary secret-keeper here, you're the one she'll open up to. It isn't that I want to lay out my own past, but if the deeper part of my story can help, I'll share."

Ruth tapped her forefinger against the rim of the mug. The other women knew Renata's husband had died of a heart attack. The reason for, and weight of, guilt is what had come from one of the nights years before when an extra bottle of wine brought forth what had ultimately been an ability for Renata to mostly purge the festering emotion. She'd felt for too long that as a pharmacist, she should have worked harder to convince him to change bad habits, to insist he go to the doctor after he'd missed his annual check-up. To have seen signs or to have done something, anything to have prevented what happened.

"It hasn't been quite two weeks yet. I mean we already understood it couldn't have been the best of marriages if he had deserted her in the way she thought. And you know Rosalinde is the quiet one among us. I think she's processing everything in her own way."

"Fair enough," Renata said and lifted her mug. "I'm on at two o'clock at the pharmacy. You need me to bring you anything?" She'd cut her hours after starting to receive social security and worked three days a week, often taking the unpopular weekend shifts. With no family, her only insistence about her time was to have a morning swim. Her volunteer work at the church foodbank and thrift shop filled her other days.

"No, I'm good. By the way, I still have a couple of pork tenderloins in the freezer I need to use. I'll put dinner together for us tomorrow and we'll see if Rosalinde's appetite has returned."

"Sounds good. I'll bring those roasted Brussel sprouts she likes and we can ask Rochelle to make her chocolate raspberry cake."

Renata finished her coffee and Ruth washed both mugs. Rosalinde had said nothing more about her husband and marriage, choosing the least expensive option for cremation. She had commented she would decide later what to do with the ashes and Ruth suspected tossing them in the outgoing garbage might be a consideration. She shook her head at the somewhat un-Christian thought, walked back to the table, and opened the envelope Renata had given her. She sat heavily, clutching the single page. Was this possible?

Little Lauren? Lauren was here? She read the note out loud, trying to imagine a young woman. She realized her hand was trembling and she laid the paper on the table and smoothed it as her mind sped through more questions. A scam? If so, how? These things happened, didn't they? After all, the single photograph of the four-year-old child wasn't likely to resemble an adult. An adult of what? Thirty-four, thirty-five? Would someone else even know about the relationship? She read the words a third time. Simply written and she couldn't say the news of Deborah's passing was a surprise. The claim of no other family was probably correct considering part of Deborah's constant pleas for money was because she wasn't even certain of who Lauren's father was. She slowed her breathing and examined her initial disbelief. What Lauren wrote was reasonable. Hadn't she wanted something like this for years until she gave up hope for reconciliation? All right, what now? Assuming it was Lauren, she hadn't shown up on her doorstep, but rather made the overture in a way to make it easy to refuse. Wasn't that a positive sign? What would that have been like for her and had she brought the envelope in the night? Had she been waiting for hours wondering if a call would come?

Ruth shoved her chair back. This was ridiculous. Of course she wanted to see the girl – the woman, she corrected herself. She hurried to the side table to retrieve her cell phone from the charger and entered the number.

The voice that answered on the second ring was almost hushed. "Hello."

"Lauren? Is this Lauren? It's Ruth, Ruth Branden, your…" She suddenly stopped.

"Yes, it is me. I'm in the library. Please don't hang up, I need to walk outside."

Ruth breathed in and out slowly, for what couldn't have been more than a minute before the woman spoke again.

"Sorry. I didn't know if you would call, and I was using one of the library computers."

Hers was a pleasant voice. Did she sound like her mother? It had been too long ago for Ruth to remember. "Yes, I only read your note a few minutes ago. You're at the library? Have you had breakfast? Do you have a car? I can come pick you up if you don't."

"You will? And no, I mean, I had some cereal, but not a regular breakfast. No, I don't have a car. I came on the bus."

Ruth felt a flutter in her stomach – a sensation she wasn't expecting. "Okay, it will take me about twenty minutes to get there. I'll pull in front and am driving a silver Ford Fusion." She hesitated briefly. "I'm glad you're here." Wasn't she?

"I…I…, I am, too. Oh, I'm wearing blue jeans, a purple top, and I have short hair."

"Okay, see you soon." Ruth's hand was shaking again, and she shook it sharply. She went into the bathroom and looked into the mirror, realizing she was a bit flushed. She splashed cold water on her face and patted dry. A quick run through of the hairbrush and she was ready. Was she? Lauren said she was in jeans and they were only going to breakfast. There was no need to change from navy-blue twill slacks and the red and navy-blue striped knit top. She did swap flipflops for a pair of dark blue closed-toe slides and put on a pair of silver starfish earrings.

She turned the radio up as she drove, allowing the lyrics to Natalie Cole's, "Be Thankful," o tcrowd out anxious thoughts. The area in front of the library was open and a slender woman was standing to the left of the library's entrance. Ruth pulled up, took one more deep breath and got out, leaving the door open. She moved around the front of the car. "Lauren?" My God, she needn't have asked. Other than chestnut hair instead of strawberry blonde, had she been clothed in a 1930s dress, she could have passed for Ruth's mother. She had expected more a resemblance to Deborah.

The woman, maybe an inch taller than her, stepped forward, nodding her head. "Yes." She smiled shyly and extended her hand. "I'm Lauren."

Ruth hesitated only briefly before opening her arms. "I think a hug is more in order." It was quick, and Lauren stepped back again, the smile wider. "Thank you. Thank you for coming."

"Right. Well, if you have everything, let's go for that breakfast. Annabelle's is close to here and a locals' favorite."

"Sounds nice," Lauren said and opened the back door to place her backpack and purse in. "I haven't been many places yet."

Ruth switched the radio off and waited for her to settle into the passenger's seat. "You're at the Gulls Nest? There aren't many of the old motels left. The owners, Traci and Gary Norton, will probably retire in another few years and we'll see what happens then."

"It's nice. I haven't seen them, I don't think," Lauren said. "The guy, Clyde, is who I talked to yesterday."

"Clyde? Yes, another old-timer. We're a small town and you get to know people pretty well. It isn't a big city for sure."

Lauren turned from looking out the window. "It was a long trip, but I'm glad I took the bus. We went through lots of small towns on the way. I haven't ever really been out of New Orleans."

Annabelle's was barely five minutes from the library on a short side street connecting the Overseas Highway to Marlin Street which was a mixed use of residential and Buddy's Marina. Six houses were to the left and Annabelle's was the first building on the right beyond a vacant lot with a fading "For Sale" sign. Built of stucco covered concrete block construction with wide plate glass windows, Annabelle's was painted yellow, the insurance office next door a complementary green and the consignment shop as the third business in the row, was blue.

"She opens at 5:30 and is popular with the charter boats crews,"

Ruth said as they got out of the car. "Just breakfast and lunch, and everything is made from scratch."

"It smells delicious," Lauren said, looking around. The 1960s diner decor wasn't intended to be trendy; the black and white checkerboard linoleum, black Formica tabletops, stainless steel tables and chairs with black vinyl padded cushions were simply updated every six or seven years. Large photographs, many in black and white, were of different parts of Verde Key dating from the 1940s when Annabelle's family came to the area.

Three men were at the counter and since the main breakfast crowd had finished, all the tables by the windows were open. Ruth led Lauren to one and raised two fingers when Angela, the senior waitress, lifted a coffee carafe. "Oh, I mean, coffee is okay with you? Would you prefer something else?'

"That's fine," Lauren said and picked up the double-sided, plastic-coated menu. "Do you have a favorite here?"

"Omelets are a specialty, biscuits and pancakes are buttermilk, and even though it is morning, pies are great. The Hungry Man's Platter is enough to keep you going for a while. Thank you, Angela."

The broad-shouldered woman placed steaming mugs of coffee in front of them. An old-fashioned sugar canister was to the side, little cups of creamer in a bowl, packets of artificial sweetener in a black wire basket. "Haven't seen you for a couple of months now, Ruth. You and the others doing okay?"

"We're fine. And you?"

"The good Lord has given me another day. Can't complain," she said cheerfully. "You both know what you want?"

"This is Lauren, newly arrived," Ruth said and passed the menu to Angela. "I had breakfast earlier, so I'm going to ignore the clock and have a slice of lemon meringue pie.

Lauren gave a half smile. "Ham and cheese omelet with biscuits."

"Welcome to Annabelle's, young lady. Good choice for your first time. Cheddar or Swiss?"

"Cheddar, thanks."

Ruth hoped her voice sounded normal. "I'm sorry about your mother. I didn't know."

Lauren blinked green eyes, the same color as her grandmother – the woman she never had the chance to meet. "You couldn't have. It was… She uh, she never got well. Not for long anyway. I wasn't with her then."

Ruth didn't need to ask why. "I'm sorry for that, too. I imagine it was difficult for you."

Lauren spoke quietly. "I grew up fast. If you don't mind me saying so, you don't look much like her. If she had any photos, she didn't keep them."

"Deborah was the pretty one," Ruth said. "I mean, yes, we were different in a lot of ways," she added immediately. "Since you didn't see photos, your mother took after our paternal grandmother. Other than your hair being darker, you look a great deal like our mother, your maternal grandmother. She was strawberry blonde."

An expression Ruth couldn't identify flitted across Lauren's oval face. "No, there weren't any pictures." She glanced down at the mug, then up and steadied her gaze. "May I call you Aunt Ruth?"

"Yes of course. I'm sorry, I should have said that before. I…, I know we have so much to talk about. Let me say I am really glad you're here. I don't want to make you uncomfortable and I'm not sure of how much you want to tell me." As soon as she said the words, she realized they were true, and it was all she could do not to reach for the girl's – the woman's – hand.

Lauren's expression of relief was unmistakable, and she edged her hand forward. "Thank you, Aunt Ruth. I was hoping this could be a good start. I'm not asking for charity or anything though."

Angela approached with two glasses of water. "Food will be out in about five minutes. Guess y'all don't need more coffee yet."

Ruth smiled. "No, we got a little distracted. Oh, by the way, Lauren is my niece. She'll be staying for a while."

"Always nice to have family in." Angela winked at Lauren. "Your aunt's a fine lady and that trio with her makes for quite the crew."

Lauren withdrew her hand to finally take a sip of coffee. "The trio? It is a motel converted into apartments?"

"Yes. A lot of people call us the *Four R's*. In order of age, I'm the oldest. Rosalinde Newton is seventy-two, Renata Lopez is seventy, and Rochelle Sancerre is the *baby* at sixty-eight. The names are a coincidence and Rosalinde has been with me the longest, then Rochelle came and Renata about three years ago." She exhaled a breath. "What's checkout time at the motel? Noon?"

"Uh yes."

"Okay, I have the only two-bedroom, two bath apartment and the one not rented has become basically an extra storeroom. There's no reason for you to keep spending money on a motel if you don't mind a sleeper sofa until we get the other apartment cleared out. We'll eat, and get your things moved over. That will give you a chance to learn more about here, about how things are." She stopped at Lauren's widened eyes. "If you want to, I mean."

"I would really appreciate it and I'm handy with DIY stuff." Her voice pitched a little lower again. "We..., we moved around quite a bit and landlords weren't always helpful."

Ruth thought back to the plaintive words of her sister's few letters and how she'd refused to bring the child and come to Florida. She trusted her instincts and even though she was certain there was more than one reason for Lauren's decision to leave New Orleans, those reasons weren't important for now. "Between the four of us, we do have some skills, but an extra pair of hands is needed at times," she said instead.

"Biscuits right out of the oven and pie which is good any time of the day," Angela said, putting their plates on the table. "You eat up, young lady. We don't listen to people fuss about calories here."

Lauren laughed for the first time and unrolled her knife and fork wrapped in a paper napkin. "Yes ma'am. I don't think I'll be needing a doggie bag."

Ruth sliced her fork through the mound of meringue into the filling which she knew was made with a mix of three different types of lemon. As with most of the recipes, this one allegedly came from Anabelle's grandmother's kitchen.

The silence that falls when eating begins was comfortable and Ruth noticed Lauren ate with a good appetite. Was that usual or had she been skimping on meals? If so, that was something they could take care of. *Appetite* reminded her of Renata's comment earlier about Rosalinde. Maybe she should call and alert the women of the new arrival. No, she would put together a charcuterie tray for the "wine time" they often shared on the beach. That was the best way for them to meet and would give she and Lauren a few hours together to start getting acquainted. Despite the many questions she wanted to ask, she didn't know what personal boundaries might exist. Lauren seemed willing to share and she didn't want to risk sounding judgmental about Deborah or whatever choices Lauren had made for her life. She didn't imagine they had included much in the way of career options. Now was for going slowly, time hopefully to discover the niece was what she seemed and not more like her mother - God rest her soul…

CHAPTER TWELVE

Bev sat quietly in the well-worn brown leather armchair directly in front of Chief Taylor's desk waiting for him to finish reading the report. His adamant position hadn't changed about he would not have a computer in the office until the day before he retired and until then, damn it, he wanted paper. Processing quarterly reports was another of the administrative tasks she'd taken on when they were in between staff hires. Their low crime rate meant, in reality, she often had extra time for mundane requirements no one enjoyed. He scrawled his signature on the last page and tossed it into his otherwise empty out basket. He lifted his mug, stained dark inside. Any suggestion he allow it to be washed was met with the same view he had of computers. "If I'm going to be a dinosaur, might as well be one about everything," he once growled at a hapless temporary administrative assistant who wasn't familiar with his habits. Bev was still stunned when he did acquiesce to quitting smoking as the only gift his wife wanted for their fortieth anniversary.

His dour expression was not aimed at her or the report he pointed to. "You and Les make any headway on the cold case?"

"Not really," Bev said, trying to keep frustration under control. "The few connections we know have passed away, are not locatable, or figure he got what was coming to him and they don't care who did it." She brushed a strand of hair from her forehead. "I haven't given up on a couple of names – just not making progress."

The Chief grunted, his brown eyes fixed on her. "I know you aren't going to let this rest and as long as we got a light caseload, spend whatever time you want to. Forty-plus years ago things were different. All kinds of problems got solved in the middle of the night in some remote spot." He held up a hand before she could protest. "I'm not saying it should have been that way. You ask your dad sometime. He remembers how it was."

"Okay, but let's say this was a situation where Newton wasn't being a son-of-a-bitch, and another guy was. That means the other guy could still be out there somewhere confident he got away with murder."

The Chief rubbed a hand across his mostly bald head. "You could be right. In all my years doing this shit, there was one case I haven't been able to brush off. You find a way to deal with the bad shit early on or you find another career. Mostly, you come to accept human nature as it is. That bad shit happens to good people, otherwise good people lose control at times, and some bastards never pay for what they do."

In these rare occasions when the Chief was willing to share old stories, Bev listened. While she often disagreed with his conclusions and methods, he was a man who believed in justice. Harder in outlook than her father, they both nonetheless accepted her desire to be on the force and supported her when it was important.

Bev searched her memory and came up blank. "Is it a case I would be familiar with?"

"No, I was a rookie. Came on the force two years before your dad. Was on night patrol and got a call about gunshots heard in a neighborhood. Had more of that then than now, but this wasn't some out of control bar fight. It was the house of a leading citizen, a bank vice-president. The houses had big yards, neighbors not on top of each other. A few of them were in their yards, and we rolled into the driveway. Outside light was on, curtains drawn, but lights on downstairs, too. Quiet though, not a sound. No music, no dog barking. We rang the bell and knocked, the sergeant identified us, waited a few seconds and tried the door. It was unlocked and you could smell the gunpowder. We took out our pistols and the sergeant motioned me to come behind him. It didn't take long, both bodies were in the living room, blood all over the place, nobody else around." His voice dropped a pitch. "Mr. Bigshot was on the couch facing the television which was off. Shot in the chest and the face. The woman was lying face up on the floor next to a chair, wound to the temple, gun almost still in her hand. She was in her underwear – her clothes on the floor, neatly folded. He was fully clothed."

That sounded odd.

"There was a piece of paper on the end table next to the woman, hand printed. *He'll never stop and no one will believe me. I had to end it.*"

The Chief recited the words, his face tight. "The sergeant grabbed the paper and told me to get my ass outside to keep everyone away and wait for the detectives and ambulance." He paused. "It was my first homicide. Fact is, I stepped out and puked in the flowerbed." He pointed a blunt finger at her. "You know how it is. Anybody tell you they don't puke the first time at something like that is a liar or cold-hearted as they come."

Bev nodded, pushing away the brief flashback to her own experience – the seasoned sergeant who assured it was a normal reaction.

"It was a goddamn circus for a couple of hours. The Chief came. Turns out he and the guy were in Kiwanis together. ME knew him, too. Me and another cop were sent to get statements and by the time we got done, the bodies were being loaded into the ambulance." He paused again. "I was a rookie, but even then, I paid attention to detail. I only saw the woman for like thirty seconds and she had bruises, different shades on her upper arms, across her stomach, upper thighs."

"That's what she meant by the note?"

The Chief nodded. "Made sense. Except on the way back to the station I said something about that poor woman. The sergeant told me to not jump to conclusions – scenes like that can be confusing. The detective would handle it."

Bev thought she knew where the story might be going.

"So, the paper carries a piece about the tragedy of depression, how the well-respected guy had tried to help his wife through her emotional struggles and all that bullshit. The Mayor gives a quote about what a good man he was for the community and how he would be missed."

Bev flared at the idea. "She didn't have family who questioned anything?"

"No. She wasn't originally from here and like I said, no kids. The sergeant buttonholed me the next day and said I needed to correct my statement. How I probably couldn't be sure of what I thought I saw. I reminded him about the note and he shrugged that off. His angle was with both of them dead, no reason to get into extra details."

"Did you change it?"

"Hell, no. Like I said, the whole thing pissed me off. A few years later when I had some seniority, and the sergeant and Chief were retired I pulled the file. Her note was gone, my statement was gone, the ME didn't include any previous injuries in his report either. If photos had been taken of her whole body, they were gone."

Bev didn't try to hide her disgust. "Christ."

"Yeah. It was a clear case of murder-suicide, and the forensic evidence supported the ruling. And the guy didn't get away with it in the sense of she killed him, but everyone involved made sure the truth never came out. To this day, I'm not sure if anyone suspected and refused to believe it of him. Maybe not, maybe he was slick enough that no one had a clue."

"Which is what the wife wrote."

"Yeah." He waved his hand toward the door. "Hard to say about your dead guy. If he was running around on his wife, could be a jealous husband or boyfriend. Or maybe he got mixed up in shit with guys he couldn't handle. Whatever it was, maybe you're correct and somebody has gotten away with murder. Or everyone involved is dead, too. Don't let it get to you if you don't find an answer."

The session was obviously over and Bev took the signed report. Chief Taylor's brusqueness was no façade, and his high standards annoyed her the times he insisted she slow down on a case to ensure she double or triple checked facts. It was easy to forget he, too, had once been a rookie and his views had been shaped over the years. She wasn't surprised he'd refused to change his statement and could easily envision the "good old boys" who decided to alter the file. The woman feeling she had no recourse, no one to turn to for help. To see no other option was tragic enough. For her to stage the scene and write the note to at least finally be heard, and then be denied even that compounded the cruelty. That was the point to pursuing and trying to close cold homicide cases. Sure, perhaps Newton got himself into a situation with a predictable violent outcome. If so, the individual or individuals had escaped punishment. Perhaps Newton, despite what they'd been told about him, was genuinely a victim. If so, he especially deserved to have his story told.

CHAPTER THIRTEEN

Les walked into the office and Bev motioned him to not take off his suit coat. "Got a call," she said and pointed to the door.

Les dangled the keys still in his right hand. "Should I be glad I stopped by the bathroom before I came in?"

"Beau and Officer Alvarez are at a house on Royal Palm. Body, male, probably at least a day, might be longer. Looks like blunt force head trauma."

"Okay. It's been quiet for a while. Guess we were due. You know the neighborhood?"

Bev pushed out of her chair. "Yeah, it's bayside, not on the water though. Matter of fact, it's a few blocks from the old motel where Mrs. Newton lives."

"The one with the older women you were telling me about? All of them named Rose or something?"

Bev grinned. "Not quite. All their names do start with an *R*. My mother was filling me in the other night. Anyway, I was in with the Chief to get a report signed. He was reminding me we might not be able to crack our cold case."

Les managed to keep a straight face. "Did he use the term *don't obsess over it* by any chance?

"Not in so many words. Anyway, that's going to have to wait a bit now."

The street was across town, similar to where Bev and her brother had grown up. Three single-story, square houses left side, four on the right. Painted cinderblock in a mix of green, blue, and sand-toned, one rectangular window on the front right-hand wall, an overhang shading the door and a shallow porch. Terracotta tile roofs, carports, and front yards defined by hurricane fences. Storage sheds by some, all but two properties well-maintained. The address they pulled up at could use a fresh coat of paint, had scraggly palms with dead fronds clinging among green ones, the faded red Silverado truck in the carport was well past the point of needing to be washed.

Crime scene tape was up and Beau was waiting outside for them. He gestured toward the house to the left. "Officer Alvarez is checking the houses, but I don't think anyone else is at home. I thought you'd want to interview the neighbor who called it in – Mrs. Godowski. She had a key, went in, realized the situation, and called us immediately. Said she didn't touch anything or go close to the body. Deceased is Trevor Moore, wife has been in Fort Pierce for about two months, no children. The ME should be here in a few minutes."

Les paused before opening the door. "The neighbor explain why she checked on him?"

Beau looked at his notebook for the first time. "He usually goes to work around eight when she's out watering her plants. When she didn't see him two days in a row, she went over and knocked."

Bev was grateful the air conditioner was running. Even in spring, it would have been warm in a closed house and the musty smell would have been worse. In fact, she was mildly surprised stale cigarette smoke was almost as powerful. Shades were closed. Overhead light in the kitchen, the single table lamp next to the couch, open floor plan and tiled floor kept the room from darkness. The matching lamp was smashed on the tile floor, an end table on its side. The body was nearby face down, blood crusted in the short brown hair, soaked into the back of the shirt, not much on the floor.

They crouched on either side. "Looks like a blow to the left temple, too," Les said.

Bev surveyed the floor. A few cigarette butts and a lot of ash were scattered between the body and overturned coffee table. "Don't see an ashtray." Three empty Yuengling bottles had rolled in the other direction.

"Detectives, the ME is here," Beau called from the door before Les commented.

Donna Sweeny came into the room trailed by Luis Gonzalez, and a technician she didn't recognize. She seemed young. Donna stopped at the edge of the coffee table. "Okay to get more light in here? How much time do you need?"

Bev rose as Les lifted his hand in acknowledgement, still looking at the body.

"We're good for now. We'll go next door to talk to the woman who found him while you and your team get busy. Not sure if cause of death is as it seems. Time is going to be especially important. Know you won't be able to tell too much initially."

Donna nodded, no one feeling the need for pleasantries. "If you're not back by the time I finish, I'll find you."

Estelle Godowski's aqua house had none of the signs of neglect as the deceased. Coral rock in the yard had been bleached by years of sun, color provided in three islands of silver palms with white and pink ginger intermingled around the bases.

The white front door opened immediately and a plump woman a full head shorter than Bev motioned them inside. "Please come in. I've made coffee and have tea or lemonade if you prefer. Would you mind sitting at the table?" Her gray eyes blinked rapidly behind gold wire rimmed glasses and her voice quavered a bit understandably considering the circumstances. "Oh, I'm Estelle Godowski, but of course you probably know that."

"Yes, ma'am," Les said politely. "I'm Detective Martin and this is senior Detective Henderson. The table is fine, and coffee would be nice if it's no trouble."

Bev and Les had a standing agreement he would take the lead whenever an older witness was involved. In nearing retirement age, his ability to project the friendly, older image when needed or quickly switch to the jaded, "Don't keep giving me bullshit answers," during an interrogation was a skill Bev appreciated.

"And you, Detective Henderson, coffee, too?"

"Yes, thank you," Bev said and they noticed the plate of cookies – homemade from the shape. A yellow ceramic matching sugar bowl and cream pitcher were next to a stack of sunflower imprinted paper napkins. From her wavy, white hairstyle to her outfit of jade green slacks with a lighter green print short-sleeve top, and the orderly rooms they could see, everything about Mrs. Godowski indicated she was a woman who cared for her home and appearances.

"I must admit, I'm a little nervous," she said in almost a question as she placed blue coffee mugs in front of them. "I've never had anything like this happen."

"Of course," Les said warmly. "It must have been a shock for you."

"Oh my, yes. Oh, please, have a cookie. I made them yesterday."

Les, not breaking eye contact with her, reached for one. "Thank you, they look delicious."

Bev had her notebook on the table, pen ready. She could sip coffee and write but juggling a cookie at the same time was more difficult.

Mrs. Godowski seemed to relax a bit and Les guided her through the basic questions. She verified the deceased's wife, Alicia Moore, was in Fort Pierce with her mother who had suffered a stroke a few weeks ago. No, she didn't see any visitors to the house, but she was usually in bed by ten o'clock and was a sound sleeper. No, none of the other neighbors were likely to be home at this hour, she was the only retiree. Yes, the Moores were tenants and moved in about four years ago. She hesitated slightly in answering the question of how they were as neighbors.

"I, uh, well, I can't say we were close friends. Alicia is a lovely woman, and she's a dental assistant. She sometimes comes over for tea and a chat after dinner. They don't have children and…" She briefly dropped her eyes.

"Yes?" Les prompted quietly. "Did the couple have any problems you know of?"

"I don't want to seem as if I'm some kind of old busybody," she said reluctantly.

"Of course not," Les continued smoothly. "I would imagine it was helpful to Mrs. Moore to talk with you."

"Oh well, yes, I like to think so. You see, Trevor had different jobs, not staying in any of them very long. I think he is – was – doing construction now. And he was always one to go out with his friends drinking. I don't mean like he was an alcoholic or anything," she added quickly. "But, I guess the last seven or eight months it's been more than usual." She drank some coffee, perhaps to stop talking for a moment.

Bev didn't want to interrupt the flow. These were things they could ask the wife about.

Mrs. Godowski suddenly pressed her fingers to her lips. "Oh dear, I just realized. Poor Alicia. I'm not supposed to tell her, am I? I mean I have her number and have spoken to her like once a week."

"No, ma'am," Les said calmly. "We take care of notifying her and we would appreciate it if you will provide a number."

She pushed her chair back abruptly. "Oh, certainly. It won't take but a moment." There was an avocado green wall phone above the short counter next to the refrigerator. Mrs. Godowski stood over a notepad beneath the telephone.

Les spoke barely above a whisper. "Think the wife will be available to talk?"

"Hope so," Bev said and her phone buzzed with a text. Donna Sweeny was ready with her preliminary.

"Oh, there is one other thing I should mention," Mrs. Godowski said, handing a piece of paper to Les. "Trevor has – had – a half-brother who is here now. He hasn't been here long, and I gather they aren't close. She didn't say so exactly, but I don't think Alicia liked him."

Bev knew Les would be thinking the same thing as she was. "Do you happen to know his name or where he's living?"

Mrs. Godowski shook her head. "I'm sorry, no. I think it was Carl or Cal, something with a *C*. Alicia didn't say much other than Trevor had no idea he planned to come here. I suppose the way she said it was what gave me the impression. Then she changed the subject and didn't mention him again." She glanced down at her wristwatch and back to Les. "I hope you don't mind. My son lives in Key West and I'd like to call him. He's a teacher at the college and I want to talk to him before his next class."

Les stood and gave her a business card. "Yes, of course. You can reach us at this number if you think of anything else."

"Certainly, and please tell Alicia I'm here for whatever she needs."

"Let's hope the wife can fill in some blanks," Bev started and saw Donna outside stripping off her gloves. She was talking to the men with the gurney, body bag folded on top. She moved to let them take the gurney inside and stepped toward Bev and Les. "Rigor mortis is lessened. Initial estimate is around forty-eight hours. I'll get to it this afternoon. Being the clever detectives you are, you probably noticed there was no ash tray close by. If there was a heavy metal or glass one, it would likely make a good match to the wound. Based on the deep laceration, whatever was used had some kind of edge. Other possibilities are golf club, tire iron, large wrench, something similar. Photos and forensics will take another hour or so."

She waved her hand toward the street where another patrol car pulled in. "Plan on tomorrow morning unless I call otherwise." She grinned at Bev. "A couple of pastries to go with coffee would be nice."

"I'll keep that in mind," Bev said and noticed Officer Alvarez had joined Beau with the two new arrivals.

Les tapped the face of his watch. "You want another check inside and I'll tell Beau what to search for? They can start in the carport and yard. We need to try to reach Mrs. Moore, too."

"Yeah, let's do that at the station. The Chief will want a brief."

He gave her a silent thumbs up and she hurried into the house. With more time to look around, lack of housekeeping was apparent. Mail scattered on the table, trashcan in the kitchen full. Dried spills on the counters, dirty dishes left in the sink, tile floor in need of broom and mop. She noticed the cell phone next to the mail and called over to the technician. "You dust the phone yet?"

He lifted his head from the bookshelf they were concentrating on. Books and other items where on the floor, little remaining on the top and middle shelves. "Yes. Checked and it's password protected."

"Okay, thought we might catch a break there. Go ahead and bag it then."

The team was experienced and reaching Mrs. Moore was the priority. Les was waiting beside the sedan. "A couple of hours should do it for the search. You ready?"

"Yeah. I'll try Mrs. Moore and you take the Chief?"

"Sure. I never mind passing on notifications."

She half smiled. "You do your share." She didn't like the idea of doing this by phone, but they needed information if Mrs. Moore was up to it. She would only ask the Fort Pierce police to make a visit If they couldn't reach her.

Forty-five minutes later, they closed the door to the office. Mrs. Moore had taken the news with no more than slight hesitation, her voice strained. She'd asked for a video call as it was close to time for the physical therapist to come for a session with her mother and there was preparation to do first.

The woman on the screen had no distinguishing features, light brown hair pulled back, brown eyes, somewhat puffy either from crying, fatigue, or more likely both. She wore no make-up and if she was in the same age range as her husband, she was in her early forties.

"Thank you for waiting," she said after Bev offered her condolences again. "I am shocked of course. I haven't called Estelle. What can you tell me?"

Bev explained the sequence of events and Mrs. Moore asked if they would notify Carl, Mr. Moore's half-brother. "They weren't close. They hadn't been in touch for at least ten years and Trev didn't know he was moving to Verde Key. Other than the first time, he hasn't been to the house. They, uh, when they meet it's mostly at Skipper's." She provided his number and her expression and tone suggesting she had nothing more to add about him.

Bev pictured the mess in the den and potential murder weapon. "Mrs. Moore, do you have a large ashtray on your coffee table?"

The woman looked startled at the question. "Uh, yes. Trev used to be good about smoking outside. Not long ago, he started smoking in the house even though he knew I hated it. There's this clunky, square metal ashtray almost as big as my hand. Trev's grandfather was a welder, and it was something he made. Trev's father gave it to him."

Bev suspected the ash tray would not be found in the house and she eased into asking if Mrs. Moore could think of anyone who might want to harm him.

She glanced away, shoulders slumping, sighed, and her eyes were distressed when she faced the screen and spoke. "Detective, there's no reason for me to waste your time. Had my mother not had her stroke, I might be here with her anyway. Things have not been good between Trev and I for almost a year. He lost a good job and hates the one he has – had. He's at Skipper's a lot and quite frankly, he might as well not be at home. He would eat dinner and sit in front of the television drinking, falling asleep in his chair half the time. I tried, I really did. He accused me of nagging and says – said – it would all work out. Just like with smoking inside again, it was if he doesn't – didn't – care anymore about me. I've been so busy with mother, who thank God, is recovering well, that we've hardly spoken at all since I arrived." She pressed her fingers to her eyes momentarily. "I'll have to make arrangements for her before I leave. Do I need to come back right away?"

"It will be at least two days, perhaps three before the Medical Examiner will release the body," Bev said quietly. "Mrs. Godowski said to tell you she would help with anything she can."

"God bless her, she's a dear." She held up her wrist and tapped the face of her watch. "The therapy session with my mother will be over in a few minutes. Is it all right if I go?"

"Yes, ma'am. You have our number if you think of anything else."

They disconnected and Bev exhaled, ready for another cup of coffee. Unless she hired someone and was an accomplished liar at least they could eliminate the wife as a suspect. She punched in Carl Moore's number. It rang five times and the automated message informed her the mailbox had not yet been set up. Great, Mrs. Moore didn't know where he was living.

Rather than coffee, if Moore was a regular at Skipper's and the brother was known there, too, they might be able to learn as much as in talking with any of the neighbors. Les might want to grab lunch and they would pass his favorite sub shop on the way. She could make do with a power bar, but Les had pointed out more than once unless they were in hot pursuit of a suspect, taking twenty minutes to gobble a sandwich wouldn't cause a case to go cold. Les could drive and she'd call their order in.

She'd predicted his response correctly and after his equally predictable order for an Italian, extra provolone, no onions, they were at Skipper's within half an hour of leaving the station. Bev had been in the place maybe once before for a friend's birthday. The weathered gray rectangular wooden building sat on an odd, pie-shaped property so beachfront on the bay was barely twenty feet, if that. Intended for locals, the simple blue painted sign was above the door, nothing eye-catching about the neon beer signs in the single front window to the left. Only a few vehicles in the parking lot was to be expected at this hour on a workday and two men sat side-by-side at the bar, an older man at the far end underneath the television turned low to a Marlins game. The two looked briefly at Bev and Les and nodded before re-starting their conversation. The man at the end didn't bother.

The bartender motioned them to the center of the bar, his hands braced against it. Bev put him in his early fifties, broad shoulders, big hands, not much paunch. His black hair was full, pulled back into a short ponytail, brown eyes with beginnings of creased lines, and a nose no doubt broken at least once. "You don't look like you're off-duty, so I'm figuring detectives?" His voice was deep, not the rasp of a smoker though. "Butch Sanders. Get you anything?"

Bev made the introductions. "Looking for information about Trevor Moore and his brother Carl if you can help."

"Trevor's been a regular about four months now. That brother of his not long. The boys got themselves into trouble?"

Bev and Les angled themselves to have their backs to the other patrons although the man watching the television didn't seem interested. "When is the last time you saw them?"

"Trevor hasn't been in as much the last week. Carl was here two nights ago with a guy I didn't recognize. Something happen?" He held up a hand before they could comment. "Of course, you wouldn't be here otherwise. Let's go to a back table." He glanced at the three men and none seemed to need a refill.

He walked a step ahead and sat where he could talk to them and see the bar. "Trevor?"

"He was found dead this morning," Bev said quietly. "We aren't able to reach his brother."

"Shit. His wife back? She's been gone for a while. Away helping her mother, I think."

"Yes, we've spoken with her. Going back to Mr. Moore. What can you tell us about him and his brother?"

"Like I said, Trevor's been coming here about four months. Working a job site close to here and lives close enough to be back after dinner at least a few nights a week. Drinks draft mostly. Watches TV, plays pool sometimes, doesn't cause trouble. My impression is he's avoiding being at home. You get to where you can tell the type."

"The brother?"

Sanders frowned. "Asshole, if you'll pardon me saying so. Whiney, weaselly, thinks the world's against him attitude. Always leaning on Trevor to buy his drinks. Not sure Carl has a job, at least not a steady one. They may be half-brothers actually."

Bev liked his willingness to talk without trying to pump them for information. "Have you seen Mr. Moore in trouble with him or anyone else?"

"Naw – it's not that kind of place." He suddenly snapped his fingers. "Hold on. Carl had some cash on him for a change and he was huddled over at a table with whoever the other guy was for about half hour, looking kind of like business. The other guy left, and Carl came to the bar for another drink. It was busy, so didn't talk to him."

Interesting. A text pinged into Les's phone. The way he grabbed it caught Bev's attention. He took a card from his front shirt pocket and handed it to Sanders while simultaneously sliding his phone to Bev, and standing. "Thank you for your time, Mr. Sanders," he said.

Sanders stood and thumped the card against his hand. "Sure thing, but if you have one more minute? Not about Trevor. Ed Newton, the guy found in the water? The one in the paper?"

They were both startled. "Yes? You knew him?"

"Not exactly. Way back when I started, I was at Half-Mast. A kid really, so did clean-up, stocking. Played ball in high school – didn't mind breaking up fights. That was a place hardly got through a night without one." He cleared his throat. "Anyway, it was just a summer job. Thing is, Nick Black was tight with Ed and he's been gone for a long time. Blew back into town and comes by here occasionally. Figure no one else except Ed's wife remembers him. I don't know where Nick is staying, but I can call you if he does come in."

Huh, that was a nice change considering what little they had been able to track down. "Yes, thanks," Bev said, anxious to return to the Moore's. Beau's text said a neighbor was in from work and had information. She hoped it included an address for Carl Moore.

CHAPTER FOURTEEN

Beau was standing in the driveway of the house across the street and one up from the Moore's, next to a red Ford F-150. The man he was talking to was a few inches shorter, stocky and balding, wearing jeans, a red crewneck shirt, and sneakers.

"Rodney Blankenship," he said, holding out his hand, his brown eyes somber. "Hell of a thing. Does Alicia know?"

"Yes, we've spoken with her," Bev said. "Do you know the Moores well?"

"Lived here for years, they moved in a while back. Mostly to say hello in passing, we've swapped tools now and then. Alicia does a lot of baking and brings things around to share sometimes."

"You know the brother though? And saw him?"

Blankenship pointed to the Moore's. "Not exactly. I'd seen the car come a few times and about a month ago, Trevor and Carl – I didn't know his name before – were out in the drive and I was in the yard doing some work. It was obvious they were having an argument. Voices were raised. Not loud enough to hear what they said and all of a sudden, Carl shoved Trevor pretty hard, shook his fist, jumped in his car and peeled out." He scratched his jaw. "I walked over to see if everything was okay, and Trevor said he was all right. Just his half-brother being a pain in the ass – nothing he couldn't handle."

"You saw Carl the other night?" Beau prompted.

"Yeah, night before last. I was late putting the trash bin out. Fell asleep watching TV and it was a little after midnight. Carl's Camaro went past me, and I didn't think too much about it, but that is the first time I'd seen him since that day. The day I was telling you about, I mean."

Les spoke up. "You said he drives a Camaro. Anything special about it?"

"Yellow. I'd say seven, maybe eight years old, in good shape. Still has South Carolina plates on it."

That would be helpful. "Do you know where he lives by any chance?"

Blankenship shook his head. "Sorry, no." He hesitated for a moment. "Listen, my wife told me Alicia's been up taking care of her mom. If she needs us to do something here, we'll be glad to. Hell of a thing for her to have to deal with."

"Thank you for your help," Bev said. "We'll pass that on." She noticed Beau had stepped away, turned his back and was on the phone. The three of them walked back to the Moore's where Alvarez was waiting at the patrol car, the rest of the team gone. Bev faced Beau. "You called the Camaro in?"

"Yeah, shouldn't be that many around town if he's here."

Bev held up her phone and Les nodded to the unspoken question. Between what they'd learned at Skipper's and from Blankenship, they would start with the formal death notification to Carl Moore and take it from there. "Okay, we'll head to the station and put in a search using his cell phone number. That will get us close."

A quick response on location and the apartment manager living on-site had them knocking on Moore's door sooner than she expected. Bev understood the bartender's description of reminding him of a weasel as soon as he reluctantly invited them into his second-floor studio. Thin face, a pointed chin, narrow brown eyes, stained teeth and fingertips of a chronic smoker. Odors in the apartment hovered on stench with dirty dishes stacked in the sink and on the short counter between the small stove and refrigerator. Empty pizza boxes and beer bottles covered the top of the bistro table against the far wall. The shade to the single window was drawn, the light over the kitchen sink cutting through the dim.

Moore swept clothes from the sofa, mumbled for them to have a seat and took the mismatched chair angled to the left. He reached for a cigarette from the half-full pack next to the blue ceramic ashtray on the coffee table strewn with empty chip packages and a glass with dark liquid in it. "What's this about?"

"We're sorry for your loss, but your brother Trevor was found dead at home this morning," Bev said quietly.

"Half-brother," he said with his eyes shifting immediately away from hers. "Heart attack or something?"

"I'm afraid not. He was murdered and a neighbor found him this morning."

Moore lit the cigarette, inhaled deeply and exhaled, no evidence of shock. "That bitch he's married to get back and smash him upside the head or something?"

Bev didn't need to look at Les to know how he was reacting. These were the times when being effective meant holding in her feelings. "There's reason for you to think that?"

He shrugged. "Probably not for real. I mean, they were having some trouble, but maybe not like that. With her being gone, maybe it was like a break-in gone bad. Was he shot?"

"When was the last time you saw him?" Bev asked instead.

Another puff of the cigarette. "Like last week. Don't remember the day. We were at Skipper's for a few beers."

"You didn't go to his house?"

"Nope, no reason to. Alicia on her way back to take care of all this?"

Bev kept his attention on her to allow Les to watch him closely. "We have spoken with her and she'll be in soon. We hate to ask at a time like this, but we do need to know where you were night before last."

He straightened and waved the cigarette in an arc. "Me? Me, I was here all night. Had a pizza, watched the Marlins game, didn't feel like going anywhere."

"You were alone?"

His voice tightened. "This place look like I've been having company? Yeah, I was alone."

Bev didn't change her tone. "Can you think of anyone who might have a grudge against your brother? Anyone he was having problems with?"

"Half-brother," Moore said again, refusing to meet her eyes. "His boss was an asshole – don't know about anyone else. I haven't been here all that long."

"You came from South Carolina? Why did you decide to move here?"

He shrugged again, grinding out the half-smoked cigarette and reaching for another. "Things weren't working out for me and I needed a change. Thought this was good a place as any. Figured Trev might have connections for a job or something. Probably move on again, haven't decided yet."

Obviously, no sentimentality for family and the smoke was starting to irritate her eyes. She rose and passed him a card. "Again, we're sorry for your loss. If you remember anything, please call or come by the station."

He heaved from the chair, cigarette in hand. "Yeah, sure."

Neither spoke until they were standing at their car parked next to the yellow Camaro. The inside looked much like the apartment with littered floorboards in back, a full ashtray, and an empty Pepsi bottle on the passenger's seat.

"Not likely the neighbor misidentified the car," Les said glancing around the mostly empty lot. He pointed to a dumpster sitting at the far end. "Knowing he's lying to us won't get probable cause for a search warrant for his apartment or car, but the dumpster is fair game."

The patrol guys will love this. "If it was the ash tray Mrs. Moore described, tossing it into the water somewhere would make more sense."

"Neighbor said it was after midnight when he saw the car and there's no water on the way from the Moore's or near here. Dumpster wouldn't be the best place, but Carl doesn't strike me as a careful planning kind of guy."

"Good point, and if the team is really public about it, that could make him nervous."

Les had his phone out to call Beau when Bev's rang. "Detective Henderson."

"Detective, this is Alicia Moore. I hope I'm not disturbing you."

"No ma'am, this is fine. What can I do for you?"

"I've made arrangements for my mother and will start early tomorrow morning to drive down. I don't think I can drive straight through but will get there are quickly as I can. Estelle said I should stay with her until…, well, for a few days. There is something you should check though. God knows we didn't have much money around the house, and I have what little nice jewelry I own with me. There is this old baseball card."

"What card, ma'am?"

"I don't know exactly. It's a card Trev's father had in one of those clear plastic cases. It should be on the bookcase in the den with some books and magazines. Trev always claimed it was valuable and if we waited another ten years, it would be more valuable." She hesitated. "I just can't think of why anyone would want to hurt Trev, but I mean, other people might know about the card and maybe it was a robbery?"

"We're looking at all possibilities. Thank you for telling us," Bev said, her pulse quickening. Les looked at her curiously. "Hold off on the dumpster for now and let's go back to the Moore's. We may have motive, and if so, we have the neighbor seeing the car, and the bartender talking about Carl having money. It's a little thin, but Judge Pickett might be persuaded to give us a warrant."

She explained as Les drove, and he turned his head slightly when they passed a convenience store close to the side street of the Moore's neighborhood. "Wonder if their cameras reach to the street?"

"Could be. I'll call the station and get someone on it." The next call was to Mrs. Godowski who agreed to go over and unlock the house after Bev assured her she didn't need to go in. At nearing four o'clock, more cars and trucks were parked at homes although no one was outside.

Mrs. Moore had asked about the state of the house and Bev provided the name of a crime scene clean-up company. Bev had been in high school with the owners. Professional and responsive, if Mrs. Moore called them, they would be able to come in quietly at night and save her from the disturbing sight she would otherwise have to deal with. They went straight to the three-shelf bookcase to the left of the desk. Paperbacks in a mix of fiction and non-fiction were interspersed with stacks of DVDs, and old magazines.

"Look," Les said, his finger resting on the edge of the middle shelf with a small rectangle of dust-free space between copies of *Sports Illustrated* and four different books about baseball. "I'd say about four by six inches. That would fit a protective plastic case like I would use for a valuable baseball card if I had one."

Bev snapped photos of the bookcase and a close-up of the blank spot. "Okay, let's check the obvious places. He might have put it somewhere else for some reason. They moved quickly through the desk, drawers in the open areas and bedroom, boxes in the closets.

"The Chief should still be at the office," Bev said. "He might be willing for us to contact the judge with what we have." A text pinged in from Officer Alvarez as Les was parking at the station. *Video has subject vehicle passing at 12:23 a.m. morning in question. Will have copy within hour.* Bev unbuckled her seatbelt and smiled grimly. "Corroboration the little weasel lied to us."

Chief Taylor placed the call to the District Attorney and put them on speaker. He sat quietly while Bev went through their list. The DA didn't hesitate. "Unless you think he's a flight risk, I'll go to the judge first thing in the morning. As soon as you personally watch the video, write up the info and send it all over. I'll be here at least another two hours anyway."

"You don't need me for the rest of this," the Chief said. "Doesn't sound like you gave this guy reason to be suspicious, but if he is guilty, he might pack up and go. More likely, he'll be another idiot and figure he's smarter than us. To be on the safe side, tell Kevin to have tonight's shift keep watch for the vehicle on their rounds and have a patrol go by the apartment on the hour. Go ahead and get the stuff to the DA."

Les went to the refrigerator in their office and took out a Diet Coke for Bev, Sprite for himself. "Think we can knock this out pretty quickly, or do we need to order dinner?"

Bev popped the tab on the cold can. "Tell you what. I'll watch the video, take care of everything for the DA and you go talk to Kevin. In addition to patrols, he can set up the teams for the morning for the search. Apartment, car, and the dumpster."

"Works for me," he said. "Pam is making chicken cacciatore tonight and has invited the neighbors. It will be nice if I'm not late again. See you in the morning. Should be a busy day."

The shot of Moore's Camaro was clear and she silently thanked the quality and range of the camera. In sending the information to the DA, she did a mental review. Barring known enemies of a victim, statistically speaking, spouses, other family members, and friends were logical individuals to suspect. The risk was focusing too closely and overlooking other possibilities. While what they had was circumstantial, and there were several reasons for Moore to lie about where he was the night of the murder, or for him to claim he simply made a mistake about the date, they were justified in doing a search. If it turned up nothing, it was still early in the investigation.

"Hey, gorgeous," Kyle said by way of greeting on the phone. "You at the office?"

"Yeah, been a hell of a day and tomorrow is likely to be another one."

"Well, if we get a table in the corner at the Macaw, you can tell me about it over dinner, or I'm close and can pick up carryout to bring home." What's better for you?

She had come in early and if Kyle stopped for dinner, she could change into tights and a tee shirt and have a glass of wine while she was waiting. "Cajun shrimp and pasta again for me does sound good," she said, thinking of the blackened shrimp and flavorful cream sauce. I have about another twenty minutes here."

"I'm on it. See you back at the house," he said, his voice making her smile. There were moments when she wondered how it was a job opportunity in Verde Key was available at the time he was considering leaving Chicago. Even though she didn't necessarily believe in fate, who was to say for sure?

CHAPTER FIFTEEN

Bev read through the confession again, Carl Moore's public defender setting up a meeting with the DA to discuss a plea bargain.

Warrant in hand, Moore hadn't been up for long, awake enough to loudly protest their action. Finding the 1935 Quaker Oats Premium Photo Babe Ruth card wrapped in a shirt in the not very clever spot of a gym bag under a pile of dirty clothes in his closet made his first claim his brother had given it to him easy to deflect. That was enough to take him into custody and begin interrogation after waiting for the lawyer to appear.

Swabs from dark stains in the trunk of the Camaro, suspected to be blood, were rushed to Donna Sweeny to be confirmed as a match for Trevor Moore. No luck with the dumpster in producing the murder weapon, but in describing what they assumed happened, Moore's body language was not difficult to interpret.

Les sent Bev from the room ostensibly for coffee and switched on "good cop." He talked about how difficult family relationships could be, especially if their father had always favored the older brother. Unfair, really and if Carl had come to Verde Key looking for help because he was a little down on his luck, and Trevor was turning him away, anybody could understand his frustration. The lawyer, sensing the proper emotional button had been pushed, tried to stop Moore from talking. No, goddamn it, it was time somebody did listen to him. It was Trevor's mother who had run off and left them, his mother the one who came in taking care of everyone. Okay, maybe he was kind of a sickly kid, but it wasn't his fault. Maybe he didn't grow out of it and wasn't the sports type like Trevor or good with his hands, but that was no reason to constantly put him down, make him feel like he would never be worth anything. Later, when Trevor left, and finally a chance for their father to pay attention to him, it was too late. Their father had started drinking more, becoming impossible for anyone to please. Where the hell was Trevor when that was happening? Who could blame his mother for taking up with another guy and running off? How did he get stuck with the old man? Why should he have stayed around?

Watching from the adjacent room through the one-way mirror with the Chief, Bev sent Beau in with the promised coffee, not wanting to interrupt the flow. She almost felt sorry for the attorney who waited out another fifteen minutes of Moore chronicling life's injustices. Les sympathetically assured him he understood he didn't mean to kill Trevor – an argument that got out of hand. Yeah, okay, they'd argued and yeah, they'd been drinking some. He hardly remembered grabbing the ashtray, not really. It was like he couldn't control himself and then, well, what was he supposed to do? He had as much right to that goddamn card as Trevor. The ashtray? Yeah, okay, he'd thrown it in the trunk of the Camaro. What? He didn't know what to do. He drove around for a little while. There was a dumpster in that park. The one near the school.

Bev called the publics works department, relieved to hear the dumpster wasn't scheduled to be emptied until Friday. Confessions could aways be recanted so the more physical evidence the better.

Les, modest about handling the interview, had gone out after for sandwiches, needing fresh air. Bev researched the value of the stolen card and found prices between six and seven thousand dollars. Jesus, killing his own brother – okay, half-brother – for seven grand and no expression of remorse. His lawyer would probably try to explain to Moore that remorse was something judges wanted to hear.

"I brought cookies, too," Les said holding a second bag in his left hand. "I put an extra box in the break room. The search team deserves it."

"Yeah, going through dumpsters isn't the best part of anyone's day." Bev remembered drawing the duty once or twice in her rookie years. "As shit as this case was, at least we have answers for Mrs. Moore. Glad she told us about the card. Saved a hell of a lot of time. Oh, he had wrapped the ash tray in the shirt he must have been wearing. Plenty of blood on it, too."

Les removed sandwiches and chips. "Why not? If he'd been stopped for some reason, a shirtless guy driving around at one a.m., wouldn't be unusual here."

"True," Bev said and swung away from the computer screen, her always tidy desk providing a space for yet another lunch eaten in the office. "Hey, how was the cacciatore last night?"

"Excellent. Pam's maternal grandmother was a young Italian war bride. Came over in the 1940s. We couldn't afford much of a honeymoon, but we did go for our twentieth anniversary. Little village near Salerno. Talk about great food. You ever been to Italy?"

"Haven't made it to Europe, but we've discussed a trip for our fifth maybe. Probably start in Scotland though. Kyle's mother was a McKinley and even though it doesn't sound like it, Henderson is Scottish. My Aunt Lorna did some research and guess that side of the family came over after the debacle at Culloden. Seems they settled in Virginia and some eventually came this way. Apparently available records are sketchy. This now exhausts my knowledge of the subject."

He grinned. "The Whisky Trail awaits you if you can swap from bourbon to single malt."

She laughed and sprinkled salt and pepper on the turkey club sub. "Kyle did several years ago. I tried. Can't appreciate it enough to justify the cost. Plus, we mostly do beer and wine."

Completing the Moore paperwork meant the case was closed within forty-eight hours, at least from their side. Under the circumstances, she didn't think there would be complications for the DA either. She was working a kink out of her neck when a call rang through. "Detective? This is Butch Sanders from Skipper's. If you want to come over, old Nick Black is here. He's the guy I was telling you about who was tight with Ed Newton."

What a day this was turning out to be. "Thanks, I will." At least she finished the report. She pushed away from the computer. "That was the bartender from Skipper's. The guy who was supposedly good friends with Newton is there, but this may be a waste of time. No need both of us going."

Les nodded. "You never know. Maybe he's been harboring a guilty secret for forty years. Two confessions in one day would be a hell of a coincidence. Call if you change your mind and need back-up."

She grinned and grabbed her purse from the desk drawer. Considering what little Rosalinde had told her, if Black had been close to Newton, he might have a suspect or two in mind. Even if Newton had run off with a woman that could lead to a jealous husband or boyfriend. They were coming up on four o'clock with a dozen or so vehicles in the parking lot. She removed her sunglasses and paused inside the front door to let her eyes adjust. Sanders inclined his head to the right where the same gray-haired man who'd been at the far end watching a Marlins game was in what she assumed was his more-or-less reserved spot, the only difference was the Rays were playing.

The man two seats from him had thinning white hair, slightly hunched shoulders that were probably broad once and a moderate paunch. Bev made the "give him another round" sign and slid onto the wooden stool to his left, as he turned toward her, his full lips in a smirk. Hooded brown eyes, leathered skin. His graveled voice was not unexpected. "At least cops are better-looking than they used to be. Didn't know they had lady detectives unless you're off-duty." He lifted the whiskey glass to his lips with his left hand and shot the bird at Sanders with his right. "Dipshit."

"Fuck you, too, Nick," Sanders said conversationally, setting the fresh drink in front of him and a glass of club soda with a slice of lime for Bev. "Detective Henderson," she said quietly. "I understand you were friends with Edward Newton."

"Eddie? Yeah. What a shit thing to find out about him. Can't say I was surprised."

Bev nodded her thanks to Sanders who moved out of hearing range as Black drained his glass and jerked his thumb over his shoulder. "Might as well go to a table long as you're buying. Knew Eddie never ran off with a broad." He swiveled to the right, gesturing to the table where Sanders had previously led them. "Read the newspaper piece. Not much to go on. His wife still here?"

"She is. She was convinced her husband deserted her."

"Never figured that mousey thing could have killed him and not likely she'd tell you her brother did, is it? Guess he must not be alive if you're talking to me."

"He's not. How much do you know?"

"Not what you want," he said flatly. "Sure, Eddie screwed around on his old lady, but didn't care enough about running off with any of them. Me and him were at Fat Jack's on a Tuesday it was. Didn't think anything of not seeing him for a day or two, then it didn't add up. No cell phones in those days and went by the Half-Mast in case he was hanging over there. Nobody seen him, but guy he worked with was there and said he was just gone. Pissed the boss off when he called Eddie's wife to see when he was coming in. Guess that's how the bullshit started about him leaving with some broad. Makes sense she would have told him that. Good story, right? Other people were willing to believe it."

Bev didn't miss the use of *any of them* to describe Newton's behavior. "No missing person report was filed."

Black shrugged. "First, I wasn't his fucking wife. Second, if I was sure it was his brother-in-law, I might of gone to the cops. Fact is, Eddie got a little stupid over something and he was messing around with some shit that could be very bad for your health. I wasn't about to get involved by asking questions or having it known I'd talked to cops."

After coming up blank on all fronts, his information was as close as they'd come to useful details. "Tell me about the brother-in-law first."

"Can't say I remember his name. Worked down *Richmond's Marina*. Comes in Fat Jack's one night – seven eight months before Eddie disappeared. We were shooting pool and this guy storms in, grabs Eddie by the shirt, gets in his face, calls him a son-of-bitch, and tells him to start treating his sister right. Eddie tells him to fuck off and they throw a couple of punches. You don't come into Jack's like that, you not a regular. Three or four guys pulled them apart and threw the asshole out. He yells something like, *you keep this shit up and you'll be sorry*. Eddie bought everybody a beer and said forget about it."

"Mr. Newton was abusing his wife?"

"Didn't know, didn't care. Not my business. So anyway, if Eddie was killed, figured the brother-in-law was good for it."

"And the other?"

Black rattled ice in his glass. "Thirsty work, remembering shit like this."

Bev half-turned in the chair and signaled Sanders. Black's memory of events had enough sound of truth to be worth the price of a second drink.

"Yeah, well, to each their own and Jack's was a place where different shit went down. Eddie didn't mind extra cash and let's just say, he was willing to provide transportation services at a price." He was quiet until he exchanged glasses with Sanders.

"Drugs."

"Never asked for details. Told him once it was fucking stupid and he told me to fuck off. It wasn't regular – he was more like a back-up. So, could he have gotten crossways somehow? People like that, don't take much."

"Same people still operating?"

Black barked a harsh laugh. "After forty years? You don't last in that business. You walk away rich or…, well, territory changes hands and it ain't because of some corporate merger. I been away a long time, Half-Mast and Jack's are gone, too. Don't know who does what anymore."

The name Richmond's Marina as where the brother-in-law worked suddenly clicked for Bev. That was the marina she and Les had been in for the O'Hara case and attempted theft of the classic Shelby Mustang. "You planning to stay around?"

Black shrugged. "Haven't decided. Place has changed a lot. Too crowded for my taste. May head back to the islands."

Bev was glad he seemed to have given her all she would get and laid a card on the table. Meeting with him the same day as Carl Moore was stretching her tolerance to the limit. She needed a hot shower to wash off the feeling and a cold beer to get the bad taste out of her mouth. "Thanks for the information. If you think of anything else, give me a call."

He held his glass up in a mocking salute.

She attempted to give Sanders a twenty on her way out and he shook his head. "One of the guys here was on the force for a while and still listens to a scanner. He came in for lunch and told us what he heard. Sounds like you and your partner made quick work on who killed Trevor. He didn't deserve what happened to him."

"True. Thanks for the call about Mr. Black."

"He was part of the old crowd. Always pretty rough. Everybody minded their own business and if deals got made, they didn't get talked about. Hey, come on back some time when it's not business. We don't do fancy, but Reynaldo's conch fritters are good as anybody's."

She smiled in answer, stood outside for a minute next to the sedan to do a couple of shoulder rolls and debated about calling Les. He might have gone home early and they could wait until morning to talk.

It wouldn't take long for her to add to her notes and the whiteboard. Black's belief about Newton's brother-in-law was reasonable and in thinking back to Zeke Richmond, he might remember the man. Black was correct, too, if Newton had been involved on any level with drugs. As Les pointed out when they found the body, the location was ideal for clandestine meetings. The Chief and her father would know who the main players were back then. She'd heard enough stories to know someone on the fringes could easily get in over his head with people who wouldn't hesitate to dump one more body into midnight waters. While the person making the decision was more likely to have Newton killed than do so personally and that individual probably wasn't still around, underlings might be. If so, those same underlings forty years later might have risen up in the hierarchy. Lots of "ifs" in this scenario, but plausible.

CHAPTER SIXTEEN

Lauren flipped the Closed sign on the door of Adventures Below and turned off the lights in the dive shop. At six o'clock, with the wide front windows and open retail space, there was enough light to complete the few close-out tasks. She could faintly hear Danny in the tank room getting ready for the morning's dive. She'd processed eight divers, all from different states and one couple from England. Learning how to register people hadn't been difficult to learn, handling the sales of items was no different than ringing up drinks. Her biggest concern when Renata mentioned her friend Walt was looking for someone to work in the shop was she knew nothing about scuba diving other than what she'd seen on an occasional television show. Assured a reliable individual was the most important thing, she felt obligated to at least go talk to him. The three other "R's" who lived in the complex had been so welcoming and generous, the chance for a job was another piece seemingly falling into place almost by magic. Not yet ready to believe in fairy godmothers, there were moments she would awaken in early morning hours wondering if everything was for real.

The remaining apartment was used for storage with each of the women insisting they'd intended to go through it for years and clear out their assorted items. Mismatched furniture and housewares still serviceable given to Lauren, boxes of clothes finally delivered to the thrift shop, filled trash bins, and a few bulk things taken by people out junking. Lauren refused to allow them to clean although the day of repainting was shared between her, Aunt Ruth, and Rochelle. A new mattress, linens, and groceries were the only purchases required. As much as she appreciated it, she did protest at being given a red used moped and refurbished laptop computer until Aunt Ruth looked at her without a hint of pity. "I was prepared to spend more than this to move the two of you here. No matter if you stay working for Walt or find another job, you aren't your mother, and I know you'll be on your feet financially as soon as you can."

"Hey, Lauren, Walt asked me to run an idea by you," Danny said interrupting her thoughts. "You want a beer and we can talk?"

Walt was as good a boss as she could ask for and Danny was a sweetheart. Since she didn't share in the tips like the boat captains and dive instructors, she probably wasn't making as much as she could as a bartender, but for now, this new environment was comfortable. Unless he had to run a boat, Walt was around to handle clients' questions about diving, and he'd given her a stack of DVDs to watch at her own pace if she wanted to. She'd started with the Jacques Cousteau ones, her curiosity growing as she learned the names of the staff, interacted with the customers, and listened to talk among them about how great diving was. Other than she and Danny, no one was salaried. The independent instructors and boat captains were a mix of ages from early twenties to much older. She had quietly asked Walt about that one day.

"You can't make a living as an instructor," he explained. "Take Mitzy – she teaches for us and works part time as a waitress, plus shares a house with two roommates. Issac was offered early retirement from his company and has that as a source of income. That's why we have a lot of turn-over in the business. It's a great start for some and a fun second career for others." He'd winked. "Or third or fourth. We get all kinds come through."

Lauren powered down the shop computer and joined Danny in the classroom. They sat across from each other at the rectangular table and she fleetingly wondered again if Danny ever had a bad day. He was human after all. His perpetual genuine grin and brown eyes glinting humor were part of why she felt at ease from the first day of coming to work.

He clinked the neck of the icy bottle against hers. "Another great day in Paradise. Did you have fun today?"

"I did," she said honestly. "No glitches with the computer, phone, or customers. Sounds like it was good on the water, too."

"Nice conditions, plenty of critters to see, and no one threw up." He leaned forward slightly. "Okay, I know Walt has told you you're doing a good job, and we hope you feel that way, too."

Lauren felt a tiny jolt. Was this for real or was there a big but on the way? She smiled. "I'm glad to hear that. I mean, having someone in this job who is a diver or at least knows something about it would be best, I imagine."

He grinned wider. "This is the Keys. Having someone who isn't a no-show because they've decided the weather is too nice to work is more valuable." He nodded briskly. "Anyway, my cousin, Oscar, comes in next week. He winters in Colorado working at a ski resort and does summers here."

She thought she kept her face neutral. "No, no, this is good news," he said hurriedly. "See, we're in the gap after Spring Break peak. Memorial Day through mid-September is prime dive season and we'll go flat out. Oscar is coming a little early this year to help Walt with the to-do list for the boats."

She wasn't sure where this was going. "Oh, I see."

"Yeah, and there is absolutely no pressure here, okay? With Oscar around though, if, and really only if you want to, we could get you in the water. We don't have a lot of benefits, and diving for free is one of them. In your case, so would getting certified."

Not what she was expecting to hear. "You mean learn to dive? I'm not even a very good swimmer."

"You like to swim, don't you?"

She couldn't deny having the bay steps away from her apartment was incredible. Even if she hadn't ventured out the distance Renata did for her morning swim, she was in the water every day. "Is learning to snorkel the first step?" She had already booked people on the boat for that and knew some boats in town were only for snorkel trips.

"Lots of people start that way, and sure, if you want to give it a try. After Oscar gets here, we can work out a time for me to take you on the boat. And look, if you don't like it, no problem for real. We just thought you might want to see what it was about."

Wow. "I, uh, this is a surprise," she said, not sensing anything other than a sincere offer. "Watching the videos has been cool. Watching is one thing. It's not like anything I ever thought about."

He touched his bottle to hers again. "Hey, I get that and it isn't for everyone. We sometimes get people who take the Discover class and what they discover is they don't like it. Most do and I was always fishing with my dad when I was a kid. My uncle, Oscar's dad, was the diver in the family and I've got to tell you, he took us and from then on, underwater was where I wanted to be. I mean, sure, I still go with my dad, and…" He stopped and grinned. "Sorry, you might think I'm trying a hard sell here."

She wouldn't exactly say hard sell. In the flash of wondering if she wasn't too old to start, she thought of the couple who'd been in the week before going diving in celebration of their recent retirements. "Like I said, I listen to people and yes – I do want to think about it."

"Super. I promise not to say anything else until you're ready. Oh, and Oscar is a way cool guy. He's great for helping with the boat and is good with the office stuff, too. You'll like him." He reached for her empty bottle. "Hey, I've got another half hour in the tank room. You go ahead and I'll lock up the back."

"Sure, see you tomorrow." Walt or Danny was usually the last one to leave. Running a business was the same whether it was a bar or a dive shop – there was always a to-do list of tasks after the Closed sign was flipped. She started the moped and thought about how she'd assumed she would find another job tending bar. She hadn't expected to enjoy the shop as much as she was, and her sense was Walt would be willing to teach her anything she wanted to learn about the business. The suggestion about diving was a surprise. Customers were often talkative as it would take several minutes to process the paperwork for diving or the charges. While most were divers, she thought about the woman who had mentioned she could see all the fish she wanted while snorkeling and didn't have to mess with the heavier dive gear. Her husband and the other couple with them teased her good-naturedly that she didn't know what she was missing. "To each their own," she'd said and stuck her tongue out at them. Lauren had smothered a giggle at their laughter.

Her thoughts turned to dinner once she pulled out of the parking lot. Every two weeks, the four women rotated cooking for the group and Aunt Ruth said Rochelle's "Snapper Everglades" was excellent. Sometimes the hostess prepared the main dish and everyone else brought a side or dessert. Apparently, Rochelle was the sole chef tonight and the menu of fish, roasted asparagus, au gratin potatoes, and chocolate bourbon pecan pie was understandably reminiscent of New Orleans. Rochelle's maternal grandmother was originally from Slidell, Louisiana and fell in love with a visiting Navy man to leave with him and branch the family into Florida.

Lauren's cooking skills were limited. Cereal, canned soup, and sandwiches on stale bread required little preparation. In one brief time of living in a decent apartment, their across-the-hall-neighbor was an older Italian woman who would greet Lauren after school, with hearty snacks and leftovers to take home. Quick cooking sausage and peppers and long simmering Bolognese sauce were the two lessons she taken with them when the inevitable eviction came. She had picked up a few other dishes along the way, making friends with the cooks in the bars where short orders were served. She would try to get Aunt Ruth alone and ask if she could host the next dinner as a way to thank the women for their easy acceptance of her. Each woman had her individual routine, compatibility forged over whatever time they'd been together.

Sunset wine and snacks on the beach might be all four or only one – no specific plans like they did with the dinners.

The degree of comfort she felt among them was as surprising as her job. She knew few details of their backgrounds, nor did they of hers. Of the three women who'd been married, none had children which seemed odd. She knew only Rochelle and Renata were widows and Aunt Ruth had quietly, briefly explained the shock of the recent discovery of Rosalinde's husband's body. There were no details, nor had there been about Lauren's sudden appearance. "My niece from New Orleans. Her mother has passed, and she'll be with us for a while."

In the initial week of Lauren sleeping on the sofa bed in Aunt Ruth's study and sharing meals together, she'd described only how she came to own the Retreat and met the women. Lauren didn't think her lack of questions was because she lacked curiosity. As a bartender, the number of people who wanted an audience for their life story and drama were balanced by those who instead wanted the proximity of others without engagement beyond polite greetings and occasional casual conversations. She'd quickly learned which was which, and she appreciated Aunt Ruth's willingness to wait until, or if Lauren was ready to talk about growing up with her mother. The darker secret though, the terrifying night that set her on the run to a place where no one knew her, was something to push deeper into her memory, hoping the scene would eventually fade to where she could think it had all been nothing more than a bad dream.

CHAPTER SEVENTEEN

Ruth had the remaining sauvignon blanc in a chilled acrylic glass – the waning crescent moon a sliver against the sky. She'd wrapped her blue paisley print shawl over her shoulders, the short-sleeve top worn at dinner not quite warm enough for the intermittent breeze. In a few weeks, nighttime temperatures would barely drop to eighty degrees.

Although each of them were good cooks with different specialties, Rochelle was unquestionably the best and like tonight, she would usually make the entire dinner and dessert was always from scratch. What a difference in Rochelle from her dark days of nearly losing her job. She knew Rochelle in the causal way of her being an administrative assistant and office manager in the insurance office Ruth used. Not one of the agents, she had little direct contact with Rochelle who was pleasant the few times they'd interacted. Shirely Cohen always handled Ruth's business personally as they'd both taken ownership of their respective businesses almost simultaneously. They'd laughed about it over the years with mutual experiences of having been mentored by the couples who'd originally established the companies.

The day Ruth's and Rochelle's lives overlapped was still fixed in memory. Rochelle was coming out of Shirley's office, a stricken look she tried to quickly hide with an attempt at a smile and friendly nod. Ruth didn't think much of it until she saw a similar look on Shirley's face. She gave a half smile and stood. "Any chance you have time to go over for a coffee?"

They'd meet there occasionally instead of in the office. Maybe it had been an especially hectic day. "Uh, sure."

Shirley's office had a private entrance to the back and Cup's Full was next door, a neatly shaped row of red tip photinia separating the parking lots. They carried coffee and orange cranberry muffins to a shaded table outside away from the only other occupied one. Shirley sighed, lifting the over-size blue porcelain cup. "Thanks. It's one of those days that being the boss isn't much fun."

Ruth hadn't pressed, allowing Shirley to choose her words as the troubling issue was explained. Rochelle was a valued employee for almost eight years, quietly efficient. Other than being a widow, no children, Shirley knew nothing of her personal life unlike the agents who easily shared their family stories. Initial lapses in her work had been minor, then more sick days taken, and a major error the month prior. Apologies and assurances it wouldn't happen again. A noticeable shift occurred as Rochelle would keep the door to her small office closed, a subtle sign but the agents were wondering at the change. One afternoon when they were alone closing up, Shirley had finally discreetly inquired if there was anything troubling Rochelle whose response had been uncharacteristically abrupt. Maxed out on sick days, Rochelle had a few mornings when she went into her office, barely greeting anyone, and emerging only briefly if necessary. With a brother who had caused intense family drama for years with his alcoholism, Shirley didn't want to jump to conclusions, but that morning when another avoidable error had to be explained, Shirley had been firm.

"She completely denied a problem, which was not unexpected. She did say she'd been dealing with some things and her landlord was selling the house she was renting. She only has thirty days to move and can't find an available place she can afford."

Ruth nodded. "That can be stressful. Maybe she had indications this was going to happen, and if she hasn't been successful, she's faced with having to leave? So, nowhere to live and maybe having to find a new job or facing a long daily commute?"

Shirely shrugged. "Possibly. Look, I don't want to lose her, but she is starting to impact office dynamics." She tapped the handle of her cup with her thumb. "I know you don't want just anyone as a tenant, and if she has developed a drinking problem, that's not good."

This wasn't quite what Ruth expected. "You know it's only a one bedroom? That's not much room if she's been in a house."

"With a lovely section of beach and a lovelier landlady. Like I said, even though I doubt this is what the real problem is, it might take some burden off her."

Ruth thought to how she'd brought Rosalinde to the first apartment, the friendship they developed, the woman using the name The Retreat, saying it was something she needed more than she realized. Could it be the same for Rochelle, or would their bond be disrupted by adding a new tenant? She remembered the look on Rochelle's face that morning. She knew Shirley well enough to know her concern was not just as a boss. "Tell her about the place and have her call if she's interested."

The call had come a few hours later, the invitation accepted to come by after work. Ruth was able to talk to Rosalinde beforehand who suggested a six-month rental as a start. Rochelle was subdued during the visit, complimentary of the apartment, and agreed short term might be best. At first, it was as if Ruth and Rosalinde were still alone. Rochelle politely declined to join them for social interaction, at least one empty vodka bottle in the weekly recyclables. Ruth did often see her on the beach in early morning, staring out before she left for what would be too soon for the office. Perhaps she had a regular breakfast spot. Shirely had called her a few weeks in to say Rochelle expressed her gratitude for the referral, her work was back to standard and while she still stayed in her office, the door was ajar rather than closed.

The night Rochelle had come to the beach was the beginning of the third month. A glass in hand, she'd sat in a chair, not speaking for the first bit. "It is peaceful like this, isn't it?"

More nights, pieces slowly revealed. Attending mass every morning, and unlike Ruth, her parents had brought them to Verde Key from North Dalota when her father's arthritis worsened to where maintaining the small ranch was increasingly difficult and the doctor recommended a warm climate. Her brother had never adapted and returned north as soon as he graduated high school. Married a few years later, Rochelle had helped look after her father, then mother, both of them passing when she was in her fifties. Ruth traded information about her background in kind, no actual details about her estranged sister. In sharing dinner with them the first time, she'd almost shyly asked about the landscaping. Minimal greenery was all Ruth could manage and Rochelle's offer to add flowering shrubs as a start was a surprise. Within another month she'd created a section for butterfly-attracting shrubs, containers of flowers and an herb garden appeared. Gentle Rosalinde, who tended to retreat each night into her preferred books and music, never inquired into their conversations, taking Rochelle's increased integration with them as something to be expected.

With the six months nearly passed, Ruth waited for Rochelle to ask the question, sensing the night when her voice was heavy with emotion. The story was more tragic than Ruth had imagined, the telling marking a passage. A marriage suitable if devoid of grand passion. Children would have filled the gap, neither thinking the initial miscarriage was to widen the cracks not far beneath the surface. Her husband, carrying baggage from the father who'd abandoned them, was denied the opportunity to be the type of father he longed to be. He'd argued vehemently with the doctor who insisted a complete hysterectomy was needed following the third miscarriage. His anger was directed at Rochelle, her own loss discounted compared to his. A sympathetic co-worker and lunches turned into the affair they hadn't planned. Not an intent to leave their spouses, snatched hours she was certain they kept concealed. Until the terrible afternoon of her husband's birthday. Dinner reservations made for later, she'd come home from work, startled to hear his car running in the closed garage. The chaos was nothing compared to the viciousness of the note. My present to myself is release from this pathetic life with a cheating, barren bitch. Thankfully, his two siblings had believed her lie that he hadn't left a note. Solace from her lover was not possible and he soon took a new job to relocate. The following years had been difficult despite moving to another house and job. Going to work for Shirely later seemed a chance to make her feel normal again.

The eventual screaming call from her former sister-in-law stripped away hope her lie would remain undiscovered. Unlike her brother, she always doubted Rochelle's claim of no note and made it a mission to find someone to verify her suspicions. Rochelle had no idea how she'd managed, but the call opened with, "I always knew it was your fault," and "You will rot in hell for what you did to him," was her closing screech.

For Rochelle, the one or two drinks at night to try to block her renewed pain became the first drink starting as soon as she arrived home after work, no longer bothering to keep count of how many. She knew she was teetering on the verge with Shirley – the uncertainty of where she would live pushing her further to the edge. "I'd like to stay here, and I've contacted the counselor my priest has wanted me to see," she'd said in the stillness. "I understand if you'd rather I go."

"Of course you can stay," Ruth said rapidly, her voice thick with sympathy. "Rosaline and I enjoy having you."

The sound of a boat moving through the night, a faint light in the distance shifted her thoughts to tonight and Lauren's surprising request to host the next dinner. Ruth took it to mean the young woman was becoming more comfortable with them and she sounded like she was satisfied with her job. She might someday explain her real reasons for leaving New Orleans. The cynical thought was she had learned of Ruth through whatever means, recognized she was the only heir, and was playing the wounded niece role to ingratiate herself. Intuition told her in this case the apple had fallen far from the tree and until proven otherwise, she would believe Lauren was different from her mother – God rest her troubled soul.

CHAPTER EIGHTEEN

Bev checked her dive computer, sensing they'd been on the wreck for about twenty minutes. Twenty-three to be precise, more than halfway through allotted time at the deeper depth of the *Speigel Grove* wreck. They were lucky with moderate current and at least seventy feet of visibility. The huge ship, sunk in 2002 to become an artificial reef, was home to a thriving ecosystem of marine plants, coral, and more kinds of fish than she could identify. A few reef sharks had cruised past and a 500-pound Goliath Grouper was around as Captain Moira had indicated. Neither Bev nor Kyle wanted to complete the training to allow them to swim inside the wreck along the corridors, but friends spoke of how at times, divers who did so would need to tuck into an opening to make space to let the hugh fish go by. Schools of yellowtail snappers and Atlantic spadefish were some of Bev's favorites and multiple barracuda rounded out the larger predators.

They would be ascending soon, with lunch at the Scarlet Macaw planned, barring no interruptions. A lack of major crimes since the murder of Trevor Moore meant she was caught up on paperwork, the weekend clear for a change. In their monthly dinner with her parents, her father mentioned he was familiar with a guy who'd done a few years in prison for smuggling during the time frame of the Newton's murder. He'd promised to see if the guy was willing to talk to Bev.

Kyle gestured to his right where a medium size turtle swam upward and indicated they should start moving toward the mooring line where the *Daredevil* waited. A leisurely final pass across the almost ninety-foot width of the ship was a pleasant way to end the dive. Moon jellyfish as small as quarter up to larger than her fist were likely to drift near them during their safety stop.

They were the second pair of divers back on board, the couple from Kansas City already stripped out of their wetsuits looking over the plastic-coated fish identification card, pointing out the ones they'd seen. The last pair of divers would be down the longest, marking their fiftieth dive on the wreck. They routinely came from Tampa, and they planned to do the flip for the afternoon trip. As much as Bev and Kyle liked diving, lunch and cold beer instead of four dives in one day was their preference.

The ride to Adventures Below was a little smoother, the occasional three-foot waves from the morning subsided and, as usual, Kyle sent Bev inside to settle the bill while he rinsed their dive gear in the tubs next to the storage shed. Bev was the first one in and the same woman – hadn't she said her name was Lauren? – was at the desk. She was average height, narrow shoulders, although not thin, chestnut hair with an almost alabaster complexion, eyes the darker green of clover.

"You're new, aren't you? This is our first time to dive this month."

She took Bev's credit card. "Uh yes, I'm still learning the ropes. Were your dives good?"

"She's being modest," Danny said with a grin, coming in with a twelve-pack of Diet Coke to restock the small glass-front refrigerator. "Lauren is catching on great and we're super happy to have her."

The woman rocked her hand back and forth. "There's a lot to learn."

Danny stepped to the counter. "By the way, Bev here is a detective and her husband Kyle used to be the assistant District Attorney. They learned to dive with us and manage to get out every few weeks."

Had Bev not been looking at the woman, she would have missed the fleeting tightening of her jaw before she slid the credit card slip and pen to Bev. Her tone was polite. "Oh, that must be exciting."

"Well, it's not like New Orleans, but things do happen around here," Danny said, folding the empty cardboard carton. "You never have to fear with Bev on the case. The bad guys never get away with it."

"We do our part," Bev said and turned her attention to Lauren again. "You came from New Orleans? Great place to visit."

"Uh yes, and yes, I relocated recently."

"Welcome to Verde Key, then. Are you getting settled in?"

The door chimed as a couple entered the shop and Lauren glanced their way. "Uh yes, I am. It's nice."

"Good to meet you," Bev said, and Danny motioned her to follow him to a rack she hadn't noticed when they checked in. "Hey, we got in these new leggings and rash guards. Water will be warming up soon and you'd look terrific in the blue."

The patterned pieces were available in blue, purple, and pink. They did look nice. "Going designer-wear, are you?"

Danny grinned again. "It was actually Lauren's idea. I wasn't kidding about being lucky to have her. She may not be a diver yet, but she's picking up on things really fast. Walt is super impressed and you know that's not easy to do."

Bev pulled a long-sleeve rash guard off the rack, liking the swirled multiple shades of blue. "True, did she just walk in?"

"No, Renata Lopez, who's at the pharmacy, remembered Walt saying he needed someone, and Lauren is staying there with her aunt I think it is?"

Bev cocked her head. Where had she heard the name Renata? "Staying where?"

Danny pulled the matching leggings off the rack. "The deal of the converted old motel where the four older women all with names that start with an *R*. Renata is one of them. Walt was telling me about it. Kind of a funny thing, but I guess the lady who owns it has been here a long time. I think she's the aunt."

Bev hadn't met the other two women the day she notified Mrs. Newton about her husband. Lauren looked to be in her mid-thirties.

Maybe her stay with Miss Brandon was temporary. Being around four women old enough to be her mother probably wasn't something Bev would care for. Well, come to think of it, if they were all like her Aunt Lorna, life could be interesting.

Danny waved the hangar. "You'll look terrific in these," he repeated with his hard-to-resist grin.

"You've turned into quite the salesman and you're right," Bev agreed. She carried the set to the counter, knowing Kyle should be finished rinsing and loading gear in a few minutes. "I haven't seen these before and they are eye-catching. I understand it was your idea to get them in," she said to Lauren.

"Uh yes. I thought they would make a nice addition to the tee shirts."

Bev passed her credit card over again. "Danny mentioned you weren't a diver yet. If you're staying around, it's great. We actually haven't been certified for long."

"Oh? Everyone does talk about the wonderful diving."

Bev was too accustomed to interrogation to not notice the small change in Lauren's body language. Picking up on subtle differences was a habit formed in the job. Lauren's tone was now more guarded, sounding almost as friendly as before and the smile wasn't as spontaneous. "So, are you getting settled in? Found a nice place to live?"

She didn't quite make eye contact. "Uh yes, thanks." She snapped her head around at the door chime, a look of relief at the interruption. Kyle and the other divers came in, conversation trailing behind them.

"We're all set and I'm starving," he said, noticing the bag Lauren handed to Bev. "Something new?"

"I'll show you," Bev said. "Bye Lauren, nice to meet you."

She barely turned her head. "Same here, have a good afternoon."

Kyle held the door open for Bev and hit the remote on his Explorer. "She's new here, I gather."

"Yeah, in from New Orleans. Danny said one of the women who lives in the same place as Mrs. Newton, the woman whose husband we found, referred her to Walt. Her aunt is the one who owns the apartments."

"Quite a difference between here and New Orleans. Wonder if she knew what a change she was in for."

"Won't take long for her to find out." Bev thought briefly to their exchange. Danny's comments about her being a detective was what seemed to cause the shift in Lauren's demeanor. Maybe she had something against police. Not *against* necessarily – maybe wariness. That wasn't uncommon, especially coming from a major city like New Orleans.

While parking at the Scarlet Macaw, a call from her father was a surprise on a Saturday afternoon. Kyle made sign language of if he should go inside and order them a beer. Bev nodded. "Hi, Daddy. What's up?"

"Did y'all get your dive in?"

"We did. Nice conditions and cool stuff. You have a charter this morning?"

"Yes, good group in from Missouri. Listen, Wayne Bannon, the guy I told you was part of the drug scene back in the day, has his boat in the end slip, a couple left from ours. I know it's a day off, but he says if you'll come around five, he's good with that. Bringing a six-pack is my suggestion."

Five o'clock would allow for lunch, a quick shower and change. "Thanks, Daddy. Should I bring extra for you?"

"Nope. Your mother has the Wilsons coming for dinner and I have to pick up a few things on the way home. Wayne has a Wellcraft 270 Coastal, the *I'm Out Now*, and yes, it probably means what you think."

Nothing like someone with a sense of irony. "Thanks again, Daddy. Love to you both."

"Tuna nachos are on the way, and their guy with lionfish brought some more if you want to go all seafood," Kyle said when she joined him at one of the few open tables. She was glad to see he'd ordered two drafts instead of a pitcher. One beer would have to hold her until after she met with Bannon.

"Great, fish sandwich for you, too?" When they were telling Donna Sweeny about lionfish they hadn't explained there were different stories about how the non-native fish had been introduced into the Atlantic and Caribbean. With no natural predators they flourished as far north as Massachusetts and throughout the islands, diminishing, or in some places decimating, native fish populations. Even though the fish was delicious, and poison in the spines rendered harmless with proper handling and cooking, catching them on a commercial basis was proving difficult. Restaurants like the Macaw served them as specials when they could get them.

"Fish tacos for me," he said and clinked his mug to hers. "Since you're having a beer, I guess the call wasn't to rush off to another body."

"It was Daddy. The guy he told me about who might know the kind of crowd Newton could have been involved with back when is at the marina and willing to talk to me at five." She raised the mug of amber ale. "I will have to stop at one."

"At least you can have a relaxed lunch. Murder and drugs are a common connection. Worth asking about for sure."

They placed their order when the waitress delivered the nachos. Diving always fueled their appetites and there wouldn't be leftovers to take home. She had an hour to spare after lunch and went through her notes again verifying dates and events leading up to Newton's disappearance. She knew the marina store would be crowded on a Saturday afternoon and stopped on the way to pick up the recommended six-pack.

Dawn's Delight, the thirty-six foot Lurhs her father and his partner used in their charter fishing business, was slipped between another charter boat and an older Chris Craft bowrider. This end of the dock was quieter and the lean man on the deck of the Wellcraft was sitting in a white plastic chair, a second one to his left, a small Yeti cooler to his right. He stood and reached for the beer, giving his left hand to Bev to climb on board. Scarred up knuckles and a firm grip, no ring, a Citizen's black strap dive watch on his wrist. Too many tattoos on his forearms to count.

"You're Frank's daughter? Have a seat." They were past the point of direct sun at this time of day, and he wasn't wearing a cap. Faded orange cargo shorts, and an equally faded green tee shirt showed muscled arms and legs, scuffed brown boat shoes. Light brown hair streaked with blonde and a deep tan made it difficult to guess his age, although his early sixties was the most likely. He placed the beer in the cooler, pulled two cans out and passed one to Bev. His brown eyes looked at her appraisingly. "Hope you're the kind who pays attention. No notes, no recording. Didn't tell your dad that, but those are the conditions."

"Fair enough," Bev said, putting her purse onto the deck and shifting the chair to be directly in front of him. "You were around in the seventies?"

"A lot younger. Wild times, lots of shit went down." He took a long swallow and tapped the can against the arm of the chair. "You're interested in Ed Newton?"

"You did know him, then?"

"Strictly business. He was on the fringes."

"An old friend of his thought he might have tried to be more and maybe crossed the wrong people."

Bannon gave a slow shake of his head. "Newton wasn't smart enough and he wasn't stupid enough," he said, and quickly raised his hand. "Not speaking paradoxically. I was on the aquatic side and in middle management, shall we say. Been on the water since I could steer a boat. Shit does have to eventually be carried by land and every once in a while, a little extra, freelance labor was required. Nothing complicated, cash in hand. That's all Newton was good for, and he understood that. I didn't deal with him much, but the people who mattered knew everyone involved. There were only three could have cut him in for anything bigger and he didn't know anyone else up the chain beyond me. Had he been asking around or dropping hints, his services would have no longer been required. Locations changed often enough, he couldn't do any damage if he was shooting his mouth off. In other words, he wasn't worth killing."

She took a small sip of beer. "Couldn't he have been also working with another group? Someone who might have had a different take?"

"Not possible," Bannon said immediately. "Back then territory was clearly defined. We were it in this area. I'm not saying shit didn't happen. It wasn't like Miami though where dead bodies showed up routinely for all kinds of reasons. It was more of a controlled business here."

He sounded credible and she'd checked his record. He was incarcerated almost three years after Newton's disappearance. "How did you get caught?"

He shrugged. "Sometimes your luck runs out. Engine quit in the wrong place at the wrong time. Patrol came along and the guys were seasoned. Didn't buy my bullshit. I managed to convince them I didn't know much and the ten years I was looking at was doable. Unlike many of my compatriots, I did not piss away my profits. Not being the kind to bulk up inside, I was useful in other ways. I finagled a job in the library, got my bachelor's degree in business – concentration in finance." He waved his hand around the boat. "This little baby has a nice mid-cabin berth, porthole windows and a skylight to let breezes in. Gally to suit me, and a head. It's built to handle rough seas, and my needs are minimal. After all, it's a hell of a lot more room than in a cell. I go where I want, when I want."

"As in, *I'm Out Now?*"

"Out of prison, out of the life, out on the water. "I cleared the deck when I got out and my old boss was headed into retirement. Gave me a hefty bonus for keeping my mouth shut." He finished his beer, reached for another. "Back to Newton. When he was needed, I'd usually find him at Fat Jack's or Half-Mast. They were the kind of places guys would mix it up regularly. Anything really bad got sent outside, but could someone have worked up a grudge instead of blowing off steam with a few punches? Sure. What I can tell you is it wasn't us." He lifted a fresh can to Bev, and she shook her head. "I don't have any real connections left and I'm headed to Bimini in a few weeks. I'll get around a bit before I go and if I run into anyone else from back then, I'll let your dad know."

"Thanks for your time," Bev said and passed him her empty can.

She walked slowly to her Spitfire – confident Bannon had told her the truth. If it *was* the truth. Maybe he wasn't as knowledgeable about the old business as he thought. On the other hand, it was only a possible scenario. So far, everyone who talked about Fat Jack and Half-Mast agreed fights were commonplace. Grudges could fester, just as the situation with Trevor and Carl Moore had spun out of control. Nick Black's belief Rosalinde's brother Reggie had killed Newton, was certainly plausible. The incident of being thrown out of Fat Jack wouldn't have helped and finding a way to get Newton alone probably would not have been difficult to do. The fact Reggie worked at Richmond's marina was interesting. The owner, Zeke, didn't seem old enough to have known him, but his father was likely to remember him if he worked there long. Unless there was a call to a crime scene, she didn't have anything on her calendar for Monday and the Pelican's Nest was a good restaurant. It was worth a try.

She waited to back out of the parking spot as a red Mustang convertible, top down with four young guys waving cheerfully passed by on their way deeper into the marina. A good reminder there was still time left in the weekend to enjoy. Thick steaks on the grill and a nice bottle of Zinfandel would make for a lovely evening.

CHAPTER NINETEEN

Lauren refilled Marvin Baranski's drink without asking, his gaze fixed as usual on the television – the Marlins playing in California tonight. His face softened without an actual smile, reminding her of Old Manny. Skipper's was so much like George's, it hardly felt like her first afternoon behind the bar. Then again, George's had been similar to other bars she'd worked.

"Most all our customers are regulars," Butch Sanders had said when she'd come in Monday. She was accustomed to working Saturdays and Sundays, and she'd assured Walt having Monday and Tuesday off from Adventures Below was fine. With routines falling into place, she realized she hadn't been out since moving into the apartment and remembered Clyde Hopkins from the Gulls Nest Motel, telling her about Skipper's. She mentioned it to Aunt Ruth who knew It only as one of the older bars. Lauren had gone for a late lunch, few others inside as she expected. Enticing scent of hot grease and grilled meat – not the cloying smell of over-used oil. Marvin, whom she didn't know then, was at the end of the bar, two men at a table by the jukebox, and an older man was settling his tab at the bar when she slid onto the second stool from the end. He gave her a polite nod, the men at the table engrossed in a conversation, Marvin fixed to the television.

"What can I get you?"

She pointed to the six taps behind him. "Draft cold?"

"Always. Got a couple of local beers – a red and an amber – rest the usual."

"The amber, please. Clyde from the Gulls Nest said you had some of the best conch fritters."

"That's Reynaldo. His grandmother's recipe."

"Sounds good."

He called the order through the window as he pulled the perfect head on the beer and set the plain pint glass on a coaster. "You're staying at the Nest?"

"I did my first couple of days."

"New in town, then?"

"Uh yes, at least for a while."

"Butch," he said and glanced past her to the table. "Be right back. The guys need another round."

She studied the bar set-up, noting the line-up of liquor, stack of plastic-coated menus and tub of napkin-wrapped cutlery on the end section of counter next to the opening. The ale was robust and she'd have to ask the name. She heard the ding of a bell in the kitchen, a hand and arm visible placing a standard red plastic lattice basket on the ledge of the pass-through.

"Give 'em a minute, coming right out the fryer," Butch said. "Sauce is Reynaldo's version and has a little kick. Got regular cocktail if you'd rather."

He had a nice voice. "I'm good with some spice."

His brown eyes were friendly, too. "Waitress or bartender?"

She cocked her head. No need to ask how he guessed. "Started tables at fifteen and made my way up. Lot of places like this. I'm Lauren."

He nodded. "You looking for work?"

"Not exactly," she said with a small hesitation. "I'm at Adventures Below if you know it.'

"Sure, Walt and I played football together. You an instructor?"

"Oh no, I'm in the office. Well, front of the house. Haven't done that kind of thing before, diving I mean. Learning a lot from hearing people talk. Walt is great and everyone has been helpful."

He nodded again and turned his head toward the man at the end. "Marvin will be ready for refill. Enjoy those fritters."

She dipped one in the remoulade-type sauce and nibbled. The fritter was a golden color, not too heavy. If others in town were better, they would be really delicious. She imagined the menu was limited to sandwiches and bar food, and doubted there were many requests for salads.

Butch drifted back to her. "You want a refill? I'll be in the office for a few minutes."

She had a third of a glass left. "Thanks, I'm okay for now."

The men from the table had moved to the bar, their empty glasses and baskets in hand when Butch reappeared. They paid cash with a, "See you later," "Take it easy, Marvin," and a vague nod to her.

"Have a good one," Butch said and turned his body away from Marvin after the door closed behind the men. "Okay, if you're interested, we could use an extra bartender Monday or Tuesday and maybe on call for some nights. Pays not much and no big tips, but it's decent.'"

She'd raised her eyebrows, his offer similar to what happened in the job at Adventures Below. "I've been here less than an hour."

His smile was genuine. "Like I said, Walt and I played football together in high school. You impressing him is all I need to know. He told me you came from New Orleans. You work in places like this there, I figure you'll be fine here. The Keys may be getting more crowded, but we're still a small community. You want to come in tomorrow for day shift, give it a try?"

With getting the apartment settled and working going well at Adventures Below, she'd started to feel a bit restless, and the truth was she wasn't accustomed to days off. She was not looking for a social life or relationships and had been earning barely enough money to keep up and try to put a little aside in savings. Even though she knew not all men were like the consistent losers her mother was drawn to, if she had a dollar for every drink she'd served because of a broken romance or divorce, she could have been retired at age thirty. She hadn't had great expectations of the few men she'd been with. It was just easier for everyone. Work was a good substitute.

"The place is still standing and you have a smile on your face," Butch said, snapping her to the present. As soon as lunch was over, he'd left to handle an annoying kind of task that could only be done during the nine-to-five hours, Monday through Friday.

She grinned and cut her eyes to the three occupied stools. "Didn't exactly have a rush while you were gone."

He chuckled. "Go ahead into the storeroom and get familiar with where all the supplies are and we'll go over any questions you have."

Lauren returned home two hours later, satisfied with the day. Renata was in front of Aunt Ruth's apartment, the two women turning as Lauren slowed the scooter. Aunt Ruth mimicked drinking from a glass and pointed to the beach. Lauren gave a quick nod. Their version of sunset Happy Hour with sometimes only one and sometimes everyone on other afternoons, was another routine she'd come to understand. Walt had surprised her with a pinot noir above the price range she would usually buy. One of their longtime customers who owned a wine and cheese shop in Jacksonville always brought him a bottle and he'd never explained he was strictly a beer, bourbon, and rum guy. Lauren changed from the khaki pair of capris she'd worn to blue shorts, keeping on the navy-blue scoop-neck cotton top she'd bought for two dollars at the thrift shop. She opened the wine, grabbed a glass, and a bag of spicy chicharrónes she'd developed a taste for.

"Rochelle is at a bridal shower for one of her co-workers," Aunt Ruth said when Lauren took the third chair. She lifted her glass "Ah, I'm drinking Chardonnay, but that one looks nice."

"I haven't opened my red yet," Renata said and held up a bottle with a screw top.

Lauren poured. "Walt re-gifted it to me. It's a little celebration."

Aunt Ruth leaned forward slightly. "Things went well at Skipper's?"

"Yes. For now, I'll be Monday and maybe Tuesday, and can be a back-up for other nights if needed."

Renata looked thoughtful. "That can mean no days off for you?"

Lauren smiled almost shyly. "True. I, uh, I'm not really used to having time off and I like the feel of Skipper's. Do you know it?"

"Only been there a couple of times. Speaking of Walt, they had his fiftieth birthday party there a few years back."

"He's part of the reason Butch offered me the job so fast, and you're the reason Walt offered me a job so fast, so I owe you another thanks."

Renata smiled widely. "As you may have already guessed, we really are a small community for things like this. People know who they can trust for recommendations." She waved her hand to Aunt Ruth. "Like me coming here. Agatha, who owned her salon, knew me from the pharmacy. I was ready to downsize and had a faster sale on the house than expected. I was telling Agatha about being in a bit of a jam and two days later Ruth called and invited me for coffee."

Ruth opened a plastic container and passed cheese, salami, and crackers over to Renata. "Agatha joked about finding me another R, and we took it from there." She shifted her chair to form more of an arc. "She hadn't planned quite this much downsizing, but there are other advantages."

"More than enough," Renata said quickly and passed the container to Lauren. "Being surrounded by older women is probably different than where you've been." She swept her hand forward to the water lapping gently against sand, sunset pinks and gold starting to develop in the sky. "Hard to beat the view though."

"For sure," Lauren said. "And I've never lived on the water. I mean except once with a swimming pool close by. I love being able to swim with you in the mornings."

The rest of an hour passed as Lauren listened to mention of people who were what were referred to as Conchs. People born and raised in the Keys and transplants, like themselves, who adopted the lifestyle. Lauren withdrew to her apartment after the sun dipped beneath the water, Aunt Ruth and Renata wishing her a good night. Not really hungry, she fixed a cold plate of smoked gouda cheese, peppered salami, multi-grain crackers, and olives to accompany the last of the wine. She ate at the mosaic-topped bistro table with her laptop and a DVD from one of the local videographers. They constantly scrolled scenes on the wall-mounted monitor at the store and Danny gave her the latest one they would start showing the next day. Watching divers move in and around the reefs nudged her closer to thinking she could give it a try.

One of the divers reminded her of the female detective who'd been in the shop. Lauren hoped she'd masked her instinctual wariness of cops. Living in the kinds of neighborhoods she had brought a clear understanding of corruption and abuse of position. Most cops were good, but those who weren't could appear to be just as friendly until you learned too late what they were capable of. Beatings instead of arrests, bagmen, willingness to plant evidence, demands for freebies from girls on the street. She shook her head sharply to dislodge the memories. This was a new place. A place, that so far, had been only kind to her. How long would that last?

CHAPTER TWENTY

Ruth refilled Rosalinde's juice glass. The small slice of quiche, two strips of bacon, and a few chunks of pineapple was all she was willing to eat. Ten pounds was Ruth's guess as to how much Rosalinde had lost and, unlike she and Rochelle, it wasn't weight she ought to lose. The dark smudges beneath her eyes were more pronounced and her skin was perhaps a bit paler.

"Are you happy about Lauren going to work at Skipper's?"

"Not having any free days is apparently not a problem for her. And as Renata pointed out, living here with no one close to her age, plus being in a small town for the first time, keeping extra busy for a while might be the best thing. Having more money will be good, too. I can tell she still feels uncomfortable with all we've done for her and wants to build up some savings."

Rosalinde glanced out the window onto the patio where a red-winged black bird had landed on the back of a chair. She turned her gaze back to Ruth. "Any idea yet of if she'll stay? I mean, here in town, not necessarily here. Oh, I don't mean she shouldn't. I think she's very nice and you seem to be happy for her." She fingered the gold crucifix and blinked. "Is she very different from your sister?"

Ruth allowed a tiny sigh. "Oh yes. When Deborah cut me off from them, I worried for a long time about what things must be like for Lauren. I finally decided I could only hope for the best and maybe someday she – Deborah – would manage to get into a program and stay clean. From what Lauren has said – even though she doesn't talk about it much – I think Deborah was neglectful rather than abusive." She tapped the edge of her mug. "I'm not saying that's good. Just the idea of beating a child..." She trailed off, remembering Rosalinde's description of her husband.

Rosalinde smiled sadly. "I know what you mean. As much as I wanted children, I have to be honest and admit I doubt it would have made things different for us. Ed was mostly verbally abusive. He kept us always short of money with his drinking and running around, and his slaps and shoves never caused me to have to go to the hospital. I suppose like many women some part of me thought I deserved that kind of treatment. That I had done something for him to change from when we were in love. Or what I thought was love. Neither of us had what you could call role models to follow. We were a way out for each other."

Maybe the crucifix was sentimental. Rosalinde wasn't overtly religious. "Did he give you the necklace back then?"

She looked momentarily startled as though she didn't realize it was in her hand. "This? No, no. Actually, my paternal grandmother. She was really the only bright spot in my childhood and gave me this for my tenth birthday. That was their tradition and I think it started with her grandmother. I'm not sure why age ten. Perhaps that was when they thought a child would be careful with it. She died not long after and my mother sold everything of hers she could and threw the rest away. She didn't even keep the few photographs we had." She kissed the tiny cross and tucked it into her top. "I, I thought I lost it once and was so glad I didn't that I've never taken it off since."

Ruth kept her voice gentle. "I understand. Look, I know our rules about not prying works well for us, but I know you aren't on any kind of a diet and you have lost some weight, haven't you? Are you feeling okay? It hasn't been very long since finding out about Ed."

"No, I mean yes, I'm fine. I've been a bit tired, kind of a cycle of insomnia, I guess, and maybe my appetite is affected, too. I might pick up some vitamins or something. I'd rather nap in the afternoons than take sleep aids. I'm sure it will pass. Don't worry." She drank the rest of her juice and scooted her chair back. "In fact, I have a couple of errands to run. Do you need me to pick anything up while I'm out?"

"No, I'm good. Leave everything on the table. I'm puttering around this morning."

"Okay." Her smile was more wistful than happy. "Thank you for caring, I know you all do and really, I'm fine."

Ruth loaded the dishwasher, leaving out the mug for a final cup of coffee. She slipped out the door sending the blackbird into flight and settled into the chair to watch a trio of zebra butterflies moving among flowering shrubs enclosing the flagstone patio rather than fencing. Rosalinde was obviously hiding whatever was wrong. Her concern did not extend to violating their rule of allowing secrets to emerge only when ready. No matter Rosalinde's claim of being okay with the discovery of her husband's murder, how could the news not evoke difficult memories for her?

She thought to Rosalinde's comment about no role model to know what a loving marriage should be led to thoughts of her own parents and grandparents. Hadn't their collective lack of open affection influenced her? Had at least some of Deborah's rebelliousness been rooted in her inability to accept a household where emotion was discouraged? Had her constant poor choices been an increasingly desperate desire for what she thought love could be? Lauren told her she knew nothing of her father other than a name and a shrug when her mother told her he'd deserted them barely a year after she was born. She couldn't help but wonder how many men her sister had brought into Lauren's life. In the same way she'd done before, she guided her mind away from the worst possibilities of what might have happened to her as a child and adolescent. She knew how well people could hide scars, yet Lauren was here now, and whatever damage may have been done to her, she was personable and there was nothing irresponsible about her. While she could acknowledge her lack of objectivity, the other three women's acceptance was neither forced nor faked.

In arriving as she had with few possessions, there was evidently no one to hold Lauren in New Orleans. Had some sort of failed relationship been a last push to leave? Two of the butterflies caught her attention in crossing paths in an aerobatic loop. There had been no mention yet of a husband or significant other. Ruth sipped the cooling coffee, considering the irony of their collective situations. One husband abusive and philandering who managed to be involved in something to get him killed. One in a failed marriage who struggled with the tragedy she couldn't have foreseen. One husband who was a good man, and nonetheless left his wife a widow earlier than expected. And her? Herself, who was hardly in a position to give relationship advice. There had certainly never been anyone in her hometown, no matter Herman Stolz's belief they were well-suited and her parents' expectations she would marry the man who was respectable and God-fearing. She smiled at the almost forgotten name. And her first years in Verde Key? Learning the business from Rebecca and Arnold Schoopman. Learning about the then common traveling salesmen whose wedding rings posed no deterrence to making advances and other men whose lifestyles did not include commitments. How many years had dissolved as she became so comfortable in her own routines that inevitable compromises to make a relationship – let alone a marriage work – held no interest for her? She'd left an environment where she'd already been declared a spinster to come to a place where individuality was nonchalantly celebrated. Lauren was not yet forty, time enough to seek – or embrace – romance if she wanted to.

Green parrots streaked overhead, their familiar squawks piercing her musings. Even though she still didn't actually know what was troubling Rosalinde, the invitation was open to her. Secrets and private thoughts were likely to be eventually shared as in times past. Perhaps what she was experiencing was simply residual shock from learning about Ed. When she was ready, their circle of friendship that seemed to be expanding to include Lauren, held whatever support she needed.

CHAPTER TWENTY-ONE

"This is a perfect day," Danny said, showing Lauren how he was setting up the dive gear. "Visibility on the reefs yesterday was at least fifty feet and should be the same today. Waves are one foot, maybe an occasional two."

"I'm pretty excited," she said, grateful the only other divers were a trio of photographers who were friendly and focused on talking about lens, housings, and other terms she assumed were related to their array of camera equipment. There was plenty of room to spread out and she didn't have much of an audience if she did something stupid. Danny had been incredibly patient in the pool the afternoon before, getting her ready for the two dives they would make this morning. He'd laughed at her concerns, promising her she was far better prepared than she thought. Maybe watching hours of video did have an effect. In her daily swims with Renata, she began to pay more attention to the small fish that would dart around them as she stood in the shallow water.

The temperature was low eighties with intermittent swaths of clouds and the sun sparkling on blue water. One of the other larger Corinthian boats passed them, divers waving. Captain Moira rang the bell ten minutes out from the dive site and Lauren pulled her wetsuit up, letting Danny help her with the zipper in back. She hesitantly repeated the pre-dive check steps, pleased she remembered each one in sequence.

Captain Moira explained they were on something called a spur and groove reef and be sure to look in the sand channels for stingrays. "You're going to be fine. Danny will take good care of you," she said and held the back of Lauren's tank as she awkwardly shuffled the short distance to take a deep breath and step out. Danny was waiting in the water, his eyes locked onto hers, as she gave the okay signal, remembering to breathe only through her mouth and everything seemed to be in place. Danny had told her they would descend slowly, swimming toward the mooring line to begin the dive. At first Lauren couldn't focus on anything other than staying as close to Danny as she could and trying to get accustomed to the sound of her breathing and feel of the equipment. She kicked as they had practiced in the pool and Danny led her forward where a school of yellow-tail snappers was so thick they blocked the closest section of reef. It was exactly like in the videos and a beautiful queen angel came into view. Lauren inhaled and exhaled more evenly now, looking to where Danny was pointing at a pair of lobsters tucked under a ledge.

This was real. She was underwater, seeing fish she would have to ask about, purple seas fans, yellow and orange corals. Now she understood why divers were always still talking about what they'd seen when they were checking out at the shop. Almost an hour passed before Danny navigated them back to the boat, Captain Moira grinning as Lauren sat and took the regulator from her mouth. 'Oh my God, my God, that was amazing."

"That's what we like to hear. You up for the second dive?"

"Oh yes, yes. For sure yes." She stopped, thinking she might be babbling.

Danny eased onto the bench beside her and held up a hand for a high-five. "You were great, Lauren. Next site has an S-shaped reef and there's a good chance we'll see a turtle. You want to swap your own gear over or I'll do it for you?"

Lauren shook her head. "No, if I'm going to do this, I need to learn everything."

Danny looked her in the eye and asked, "You're in then for the whole course? Get you officially certified?"

Captain Moira was at the ladder with the first of the photographers coming up.

Lauren tried not to sound too eager. "It really is okay? Taking the training for free? I mean I know how much it costs. I don't mind working extra in trade."

Danny laughed. "Hey, basic and the next one which is advanced, plus the rescue course if you're willing, come with the job. You decide you want to become a divemaster or all the way to instructor, that's a little different."

"Ah, don't forget she might want to learn to drive the boat instead," Captain Moira said. "Good boat captains are always in demand."

"One thing at a time," Lauren said, feeling a rush of warmth. Jesus, it really was like being part of a family. The second site was either better or with her initial hesitation over, she was able to see more, and included Danny finding the promised turtle and a blue-tipped anemone. She did draw closer to him when a pair of big barracuda swam less than an arm's length away. She remembered she'd been told they weren't aggressive, and she supposed she would get used to them. Despite the photographers expressing disappointment with no sharks, she didn't mind.

She showered at the shop and changed quickly so Oscar could take over as mate on the afternoon boat because Danny had to service several regulators before the next morning. Once the customers were out of the shop, she gobbled the sandwich she'd brought for a late lunch and grabbed the thick, well-thumbed copy of, Reef Fish Identification, Florida, Caribbean, Bahamas they kept on the counter. Good Lord, so many different fish and other things to learn. Oh, the long odd-looking one she'd seen was a trumpet fish.

Aunt Ruth sent a text a few minutes before closing. My place at 7:00. A special dinner to celebrate. You don't need to bring anything.

How sweet, especially since none of the women were divers. Lauren had questioned them at their Happy Hour a few evenings before. Renata said she had tried and preferred swimming. It was easier and much less expensive. Rochelle admitted she didn't like the idea of being underwater, and Aunt Ruth said it was one of those things she'd considered and never got around to making happen.

"We're on the terrace," Renata called out when Lauren opened the front door to see a bright blue Congratulations balloon attached to the back of one of the chairs at the round table, four small plates of shrimp cocktail set out. A bottle of pinot grigio was in the clear acrylic wine holder.

"Rosalinde is a bit tired and sends her love," Aunt Ruth said handing her a glass. "We want to hear all about your adventure. "The casserole will be ready in about twenty minutes."

"Please tell me you didn't see sharks," Rochelle said as they sat and leaned in to clink glasses. "I was a little worried."

Lauren grinned. "Not a one in sight, but it really was incredible. I was less anxious than I expected, and Danny was wonderful."

"He's a good kid," Renata said dipping a shrimp into cocktail sauce. "You're going to take all the lessons?"

"Yes, and if the schedule stays light next week, I'll be able to get the basic course finished."

"How nice," Aunt Ruth said. "Tell us your favorite part, then we'll have dinner."

A casserole of chicken and saffron rice in herbed cream sauce, honey and mustard glazed baby carrots, and sourdough rolls were followed by lemon poundcake drizzled with blackberry sauce and Guatemalan coffee. Lauren insisted Renata and Rochelle go home to relax while she helped Aunt Ruth clean up. After a round of goodnight hugs and the dishwasher was loaded, she and Aunt Ruth took the final mugs of coffee outside.

Lauren cleared her throat to avoid tearing up. "Aunt Ruth, I can't thank you – all of you - enough for tonight. It was very special."

"Renata came up with the idea and of course everyone agreed. We sometimes think it must be a bit odd for you to be among only old ladies."

"Okay, I admit I didn't know what the arrangement was here at first and I'm still sort of in shock – and I mean in the nicest way – how y'all have taken me in. With, well, with everything. I mean from the minute I arrived."

Aunt Ruth's voice was soft. "You and I are family, and no matter how much I regret what happened with your mother, and no matter what you ultimately decide to do, I'm glad you're here. I think you can see that even though we Rs aren't related by blood, we're close in our own type of sisterhood."

Lauren smiled. "Anyone who spends more than about an hour around y'all can see that."

Aunt Ruth extended her hand. "Each of us understands about starting a new phase of life. You and I have talked a lot now about how I wish things could have been different and in time, the others will probably share more of their stories. We all have regrets. Feel remorse for mistakes we made. We also know we can't change any of what happened in the past."

Lauren reached out for a brief squeeze. "You're right about not knowing yet what I might do say six months or a year from now. I am glad to be here and for the first time since, well, since I knew mother was never going to stay clean, I can learn what having family is like – blood or otherwise." If she didn't stop, she was going to break into stupid sentimental tears. She withdrew her hand and lifted her mug. "It has been a full day. Thank you again for tonight."

Instead of going directly to her apartment, she wandered to the beach, slipped off her sandals and stood in ankle deep water looking outward. How could so many good things she'd never imagined be happening to her in such a short time? Well, yes, when she was young she had thought maybe someday she and her mother would go away and start a new life. She couldn't remember exactly when she came to accept what she had to do to manage on her own. And she had managed, if not in a way many people would consider successful. It was a damn sight better than where she'd started. She thought about Aunt Ruth's comment of learning the other women's stories in time. No, she didn't know the specifics, but she doubted she would hear anything she hadn't heard in years as a bartender. Broken dreams, broken hearts, betrayals of trust, sighs of regrets for poor decisions made, or refusal to see their own blame in whatever disappointment they were sharing.

She did wonder about Rosalinde. In the few times she'd been with all of them, she hadn't stayed long, always pleading fatigue. Were Aunt Ruth, Renata, and Rochelle too close to see the almost translucent tone to her skin, darkened circles under her eyes? Or they were aware, and were allowing her privacy rather than trying to intervene? Lauren had watched customers drink themselves eventually to death and while Rosalinde wasn't showing those physical signs, there seemed to be something wrong. Since Lauren didn't know her, she could possibly be struggling with emotions because of the news her husband had been murdered instead of deserting her. Were her regrets for having doubted him all those years? Probably not. She must have had reason to assume he'd left her in the first place.

She stepped sideways to reposition her feet, moving her thoughts to the excitement of the morning and planning to become fully certified to dive. Danny, Moira, Oscar, and Walt had been genuinely happy for her. What another seemingly impossible thing this was. Impossible wasn't the right word. Completely unlikely and nothing she'd ever imagined were accurate. Less than a month ago, she'd huddled, terrified on the floor in the dark, then ran in desperation with no real plan. There was more than the distance of hundreds of miles between New Orleans and Verde Key. There was the kind of hope she'd set aside in creating enough satisfaction to get by. Here though, was it a place where it was going to be different, not just a place to temporarily shelter? There was no doubt Auth Ruth wanted her to stay and for now, being around the other women was not as odd for her as they seemed to think. With the addition of work at Skipper's, she could build up savings for a deposit somewhere else if she did decide to look around.

She exhaled deeply and a yawn reminded her it had been a long, full day and she'd be starting her morning again at six-thirty to join Renata in her early swim. She thought tonight could be another one where she might sleep without troubled dreams.

CHAPTER TWENTY-TWO

"I appreciate you seeing me," Bev said, needing no identification of Melvin Richmond as Zeke's father. Eye color, shape of face, and build were the same. He might be retired, but he was fit and his calloused hands bore the signs of a man who still worked. Unlike his son, he did have a classic *U.S.M.C* and anchor tattoo on his left forearm and a mermaid on his right.

His voice was deep. "Reggie Mosley. A name I haven't heard in years."

When Bev called Zeke, he'd vaguely known Mosley. He was around the summer before Zeke reported for basic training, following in his father's footsteps of joining the Marines. He'd been in service for six years and remained in Hawaii another four years after. Reggie had moved on by the time he returned to continue the family business. He told Bev his father was out for the morning and could meet at two o'clock. They were at a back table in the bar of the Pelican's Nest, a draft for him, coffee for her.

"Got a couple of hours before the early drinkers show up," he said waving his hand around the nearly empty bar. "This is my office now. Zeke has a good handle on things in the yard. What's this about?"

"Was Mr. Mosley working for you in February 1977?"

"Yeah, sure. Hired him on in '73, stayed with me for right at ten years. One of my best mechanics, good welder, too. Could run the forklift as back-up."

"And Edward Newton, his brother-in-law?"

"Ah shit. Hell of a thing," Richmond said, a note of recognition. "That body, the guy in the news not long ago. Couple of guys fishing found him, right? Yeah, okay, I got it. Hauling that one in must have been a shock."

Bev nodded. "Yes, his widow never reported him missing because she thought he had deserted her. We've spoken with a few people. Not many here anymore who knew him."

"Huh, Ed Newton. Hell of a thing to find him like that," Richardson repeated. "Let me start with Newton then because you remember the problem ones, don't you?"

Interesting response.

"See, we're bigger now than back then – well, I guess all the marinas still open are. Anyway, I had about a dozen guys working, most with specific skills and like I said, Reggie was really good. Came to me one day, kind of reluctant. Wanted to know if I'd be willing to give his brother-in-law a chance. They'd just moved from up somewhere and he was mostly in construction. No jobs open in Verde Key and yeah, there are some general skills kind of things we need. Plus, I was always willing to let somebody apprentice in another area if they had an interest. I'd had a guy leave, so I figured what the hell."

He lifted his left hand toward the bar in what Bev assumed was a signal to Gabby, the young lady who waited on them when she and Les were there before.

"Ed started out okay, not a big guy, but strong enough. Did general stuff like I said, plenty to be useful. Lasted about two months. Started coming in late, then coming in with a hangover. Got a little mouthy with some of the guys. I was cutting him as much slack as I could, but with everybody else getting along, that's not the kind of crap you need to put up with."

Gabby deposited a fresh beer, the coffeepot in her left hand and Bev nodded to a refill.

"I quietly warned Reggie and he said he would talk to Ed, but I should fire his ass if he didn't straighten up."

"So, they didn't get along?"

"I wasn't going to ask for details. Things were good again for maybe three weeks, then he comes in late, tangles with my supervisor. I cashed him out and sent him on his way. Reggie apologized and I told him not to worry about it. I mean, shit – pardon my French – he was just trying to help his sister. Kind of a pain, but no real harm done."

"Newton did cause problems in the yard?"

Richmond raised his eyebrows. "Are you asking if anyone would have taken it beyond the yard? No reason to. Got rid of him and that was that."

"Other than a pissed-off brother-in-law."

"Yeah, well, like I said, one of my guys got a personal problem and wants to talk, I'll listen. Have helped in the past with some. Their personal life is not my business though and my take is Reggie felt like he did the best he could getting Ed the job. Not his fault the way it went."

Except if she added some of the other information she had about Reggie. "Okay, tell me more about Reggie. You said he stayed on."

Richmond scratched the back of his left hand. "Yeah, but now that I think about it, he did take some time off, what, like a year or so later? Had to help his sister move to a new place. You said she thought Ed had run off, huh? Must have been about that time. Sure, I guess she would need help. Can't say I saw anything different in how Reggie was here though."

"Why did he quit?"

"Bad luck kind of thing. Back started giving him trouble, couldn't put in the hours like before. Would have like to have kept him, but didn't have a desk job to offer and Dolphin Marina did. We gave him a nice going away party. Saw his obituary, what, about ten or twelve years ago? Didn't keep in touch with him."

Bev thought to the way Newton's body had been wrapped and dumped. "Did Reggie own a boat?"

"A boat? Don't think so. He never talked about one." Richmond paused. "We did have a couple Contenders the guys could use if they wanted to. Stripped down, nothing fancy. Center console for offshore, flats for backcountry."

Another interesting tidbit. "Were they used much?"

"Yeah, some. A few of the guys did have their own. We pay top of the scale, give what benefits we can and treat them right, but not a lot of perks to this job. They had their own boat, they needed parts for repair or maintenance, they got them at cost and could fuel up any time they wanted. For the guys who didn't, letting them have access to the spare boats was an easy one to offer."

Bev was fitting pieces together. She didn't think Richmond had much else to say and she wanted to catch Les before he left the office. She quickly finished her coffee. "Thanks again for your time."

Richmond stood and extended his hand. "My pleasure, and look, back in the time you're talking about, I got rid of Ed before he got to be too big a problem here. Mouth like his, depending on where he hung out, I could see him stepping into some serious trouble. You know what I mean?"

"Yes, thanks, and you have my number if you think of anything else."

She called Les, gave him a quick summary and he said he didn't have plans to leave early. Traffic was light and she worked through three scenarios while driving. The station was quiet, not time for overlap of changing shifts. Bev grabbed a Diet Coke from the refrigerator and Les swung a chair around to sit as she picked up a marker to add to the white board. She'd already filled in notes about her conversation with Wayne Bannon. She relayed Richmond's comments as she jotted key words, then stood at an angle taking everything in.

"Okay," Les said. "How much credence are you giving the tangling up with drug guys theory?"

"I'm inclined to put that low on the list."

"Right. Don't forget, he was messing around on his wife and from what we know, he probably wasn't careful about whoever it was being married or otherwise unattached. Jealous husband or boyfriend can't be discounted."

"True, although we don't have any names to associate with that or an as-yet-to-be-identified individual he pissed off for some other reason."

Les rubbed his hand across the back of his neck. "You starting to like the brother-in-law?"

Bev held her left hand in a fist, then opened her thumb. "One, even though Mrs. Newton claimed her husband was controlling and verbally abusive, Mosley came after Newton at Fat Jack for the way he was treating his sister. She might have been reluctant to tell us about physical abuse." First finger up. "Two, Newton screwed up the job Mosley got him and might have caused more grief than Richmond realized." Next finger went up. "Three, stuff used to weigh down Newton's body could all be found at a marina." Fourth finger. "Mosley had access to at least the boat in the marina and maybe from a friend for all we know." Last finger. "Mosley takes time off to help his sister move, allegedly after being deserted."

"More links there than we have with anyone else," Les agreed. "Circumstantial and quite a few *if's*. You trying to make facts fit theory?"

Bev wasn't offended at the logical question. "You telling me you're not feeling it?"

"Didn't say that. What are you thinking about doing next?"

She took a swig of Coke and glanced at the clock on the wall. "I want to go talk to Rosalinde again. If I call now, we can maybe set for tomorrow morning."

He swiveled his chair. "Yeah, but I have to take Pam for an appointment. If you need me with you, it will have to be afternoon."

Bev shook her head. "No, I'm going to come at her with the angle of trying on the drug thing first and ease into the other. She might be willing to open up more about abuse if I'm alone."

He looked at her quizzically. "If she does admit abuse, we have a shift then. We know she couldn't have gotten rid of the body by herself. Doesn't mean she didn't kill him and call her brother for help. Or maybe put him up to it, or they were in it together all along."

"I know. She's had a long time to perfect her story, Mosley is dead, and it isn't like we have physical evidence to back us up."

He stood and stretched. "Okay then, see you tomorrow afternoon."

Bev stared at the whiteboard for a few minutes before she remembered Mrs. Newton wasn't easy to contact. She reached Miss Branden who assured her Mrs. Newton was at home and would call the detective. Arrangements were made within a half hour and the woman's soft voice didn't indicate reluctance to meet although she did say she would like to have Ruth with her. Bev could hardly object. She would watch her body language closely and listen for subtle changes in her tone of voice. Would the fact she had tracked down Black, Newton's old friend, and spoken with Richmond come as a surprise?

Bev tossed her empty can into the recycle bin on the way out. Les was correct. They still had only theories. While Mosley was shaping up to be the most logical suspect, there was no evidence.

CHAPTER TWENTY-THREE

Ruth felt as if they were in the replay of when Detective Henderson had come to notify Rosalinde about her husband. When Rosalinde telephoned the detective to set a time to meet, she said only the detective had some news and a few more questions. Rosalinde asked if she would be with her for the second visit, and Ruth didn't think her presence would be a problem. Surely the detective would expect Rosalinde to want a friend to support her.

They were seated again with the detective in the armchair and she and Rosalinde on the sofa. The plate of oatmeal raisin cookies was untouched, and the detective drank some coffee before setting her notebook next to her cup.

Rosalinde placed her cup on the saucer and moved to the edge of the sofa, her knees touching the coffee table. "You have news?"

"Not news exactly – more information that raises some questions I'd like to ask," she said with a neutral expression. "We did locate Mr. Black and also spoke with Mr. Richmond at the marina. He's retired now but remembers your husband."

"Oh my, I didn't know if Nick was even still alive. As for Mr. Richmond, Ed didn't work for him very long."

"He mentioned that, but first, Mr. Black provided some information that caused me to meet with another source. Were you ever aware your husband was involved with drug smuggling?"

Rosalinde drew back slightly, her eyes widening. "No. I mean Ed did have different jobs, but are you sure? Do you mean like he was a dealer?"

"Not to that extent. He was more a courier and it wasn't all the time."

"Are you saying his involvement may have been why he was killed?"

Ruth sat silently, her hand next to Rosalinde.

Detective Henderson tapped the still closed notebook. "That doesn't seem to be likely at this point unless we uncover other information. I know some of my questions will be difficult, but you thought your husband had left you. Perhaps for another women? If so, did you know who?"

Rosalinde lifted her left hand to finger the crucifix in the unconscious gesture Ruth now understood. She was still looking at Detective Henderson. "The simple answer is No. I can't honestly say when I began to suspect, but I never confronted him about it."

The detective's voice was softer. "You mentioned before him being verbally abusive and controlling. He was physically abusive, as well, wasn't he? At least somewhat?"

Ruth flicked her eyes to Rosalinde, uncertain of how truthful she would be.

"I assume in your work you have seen women who have been terribly abused?"

"Yes ma'am, and I know how difficult it can be to seek help."

Rosalinde released the necklace and reached for her coffee cup, her hand steady. "Slaps, shoves, not the kind of horrible beatings I've known other women to endure, and it was infrequent enough I could do like so many women do and make excuses for him. I'd believe him when he said he was sorry."

"Did your brother know?"

"No, no, I'm sure he didn't," she said quickly.

Ruth felt a surge of nervousness as the detective cut her hazel eyes briefly to her and there was an undercurrent in the glance. Did she suspect Rosalinde had confided in her and she would be willing to be more forthcoming? She had nothing else to add though since Rosalinde had described the abuse in the same way to her.

The young woman tapped the closed notebook again. "Then you aren't aware of the time your brother attacked your husband at a bar, warning your brother to treat you better?"

"What? No, Reggie never said anything to me and neither did Ed." Rosalinde's voice seemed to quaver. Or did it?

"In going back to Mr. Richmond, do you know the real reason your husband was fired? And it was your brother who arranged for him to be hired in the first place."

Rosalinde dipped her head momentarily before she straightened, more rigid than since the conversation started. "Detective, I may not have been willing to openly admit my husband's weaknesses, having been raised at a time when 'for better or worse' was expected – especially of a wife. But it didn't take me long to understand Ed's excuses for losing jobs couldn't always be someone's else's fault."

The detective's tone shifted slightly, her posture not changing. "Your brother knew your husband's routines, how to find him late at night, and had access to at least one boat. He also knew you would easily believe you'd been deserted. And he was correct in you never reported him missing. No one was looking for him."

Rosalinde's eyes flashed and she vigorously shook her head. "No, no, no. Reggie would not have killed Ed. He wouldn't do that. He wasn't like that." Her hand started up to grab the crucifix. She stopped, clasped her hands in almost a motion of praying. "No. I understand why you might think this, but no, Reggie would not have killed Ed."

Ruth realized the detective was watching Rosalinde closely. She gave a tiny nod, and stood, her voice still neutral. "Yes, well, then you understand we are pursuing all lines of inquiry. You have my number and as difficult as it may be to go back to that time in your life, please call if anything we've talked about today brings other details to mind."

Rosalinde rose shakily, reaching for Ruth's hand to steady her. "Of course, and I apologize if I snapped at you. It is difficult and I…"

"That's quite all right, ma'am, and I'll see myself out," she said, retrieving her notebook, not looking at either of them as she left.

Rosalinde turned into Ruth's open arms and laid her laid against Ruth's shoulder. "I just need a second. God that was awful. Reggie, for them to suspect Reggie. He wouldn't have done that." There were no tears and she pulled away in a moment, a tremulous smile. "Not the best way to start a day, is it? Thank you so much for being here."

"I wouldn't dream of letting you do this alone," Ruth said immediately. "Do you want to talk some more?"

Rosalinde sighed. "Actually, I feel drained." She waved her hand across the coffee table. Let's leave this and I think I'll go lie down for a bit if you don't mind."

"You go lie down and I'll have this cleared up in two minutes," Ruth said firmly. "Come over later if you feel like it. I plan to be home all day."

Rosalinde held out both hands and squeezed Ruth's gently. "How lucky I am to have you. Well, all of you."

"Go on, now. Rest and don't forget to eat later. I have lovely leftover chicken and dumplings, plenty for two. Or I can make a nice omelet and salad for something lighter."

Rosalinde's smile was a little stronger. "I may just eat all the cookies. I have milk to make it nutritious."

Ruth kept her thoughts in check until she was in her apartment. She poured the last of the coffee into her mug, placed it in the microwave to reheat and recalled the morning. Detective Henderson had been polite, her body language controlled. Was that personality or technique? Not one for watching true crime shows, or any crime shows for that matter, she did know murders were often committed by relatives or friends. To her, it sounded as if there were multiple possibilities for who killed Ed. Of course, Rosalinde didn't want to believe her brother was guilty, and the detective was the one who brought up Ed's involvement with drugs. Weren't they all violent people? She did say they weren't thinking that was likely and if her brother had been in one fight with Ed, could there be more to it? That's what she took from the detective's comments.

She shuddered as the microwave beeped. Poor Rosalinde. Was it any wonder she didn't seem to be sleeping well nor have much appetite? And how long would the investigation continue? With forty years passing, what was there to find? She removed the mug, a decidedly un-Christian idea taking hold. Rosalinde was a good woman, who had undoubtedly suffered more at her husband's hands than she was admitting. With her husband gone, she'd managed to make a new life for herself. Sure, maybe she would have eventually had the courage – with maybe her brother's help – to leave him. The detective was too young to realize what the culture was like then, how women were too often expected to remain in bad marriages, feeling trapped. Whether it was Rosalinde's brother or someone else, it's not as if Ed's death was really a loss to anyone. Couldn't it just be left at that?

CHAPTER TWENTY-FOUR

"I think she's lying," Bev said bluntly, almost before Les could sit down.

"Good afternoon to you, too. Yes, I'm fine, thank you."

Bev snorted. Despite rarely openly acknowledging Les's methodical calmness counterbalanced her tendency to go in speedy bursts, they did make a good team. "Fresh coffee if you're interested."

"Of course, and does this mean you actually learned something, or your instinct is kicking in?"

Bev moved to the coffeepot, talking over her shoulder as she prepared the drinks. "A finely honed instinct you know good and well is pretty accurate."

Les accepted the mug. "Thanks. Accurate more often than not, however, not infallible."

"True. I'll start with what she said that I believed. By the way, she did admit to physical abuse and claimed slaps, shoves, that level. We sadly know there's a whole other range of abuse, and based on what else we've been told, Newton might be the kind to lose his cool and lash out rather than inflict deliberate sustained beatings." She perched on the edge of the empty desk next to Les. "I also believe she didn't know about the drug part. Aside from the fact it wouldn't make sense to tell her, with him being frequently unemployed, extra cash in his pocket took care of his booze – you know. As for the other woman – or women if Nick Black is to be believed – again, she didn't know who nor want to. Plausible."

"Which brings us to the brother?"

"Oh yes. Definite immediate emotion and reaction. Adamant it couldn't have been her brother. Swears she never told him about the abuse and didn't know about what went on at Richmond or the attack at the bar."

Les took a couple of sips of coffee. "Maybe we're talking denial, rather than knowing and lying about it. That fits our scenario of Mosley attacking Newton late one night, getting rid of the body, then being there to support his sister after she thinks she's been deserted."

Bev rocked her hand back and forth. "Yes. The lying part could be she did tell Reggie and knows or at least suspected he took care of the situation. Or she killed Newton, called Reggie for help, or they were in it together."

"Which puts us no closer than we have been."

Bev ran her hand through her hair. "Yes."

Les smiled wryly. "I'm not saying you're wrong. Family and friends are the first suspects for a reason. Short of hauling Mrs. Newton in for questioning – based on nothing concrete – and hoping for a confession, what's your plan?"

"Go through the file, doublecheck with Donna Sweeny to see if there's any forensics we might have missed. Talk to Nick Black again. Remember, he was sure it was Mosely if not the drug connection. Maybe he's remembered something else."

Les looked thoughtful and pointed to the white board. "Shit, Newton's truck is a missing piece. Someone had to do something with it. Let's stick with Mosely for the moment. He waits for Newton to come out of whichever bar late one night or somehow lures him out to the site. Bashes him with a baseball bat or whatever. If he's at the site, he already has the boat and everything pre-positioned and has his truck. He dumps the body, then still has to get rid of the truck."

Bev pursed her lips for a moment, thinking how her father had speculated about Newton's truck, too. Why hadn't that clicked to her at the time? "Okay. If it was at one of the bars though, Mosley puts the body into Newton's truck, takes it, then after getting rid of the body, makes his way back to his own truck somehow. Even if he has to wait until the following morning to retrieve it, leaving a vehicle in a bar's parking lot after closing time isn't unusual."

"And if Newton is killed at home by Mosley and/or the wife, she drives the extra truck."

"I'm having trouble picturing that if killing Mosley wasn't planned, but maybe if she was in a panic, Mosley talked her through it. Works for sure if premeditated." Bev said. "Look, no matter how the truck gets there, the water around Palmetto Paradise isn't deep until further out. Taking Newton's body by boat is one thing. There's no easy way to get the truck deep enough. There's like ten acres or so to the property though and growth is pretty thick except in the developed area close to the water. Add in the years of neglect and no one is likely to have gone beyond the sections they maintain." No reason to kick herself too much for not thinking about the truck before now. Even exposed to weather and time, the chance for forensics was better than forty years underwater.

Les scratched his head. "You think the Chief will allow manpower for the search?"

Bev snapped her finger. "The Community College. It's a good exercise for their Police Academy students. We'd only need one or two for supervision, and Kevin and Beau have both worked with them – the staff I mean."

Les looked at his watch. "Chief is already gone. You want to contact them and see if they're willing and we talk to the Chief in the morning?"

Bev set her mug on the desk, went to the white board to add the entries. "Yeah, I've got the name of the contact somewhere. Damn, I'm liking this."

"Should be worth a shot," Les said. "Tell Kyle hello for me."

"Will do. See you tomorrow. I'll catch the Chief as soon as he comes in. Hell, I'll brew an extra nice coffee to greet him with."

Les laughed. "Can't hurt."

Bev had arrangements made within an hour, realizing there were other ways Mosley – or whoever – could have disposed of the truck. Particularly if there had been more than one individual involved. It was a logical step to take, and the search could be completed in no more than several hours. If they were wrong, they wouldn't be any worse off than before.

Kyle's text came in while she was leaving the station. *Running late. Bring take-out home instead?*

Sure. Anything special?

Surprise me. Be home about 8.

Another plan for an evening disrupted by work. Nothing new and she would enjoy a drink and maybe an appetizer while waiting for the carry-out. Her stomach was reminding her a container of yogurt and small packet of trail mix wasn't a lot of food. The usual chatter of the Happy Hour crowd at the Scarlet Macaw blended with sounds of Jimmy Buffet, whir of blenders and the ding from the kitchen bell to signify orders were up. Bev spotted Donna Sweeny at the far end of the bar, two stools to her right empty. She was staring at a man talking to George who was shaking his head. She didn't notice Bev at first and the look on her face was uncharacteristically pensive. She turned as Bev approached, seeming to make a concentrated effort to smile and patted the bar top. "Kyle on his way, too?"

In the weeks since meeting, they'd socialized several times and Bev wondered if it had been a difficult day at work. "Not as it turns out. We planned to have dinner here and he's getting back later than expected. I'm going to take stuff home instead." The highball glass rather than beer or wine was unusual, too. Bev slid onto the stool and glanced at George who was now shrugging and taking a bill the man passed to him with a "keep the change" gesture. He downed the rest of his drink and left.

"How about you? Dinner, I mean?"

George placed a fresh drink in front of Donna. "Hey, Bev. Beer or wine? Want a menu?"

"Beer and yes. I'm ordering take-out but was kind of light on lunch."

"Ocean Bounty Sampler is always a good choice when you're hungry. Might not leave much room for dinner though."

"Not a problem if I have a friend to share it with," she said and bumped Donna's shoulder. "Unless you have something else going."

"No, just not much of an appetite." She poured the remaining ice into the new glass of what looked to be a double with minimal amount of water.

Bev raised her eyebrows. Donna turned slightly and grimaced. "Yeah, you're right. Food is a good idea."

"Tough day?"

"You mind moving to a table?"

"Sure, that's good."

Donna reached for her purse hanging on the back of the stool. "Go ahead and get one and order and I'll cash out here."

"Sure," Bev repeated, catching Natalie's eye and indicating their usual back table. Whatever was bothering Donna, it would probably be best to be in the corner. Natalie followed her with two glasses of water – a bowl of sesame straws and peanut mix already in place. Bev sprinkled a handful into her palm and pushed it close to where Donna would sit.

"Primary cause exacerbated by another I will get to. I'll give you the short version." Donna sat and said without preamble. By-passing small talk was another trait the women had in common.

"Kyle won't be home until almost eight," Bev said. "I have time for the long version if you'd rather."

"No need. You'll understand. Three years and each year, I think it won't affect me. Well, this year is a little better. I made it all day through work. You ever have a stalker case?"

"No; have read case studies about them. Was it in *Cleveland*?"

"Part of the reason I came here. Guy I met at a bar one time. One of those things where you're sitting next to someone and a conversation starts – not with some lame come-on line. Know what I mean?"

Bev nodded, knowing of it more from listening to friends than personal experience.

"Devon Sanders, and yes, the hey-same-initials, coincidence came early in the conversation. He was in human resources for one of the banks and a bit of a techy. Nice enough looking, had another drink and exchanged phone numbers. He waited a couple of days, called about an art exhibit opening."

She paused for Natalie to deliver the laden platter and a beer for Bev. "Here you go, ladies. Bev, you know what you want to-go? I'll wait to put it when you're ready."

"Stuffed shrimp for one and Snapper Everglades for the other. Lime-cilantro rice and veggies with both. Thanks."

Donna drank half a glass of water, not yet reaching for food. "You eat," she said, almost allowing a smile. "I will in a minute. Sticking with the short version. By second date, it wasn't happening for me and he seemed to take it okay. Maybe a month passed, then little things at first. Phone calls in early morning hours – no voice, only a few seconds. Okay, some wrong number drunk dialed. A romantic card to my apartment declaring I have a secret admirer. A small bouquet to the office – same thing."

Bev ate some of the calamari, listening to bleakness set into Donna's tone.

"The package with a pair of sexy panties in my size and a photo of me getting into my car was what sent me to the police. They had an advocacy program, but that still left the problem of I had no idea who was doing it. One of the three men I'd dated in the past year? Someone I ran across and didn't remember? Someone I never met? I wasn't very active on social media, but there are strange people out there." She swirled ice cubes in her glass, taking a small sip. "Six months. Texts and emails increasingly with the theme of how I'm the one and as soon as he gets up courage, he'll make himself known. I started to feel like I was being followed and couldn't tell if it was real or paranoia. The statistics are eye-opening although finding out more than thirteen million people in the country are stalked every year wasn't exactly comforting."

Bev wiped the corner of her mouth with a napkin. "Jesus, a bigger number than I would have imagined."

"Yes, and twenty percent of the time the stalker uses a weapon as a threat or…" She ran her finger around the rim of her glass, her voice strengthening, the pain flashing through her eyes. "And things can go horribly wrong." She straightened and exhaled deeply. "Three years ago tomorrow. I was at my car after work, never saw him coming, he had a pistol. I would say things were a blur after that and maybe they will be some day. Someone was quick to call 911, a patrol was nearby. Devon was out of control, ranting about how I should have known it was him, cared about him the way he cared about me, refused to surrender the gun. Not surprisingly, the family immediately claimed the cop was at fault, internal investigation ultimately cleared him and every rational part of me knows I have nothing to feel remorseful about. I didn't lead him on and nothing I could have done would have changed the outcome." She managed a half smile. "Still, emotions will war with rational thought, won't they? So yeah, tough day. Maybe next year will be better. Sorry you asked?"

"Hell no," Bev said and touched her mug to Donna's glass. "Glad I did."

Donna reached for a shrimp. "Yes, getting something besides scotch in my stomach is a good idea. Thanks – for both the food and the shoulder." She half-turned in the chair, then brought her gaze back to Bev. "Bringing me to the genuinely odd addition to the day. Did you happen to see the guy who was talking to George as you came in?"

"You mean the black guy with the shaved head, about five nine, put him around hundred and sixty pounds, late twenties? The one you were staring at?"

"Ah yes, your keen observation skills at work."

"They don't shut down when I leave the office and your stare was hard to miss. Did he remind you of the guy, Devon?"

Donna shook her head. "Not exactly. Last night I was at the bar at Bojangles. Woman I go kayaking with wanted to talk about putting together a group thing. Anyway, this same guy comes in, sits one stool away from me. Orders a drink and asks the bartender if Laura, Linda, something like that was working there now. I wasn't paying attention at first, but when she told him they didn't have a bartender by that name, he kept at her a little bit. Said she would be new in town, and he'd forgotten which bar she told him she'd be working at and he'd lost her phone number. The girl finally said something like, *can't help you on that*, and he finished his drink and left." She hesitated. "I can't tell you exactly why it bothered me. Still, I see the same guy talking to George who seemed to be reacting in the same way as the other bartender did. The guy has the one drink and leaves after. it just seemed weird." She put more food on the small plate. "You know, I do feel a little hungry now. Let's see if we can handle this between the two of us."

Bev understood her need to change the subject. "How about discussing the potential for forensics in a truck abandoned in a heavily foliaged area for forty years?"

"Not much is likely to be recoverable left in the open in this environment for so long. I can't imagine how much rain would have fallen and humidity is a bitch when it comes to deteriorating different materials. A new lead in your cold case?"

"Possibly. We've managed to track down a few people who knew the guy. Enough to develop a couple of viable theories."

Natalie led a quartet to a nearby table and pointed to the platter. "You ladies need another drink to polish that off? Bev, your to-go will be ready in about five minutes."

"I'm good, thanks," Donna said and looked at Bev. "You?"

"This one will get me through." She passed a credit card to Natalie. "Go ahead and run this." Donna looked relaxed for the first time since Bev walked in. "Okay, five minutes to clear the platter?"

Donna's voice was normal again. "Oh yeah, we got this."

Bev drove home slowly, glad she'd been at the Macaw. She had no doubt Donna would have been okay without unburdening, but sharing with the right person usually does help. Alone in the car, the memory of the first time she'd been forced to shoot surfaced. How could it not? She was in her second year of patrol and a tense scene had escalated rapidly. A drunken man with a shotgun, enraged about his ex-wife, had assaulted the ex's new boyfriend in the parking lot of Gill's. The victim on the ground, bleeding, orders and pleas to lay down the weapon ignored. Jesus, what a mess. Months of broken sleep despite assurances she'd had no choice. Hell no, she hadn't wanted to go talk to some counselor and the Chief hadn't insisted. Sort of like tonight with Donna, her father finally invited her to come out on the boat, the two of them anchored in a secluded spot, a magnificent sunset, a bottle of bourbon instead of beer. The timing, the place, the quiet telling of her father's own experiences had cleared the lingering feeling she should have been able to defuse the situation.

She exhaled sharply to shift her thoughts to the coming morning and the chance of finding Newton's truck rusting away under decades of plant growth. The odds of course were Mosley, or whoever, wouldn't have left the murder weapon in the truck conveniently encased in something to preserve fingerprints and blood samples. Whatever had been used would have been hauled away with the body and dumped in the water in a separate spot. People did make stupid mistakes, but unlike Carl Moore who fled the scene when he killed his brother and by-passed several better places he could have disposed of the murder weapon, the way Newton had been wrapped and carried out wasn't the mark of someone panicking. Even if Newton's death had been the result of an assault that went wrong rather than premeditated murder, disposal of him had been carefully planned. What the hell, it was worth a try. Maybe they would get lucky.

CHAPTER TWENTY-FIVE

"Oh, hi Butch," Lauren said, looking up from the computer screen when the door chimed. "A surprise to see you here."

He held up what looked to be a liquor bottle in a brown paper bag. "Called Walt a little while ago. We'll be in his office for a bit, you need him."

"Sure, kind of quiet today – didn't have an afternoon trip." The morning had been busy and she'd taken several calls earlier for bookings later in the week. No one else had come in for the past hour and she was doublechecking the schedule to verify if Ladd was available to teach the one wreck diving class. One of the things it had taken her some time to understand was being an instructor didn't mean he or she could teach all the specialty courses. Danny was gone for the afternoon, picking up some part for the older boat, the Daredevil.

Half hour later, Walt and Butch came out of the office and went into the training room. Walt walked to the front door, turned the lock and flipped the Closed sign over. "Hey Lauren, go and ahead and shut down and then come into the training room, please. I'll be there in a minute."

She was startled and couldn't read the expression on his face. "Uh, okay, sure. Is there a problem?" Shit, had she done something?

"Not exactly," he said with enough of a smile to help stop her thoughts from running away. "There's a situation we need to discuss. We'll explain."

Why in the hell were both her bosses together to talk to her? She inhaled and exhaled slowly in logging off, trying not to jump to conclusions. Walt waited while she came around the counter. He had three glasses of ice and motioned her into the room where Butch was seated across the table, a bottle of Knob Creek bourbon open. What the hell?

"First, we're here as your friends," Butch said pouring bourbon over the ice. "You want water?"

Lauren kept her voice steady. "From the looks on your faces, I'll say no."

Walt was calm. "Before we explain why Butch is here, let me give you some background. The Keys have changed a lot since the old days, those being back when we were in school. To be honest, as wild as things were then, it had been more so, but that's for another story. My point is, people could come here and drop out of sight if they wanted to. Plenty of places to live tucked away on a boat, on land, not mingling. People were friendly and laid back if you wanted and left you the hell alone if you didn't. Questions didn't get asked about where anyone came from or why." He turned his glass in his hands. "Coming here to reinvent yourself is still common. Just people are more likely now to want to tell you about the divorce, business screwing them over, whatever."

He looked at Butch, whose tone was somber. "What he's saying is we know you're running from something, Lauren, and it's not our business. Neither of us would have hired you if we thought there were serious problems and nothing we've seen changes that."

Lauren clutched the glass to keep her hands from trembling. "Until?"

"A couple of hours ago a guy came in looking for you," Butch said gently. He held up his hand. "Hold on. I didn't talk to him. You haven't met Gabe yet. We're a second job for him, too, and he's in two days a week. He's been gone almost a month which is why he doesn't know much about you. I was out and when I got back, he told me this black guy, shaved head, in his twenties, asked when you'd be at work. Gabe said he didn't know who the new woman was, but he's been gone, and he'd have to check back with me tomorrow. This sound like anyone you know?"

Lauren shook her head rapidly. Jesus! How?

"Lauren, listen to us," Walt said gently. "We're here to help you. Who is he?"

She took a large swallow, their eyes comforting, not questioning. "I don't know," she said. "I don't know how they found me either and no, I didn't come here running from an ex. Tyrone Baxter is who would have sent him. I was closing up at George's one night – place in the Quarter – and was in the alley. I saw and heard something I shouldn't have and ducked inside so I wasn't seen. Or hoped I wasn't. I thought maybe it would be okay and the next night, Tommy Blue, one of Tyrone's men, came in with a strong hint it wasn't safe for me to stay." She shoved her glass forward. "I had forgotten about Aunt Ruth and wasn't sure if she was even still here. I was a kid when the final break happened between her and my mother. I managed to find the old envelope with her old address and figured if she wasn't still here, at least it would get me far enough away." Butch poured another splash of bourbon in the glass. "Guess I was wrong."

Walt frowned in thought and turned his head to Butch. "You think he'll be back?"

"Yeah. Don't know if it will be to talk to me or assume Lauren is who Gabe was referring to." He tapped his forefinger against his glass. "Does your aunt know any of this?"

"God no. I… I'm sure she didn't buy my story of being at a crossroads in my life, but like y'all, she hasn't pressed me."

"Okay," Walt said matter-of-factly. "The way I see it is this. Assuming you're right, and no reason to think you aren't, apparently they've only been able to track you to Verde Key. If we have until tomorrow, that gives us time to plan, and the plan includes calling Bev Henderson."

Lauren dropped her head into her hands briefly before looking up again. "Or I…"

Butch was firm. "No. Look, I don't know the detective the way Walt does, but he was with her on something really sticky a few years ago and she's kind of famous around here, plus her boss Claude Taylor is someone we do know. She's kickass and he's the kind you want to have your back."

Lauren drew in a deep breath. "What do you have in mind?"

"We can get her here to talk and lay everything out."

Lauren shook her head. "If I've put Aunt Ruth and everyone else in danger, me leaving is going to be the only way. This guy must know where she lives since he's here."

The men exchanged looks. "It may be that he's seen the place, but not you and so thinks you might be staying somewhere else." Walt swirled the drink in his glass. "Let's do it this way, Lauren. You call and see if Ruth can come here. I'll call Bev. Butch, you cap the bottle, go to the break room and make a pot of coffee."

Lauren saw their resolve and spread her hands on the table. "Why? It will be better for everyone if I go. I can be on a bus tonight."

Walt's face was set. "Butch and I did more than play football togetherl. We went to the recruiting station together, too. One of those join-with-a-friend deals. Boot camp, even managed to get assigned to First Infantry Division together. Didn't plan on Desert Storm, but shit happens. One thing you learn is bad guys don't quit because you run. We know you still don't really understand why all of us took to you as quickly as you did, but you'll get it someday. In the meantime, you are one of us and your Aunt Ruth is going to tell you the same thing."

Lauren exhaled loudly. Goddamn it, she wasn't going to cry. "I'll call," she said as soon as she could trust herself. "But if Aunt Ruth wants me out, I go. No arguments."

The men shrugged and left her in private, taking their glasses. Her hand shook as she punched Aunt Ruth's number, trying to think of what the hell to say. Her blunt statement of being at the shop with Walt and Butch because of a serious situation that might involve the police and needing her help was met with a single question. "No, no one is hurt, but it's complicated."

"Bev will be here in thirty minutes," Walt said, sitting at the head of the table again. "Butch is right. She is on the no-shades-of-gray side. It's either right-or-wrong, but she's tough and she's smart."

"Aunt Ruth is on her way." Lauren's mixed emotions of despair and gratitude were difficult to separate. "I haven't even opened a bank account since I arrived," she said bleakly, "and I still have a pay-as-you-go phone. I didn't think I had a trail to follow."

"You remember you asked me once about older instructors? All of ours had pretty high-level previous careers that provide their real income. I can barely manage my way around a computer, but Ladd was a techy. He'll sometimes talk about how easy it is to find and track people. I mean real Big Brother shit. Anyone in New Orleans know about Ruth?"

"No, they couldn't. Like I said, I'd forgotten about her, and I took the envelope with me. I…," she stopped as Butch entered carrying three mugs in his big hands. "Didn't know how you took yours, Lauren. These are all black."

"Black's good," she said, her hands no longer trembling. "Thanks."

Butch set the last mug down and straightened at the sound of knocking on the front door. "I'll get it, I'm already up."

"Since I've met Butch now, you must be Walt," Aunt Ruth said, carrying a plastic container. She kissed the top of Lauren's head and set her purse on the table next to the container. "Brownies. I've never known a problem yet that wasn't helped by chocolate."

Lauren rose and wanted to smile. "This might be the exception."

Aunt Ruth searched her face and Walt cleared his throat. "Butch and I will get you some coffee, Ruth, and give y'all a few minutes."

"Thank you," she said and spun Lauren's chair where she could face her and reached for her hands.

Lauren gulped, not able to stop the tears this time. "I'm so sorry, so sorry. I've ruined everything by coming here."

Aunt Ruth didn't break eye contact as she grabbed a packet of tissues from her purse. "Listen to me, sweetheart. I never once believed you decided to leave and find me because you had a sudden burst of sentimentality. I always thought you might eventually tell me the truth. Is it an obsessive ex-boyfriend or husband? A man you thought couldn't find you and has?"

Lauren swiped the tears roughly. "Worse. I mean I think it's worse. I crossed someone in New Orleans I shouldn't have. Butch came to see Walt because earlier today there was a man in the bar asking about me. I didn't recognize him from the description, and I don't see how it could be anyone else. I don't mean the man I crossed. But someone he's sent."

"What did Butch tell him?"

"Uh, no, I mean Butch didn't actually see him. The guy talked to a bartender that I haven't met yet and he told the guy he didn't know the new bartender. He suggested he come back and check with Butch."

Aunt Ruth tried to erase the worry in her eyes, but she was an intelligent woman. "You said the police would be involved?"

"Detective Henderson. Funny enough, she and her husband dive with us. I don't quite understand it, but Walt has known her for a while and she'll be here soon."

Walt's voice carried from the doorway. "Okay for us to come in?" He had the extra mug of coffee, Butch carrying a caddy with sugar packets and containers of cream.

Aunt Ruth released Lauren's hands. "Yes, please. I think we all need to catch our breath since I gather Detective Henderson is on the way."

"Yes, you know her?"

"Only recently. Rosalinde Newton is one of my tenants."

Butch gave a low whistle. "I'll be damned."

Detective Henderson arrived as he was explaining his comment about how he knew Ed Newton. She was quickly seated across the table from Lauren, notebook open, a coffee and a brownie. "Let me explain what we're going to do here. First, I want to get a clear understanding of why Butch came to see Walt. Walt, you can fill in after. Miss Branden, I'll need to know a few things from you as well. Lauren, we'll save you for last because I'll need you to go all the way back to how everything started. Now, there is only so much I can discuss with you here because I will take this to the Chief. Detective Martin would be with me, but he's working another case."

She looked directly at each person – her hazel eyes intent. Lauren was glad she wasn't trying to hide anything from her. Butch and Walt were through in less than ten minutes. Aunt Ruth was listening carefully to them.

"Miss Branden, have you seen anything unusual the past few days on your property? The sense of anyone watching?"

"Please call me Ruth, and no, and none of the others has mentioned anything either."

"What kind of security do you have? Cameras by any chance?"

"No cameras. The gate you come through is locked each night after dark and I open it in the morning. Well, whoever goes out first does. We're all early risers."

Detective Henderson seemed able to make notes with barely a glance at the paper. "If I understand correctly, Lauren's apartment is the farthest from the front?"

"Yes, and the landscaping we added over the years has been to break up the original motel look of just open space for parking. If what you're asking is can Lauren's apartment be seen without coming all the way in from the street, the answer is no."

Lauren was surprised at the detective speaking to her in a softer tone. "I can't imagine how you're feeling, Lauren. First though, do you need a few minutes' break? Are you certain you want everyone here? I may have to ask you some very personal questions."

Lauren sensed them starting to rise and she held up both hands, edging closer to Aunt Ruth and looking at Walt and Butch. "Wait, please. Detective, it's hard for me to describe how kind everyone in this room has been to me. Why I came was all I was really hiding. Nothing you can ask is going to bother me and if I have put them in danger, they have a right to know why. So no, I don't need a break."

"Butch and I are older," Walt rumbled. "Give us five minutes. Lauren, you know where the coffeepot is."

"Actually, I'll step out for a call," the detective said.

Lauren pushed away from the table to face Aunt Ruth again. "No matter what else is said, the safe thing for everyone will be for me to leave. As soon as…"

"Stop that," Aunt Ruth said firmly, her eyes determined. "I'm not going to pretend I'm not concerned. Of course I am. You haven't done anything wrong and running again can't be the answer. I also can't pretend to understand what it's like living in a big city where maybe you can't trust the police. I don't think that's how it is here. Now, take me to the coffeepot and we'll get refills for everyone."

"I need to add something," Detective Henderson said after they reassembled. "Butch, if you could call your bartender, Sergeant Blackwell is on his way to get a statement from him." She looked around the table. "Sergeant Blackwell will come here after and be joined by Officer Alvarez. They will take official statements from everyone to save coming to the station. Lauren, if you're ready, it will be helpful to start with a little background about the neighborhood of the bar where you worked."

Perhaps because she'd relived that night and next day literally every hour on her crisscrossing journey to Verde Key, she was able to lay out the details in a surprisingly short time. She hadn't noticed Aunt Ruth's hand until she felt a comforting squeeze on her forearm when she explained how she'd found the envelope with the address. She paused long enough to give her a wan smile before continuing. She stopped speaking once she'd described the precautions she'd taken in leaving. The room was silent for what was probably no more than thirty seconds.

"Son-of-a-bitch," Walt said with no inflection. "What's your plan, Bev? What do you need us to do?"

The detective's lips twitched briefly and she held up one hand while she checked an incoming text. "First, I need everyone to understand we are developing a plan, and the information from all of you has been helpful," she said briskly. "Next, we agree it's most likely the man in question does not know for certain Lauren is living at her aunt's place. I can't explain more about this at the moment. However, we will ensure frequent patrols come by Miss Branden, and if anyone does see anything suspicious, call 911 immediately. Butch, if he does not come back to Skipper's tomorrow, it's likely he's sure he's found Lauren." She took three business cards out of the notebook, slid them to the center of the table, and looked at each one in turn. "I'm headed to the station because we need to use this information to finalize our plan. Sergeant Blackwell and Officer Alvarez should be here within about fifteen minutes. Walt, you already have my direct number. If anyone remembers anything else, you can call me no matter the time. Do you have any questions before I go?"

Lauren felt a surge of emotion, fear and anxiety giving way to recognizing she wasn't alone in this. She still didn't understand why, but she could accept it as true. "I… I want to say… I mean, I don't know what to say."

"You haven't done anything to deserve this," Walt said looking more at the detective. "And this son-of-a-bitch and the one who sent him is going to find out we take care of our own here."

Detective Henderson did give a half smile and stood. "Okay. All of you please keep your eyes open and call if you see anything unusual, even something small. I'll let myself out, Walt."

Butch picked up his coffee mug. "Guess we'll be here for a little while longer. I'll make another pot of coffee and, Ruth, I've been eyeing those brownies."

Aunt Ruth nudged Lauren. "You see, I was right. I've never known a problem yet that wasn't helped by chocolate."

CHAPTER TWENTY-SIX

What a hell of a change to the day. Bev's morning had swung between hope for the best in the Newton case to utter frustration.

Les's suggestion they talk to the property maintenance company about site plans had resulted in pinpointing a rutted road screened behind a tangle of vegetation that was cleared quickly. Newton's truck – or rather a truck – was found within an hour. Bev's optimism plummeted as they surveyed the rusted heap partially covered by two fallen trees. The state of their decay indicated bad weather hitting it several times. Hardly a surprise considering the number of hurricanes and lesser storms that would have occurred over forty years. A mass of vines and shrubs grew from most of the exposed parts. Beau and Julio Garcia, a retired police sergeant who taught at the college's Police Academy, had stood with her.

Julio stated the obvious, not caring that she didn't want to hear it. "Jesus Bev, I doubt the damn thing can even be extracted in one piece. I don't care how much forensics has advanced – I don't see how they can do anything with this mess." He'd flashed a sympathetic smile. "On the other hand, they might see it as a challenge."

"Yeah, I know. The team is on standby." She'd called to Beau who was already snapping photographs. "Okay, get it from every angle and we'll send them to forensics. That way they know what they'll be looking at." She'd sighed and gestured to eight students clustered around the one who'd made the find. "Well, there are plenty of beverages and pastries at the control point. You want to take your bunch back and help yourselves? Might as well use it as a teaching lesson while you're here. Appreciate the quick response to this."

"Anytime," he said. "Field work is good for them. I'll step in there with Beau. We ought to be able to find the VIN on something so you can make an identification. Based on what you told me, hard to believe some random truck got abandoned in here in what looks like about forty years ago."

"That would be a hell of a coincidence," she said, shook his hand and went to thank the students. She spent a few minutes with them answering questions, impressed with their enthusiasm. Chief Taylor had been philosophical, agreeing with Julio. "Good practice for the students. We'll see what forensics has to say. Maybe they've got some new gizmo we've never heard of."

Les had insisted they go to Annabelle's for a calorie-laden lunch and the grilled chicken and bacon sandwich smothered in three-cheese sauce with seasoned fries did qualify as comfort food. They hadn't been in the office long before Walt called. In listening to him, she'd immediately thought of the man at the Macaw and what Donna had told her about seeing him at Bojangles. She'd called the Macaw and rushed over when Steve said George was on duty and yes, they still had CCTV cameras covering the parking lot. Those had been installed last year when a group of adolescents had been vandalizing vehicles. She gave Steve the time frame she wanted, and he had the image up on the screen waiting for her, after she spoke with George. He gave the same version Donna had related she overheard about the man asking if Lauren Smith was working there.

Dispatching the man's image to Kevin and Les, she had asked Les to give the Chief a heads-up and gone directly to Adventures Below. Staying focused on what the group told her while her mind was mapping out possibilities had been the difficult part. She understood now why Lauren had reacted the way she did in finding out Bev was police and Kyle a former prosecuting attorney. The kind of place she came from wasn't what could be considered a trusting environment.

As unanticipated as the session had been at Adventures Below, there was no doubt in her mind they were facing a credible threat. How serious was the real question. Her comment to the group she couldn't tell them more until she spoke with Chief Taylor was certainly an understatement. The text from Kevin pinged in. *Yes! the bartender confirmed the guy was the same one from Scarlet Macaw.* Bev called Les from her car. "Kevin sent a text and I'm on the way back. Did you get the photo in to the Florida database?"

"Yep, no response yet. The Chief wasn't as skeptical as I've seen in the past. My guess is, he'll have his head wrapped around it by the time you arrive."

Bev didn't feel her customary surge of annoyance at the Chief's reaction. This was coming at him – well, at them – with no warning and no lead-up. She hurried inside the station, halting abruptly seeing Chief Taylor standing in his doorway. "Get Les and come in here," he said and turned away.

Shit! She wanted a few minutes to get organized. Nothing she could do about that now. She took out her notebook, threw her purse in her chair, and motioned to Les.

"Someone called him while we were talking and he threw me out," Les said calmly. "Not in a bad way though."

Christ, what was the Chief thinking? This was no time for him to lecture her about slowing down. They maybe had a day to figure out what to do. Les closed the door behind them and they took their usual seats.

"Sit and listen to me, Bev," he said with a hard stare. "I know your brain is going in a dozen directions at once. First, I understand the situation. Second, I think even you realize we may not have the resources to handle this alone depending on what the hell we really have. Walt called me," he finished and shifted his stare to Les. "When can we expect an answer from the facial identification database?"

"Not sure yet, but soon if he's in it."

Bev was struggling to control her impatience. Goddamn it, she…

"Okay, good. Bev, Walt said you handled the session with them perfectly. He's chomping at the bit to do something, and I told him to hold his horses. What have you promised so far?"

His tone was the note of respect he used sparingly. "Gave everyone my direct number and ensured an hourly patrol going by the residence. It's logical he doesn't know for sure she lives there or he wouldn't be asking around for her. Lauren is scheduled to work tomorrow, three o'clock until closing. If the guy does show up tomorrow to talk to Butch, denying the new woman is Lauren might work. He's been to two other places we know of. If he strikes out all around, maybe he gives up and thinks she didn't come here after all."

"That's not what you expect."

"No."

Les's phone rang before she could continue. He looked at the number and gave a thumbs up. "Martin, Verde Key Police. Thanks for calling. I'm in with our Police Chief Taylor and Detective Bev Henderson. I want to put you on speaker." He set the phone on the Chief's desk, and they all leaned forward.

"Sure. This is Captain Ernesto Sanchez, Miami Dade Police Special Investigations Section. Your match is for one Calvin Dumond, street name Cracked Calvin. What's your interest?"

"Detective Henderson will fill you in. She's the lead on what we think we have."

Bev didn't pause and Sanchez listened with few questions.

"Okay, good rundown, thanks. If y'all don't mind, can we go to a video call? I'd like to get Sergeant Dieon Hayes in, and it will take me about twenty minutes to round him up. I'll send you the info, Les."

"No problem," Bev said and looked to the Chief after the call ended.

"Kevin should be done by now. Alvarez can finish if he isn't. We need him in on this," he said and waved toward the door. "Get us set up in the interview room. That way we're all hearing the same thing. I don't know what the hell the connection is with some guy out of Miami and New Orleans. Guess we'll find out." He paused. "Since we're not sure where this is going, I'll give the DA a call, see if he's got someone to send. Whatever it is, I suspect we'll need to be solid from the legal end."

Les stopped at the hallway leading to the restrooms. "We've uncovered some tangled shit in the past. This one sounds like it could be right up there. Be back in a few."

Bev nodded. How *would* someone known to Miami police be connected to Lauren and New Orleans? There was no use speculating and she took a cold Diet Coke and the spare laptop into the interview room. When the call connected, Sanchez looked the way she'd imagine from the conversation while Hayes was in civilian clothes of a plain black tee-shirt, close cropped hair and a gold stud in his right earlobe. Sanchez was probably average height and build but seemed smaller next to Hayes's muscled bulk. Introductions were made and Hayes got straight to the point.

"To answer what must be one of your big questions, Dumond came here couple of years ago. He was a person of interest in a homicide in New Orleans and his cousin, Deshaun Baxter, had some kind of personal connection with the head man here. We found this out after we picked Dumond up as a person of interest in another homicide. We couldn't pin anything either, New Orleans didn't have enough to request extradition, and he walked. The bad guys have some good lawyers."

"Why would Miami be involved with this?"

"We don't think they are," Hayes said immediately. "I don't want to sound condescending, but are y'all familiar with gang hierarchy?"

"Not something we have to deal with," Chief Taylor said.

"We have enough of a file on Dumond to know he's a thug and useful. A soldier, not far up the chain. Our guess is Baxter is calling in a family favor and it's independent of what goes on here." Hayes turned slightly to Sanchez.

"To answer your other big question, your young lady probably thought she witnessed a mid-level dealer caught stealing from Baxter who took him out as a lesson. Problem is he was a New Orleans undercover cop."

"Well, that's a goddamn pisser," the Chief rumbled.

"Yeah. The arrangement here for Dumond was between the head man and Desaun, not Tyrone, which means they owe nothing to Tyrone. There's no way they would dispatch Dumond to go out of territory for something they have no part of."

Bev was processing the information which at least now was making more sense. "Do you mean Dumond is in this strictly alone? He's the only one we have to deal with?"

"That's our assessment. What you do need to know is his street name of *Cracked Calvin* comes from him being high a lot and we know he's was in on the one homicide but could be more. He's dangerous and unpredictable."

"I spoke with my boss and even though this is outside our jurisdiction, not to mention New Orleans is obviously interested, we'd like to offer assistance, especially as time is critical," Sanchez added.

Shit, were they looking to take over the operation?

The Chief gave her a glance to stay quiet. "Fact is, we haven't had a chance to fully develop our plan yet. We're having extra coverage on the residence as a precaution. Working on the idea he'll try for her after closing which is 1:00 a.m., we want to have someone inside from the time she comes on shift tomorrow at three in the afternoon and that stretches us a little thin considering we probably need to swap someone out every two hours."

Bev pressed her lips together tightly. In all fairness, the Chief hadn't had time to share anything about an actual plan, but there weren't many options.

"Tentatively include an undercover van and three to four officers for support," Sanchez said. "We'll get details back to you within the hour." Sanchez hesitated. "You need a female who can pass for Smith?"

"I think we have that in hand," Chief Taylor said. "Appreciate the help and unless you have something else for us, we'll get back to work."

What the hell? Who the hell was he thinking of? Kevin had slipped into the room for the final few minutes and given Bev a thumbs up. She powered down the laptop. "Uh Chief, I…"

"I have to make another phone call," the Chief said and stood. "You two fill Kevin in, and we'll use the training room for an operations center. Move whatever you need in there. It's going to be a long couple of days."

They waited for the Chief to be out of range for mutterings he was known to hear from a remarkable distance. Les broke the silence. "From the look on your face, I'd say you don't know who he's talking about either."

Bev threw her hands up. "No. But first, Kevin, talk to us about Gabe and then if anyone told you they were adding something more than what we all discussed."

"Gabe identified the guy right away. Said the only other person in the place at the time was one of the regulars who was watching TV. Gabe thought the guy was acting a little odd, so he figured telling him to come back tomorrow to talk to Butch was the right thing. Alvarez was great with taking statements, by the way, and the lady, Lauren, told her aunt to go ahead. As soon as she left, Lauren asked me to go outside to give me a message for you. Said they – not sure who they are – will take a vote. If they want her out, she goes. If not, she'll do whatever needs to be done. That make sense? She was looking pretty determined."

Bev picked up the laptop and inclined her head to the door. "Yes. The Chief will have to come clean with us soon. We don't have a lot of time here." She was startled to see Kyle waiting at the doorway of their office. "Uh, this is a surprise." He was in his navy-blue suit, tie loosened.

He lifted his briefcase and followed them in. "I was almost at the house after the meeting in Key West and my old boss called. He and the assistant are tied up in separate courts until tomorrow afternoon. Asked me to lend a hand. Said Chief Taylor needed help tonight. What's going on? You found something significant this morning?"

Bev blanked for a moment. "What? Oh wow… That was just this morning, wasn't it? No, completely different. Come with us to the training room and we'll explain."

Chief Taylor entered as Bev was making the last entry on the white board. "Good to see you, Kyle," he said. "Bev and Kevin get you up to speed?"

"Right, looks pretty straightforward from a legal point of view. Not sure how you're going to handle it."

"You mean we got goddamn nothing until he actually goes after Lauren. Not but one choice as I see things," the Chief said, motioning Bev to the table. "The son-of-a-bitch hasn't done anything we can pick him up for. The easy solution would be him having an outstanding warrant in Miami, but he doesn't." He jerked his thumb over his shoulder to the whiteboard. "In the most likely case, we've got thirty-one hours before Lauren is alone at closing. We know we can't expose her and fortunately, we have a resource to help."

Finally. Bev was trying not to show her impatience.

"Stephanie Bryce, Arnie's daughter if anyone knows him, was with Atlanta DEA until a little over a year ago. Doesn't matter why she's here now and she's going to be on the staff at the college in the Police Academy in the fall. Walt sent me a photo of Lauren. Stephanie's hair's all wrong, but she's close enough in height and build to pass for Lauren with them wearing the same clothes."

Drug Enforcement Agency? Huh, no wonder he turned down Captain Sanchez's offer. Bev broke the brief silence. "She's done undercover?" Okay, that didn't come out the way she intended.

The Chief's look was acerbic. "No Bev. She's a goddamn desk jockey I thought I'd give a shot to." He relented with a wave of his hand. "Look, we're all scrambling some on this. Our two biggest advantages are Dumond doesn't know we are on to him, and if Miami is correct and he's in this solo, he's all we have to focus on."

Kyle spoke quietly. "You are planning to deputize Ms. Bryce? Keeps this clean."

The Chief rolled his eyes. "That's why you're here. Last thing we need is screw this up on some goddamn procedure. Oh hey, Beau. What have you got?"

Bev stood as he hesitated, a piece of paper in his hand. "We had Dumond's car from CCTV. Did a BOLO," he said.

The Chief nodded. "Good thinking. Come on in, you'll be part of this anyway."

"Car is registered at the Holiday Inn, paid cash under the name of Carlton Deleon. Do we do anything else?"

"Across from the hotel is one of the spots we set up sometimes for speed checks. Get one put into place. Make sure they're positioned to see his car and get the photo out to everyone. Then come back in and we'll get you caught up." The Chief shifted to Bev again. "You spent enough time with Lauren to assess her?"

Bev gestured to Kevin. "She comes from a tough background. My take is she'll be able to deal with it. There's a chance she's going to run instead. She's feeling guilty about putting her aunt and maybe the others at risk."

"What odds are you giving it?"

Kevin cleared his throat. "If I may. Like I told you, Alvarez was great with the group and she agreed with me after that Miss Ruth, Walt, and Butch seemed to be united in telling Lauren she could trust whatever we plan."

Bev's phone pinged a text. *Can you come to Aunt Ruth's? Everyone's okay.* She held her phone up. "Sounds like Lauren is ready with a decision."

The Chief grunted. "Get going then. Stephanie is on her way here and we'll take a fifteen-minute break. Call as soon as you're done. I hope the girl has enough sense to understand we're her best bet."

With fear and guilt mingled, Bev wasn't sure how much sense would count for. She guessed they were about to find out.

CHAPTER TWENTY-SEVEN

Lauren opened the front gate remotely and waited with the front door cracked rather than have the Detective knock. She was still trying to fully grasp how united Renata, Rochelle, and Rosalinde had been. Aunt Ruth had insisted she explain her position before Lauren spoke.

Lauren had barely begun to apologize when Rosalinde, usually the quiet one, was as firm as she was gentle. "Lauren, dear, you made the best choice you could. With the police providing extra protection and the belief they can make an arrest soon, I don't see you leaving as what you should do. All of us here have been through things in our lives that aren't the same as you. But we've come through difficulties and the regrets we've learned to deal with. You did nothing to deserve this." She'd looked at Aunt Ruth with affection. "While I may have been the first one to refer to this place as a personal Retreat, it has been and is for everyone. Ruth, if you feel the police have this under control, I'm comfortable with it."

"Agree," echoed Renata and Rochelle smiled warmly at Lauren. "So, that should settle that. I expect you and Ruth need to finish what should now be a very short discussion and, unless I'm mistaken Ruth, you were in a baking mood earlier. I for one will take goodies to go."

Lauren had furiously blinked back tears of gratitude as Aunt Ruth patted her arm, rose and gestured to the kitchen. "The brownies went to a good cause, but the apple caramel cake is ready to slice. Lauren, please call or text Detective Henderson and I'll get everyone on their way with cake."

Their conversation had indeed been short, Lauren prepared to play whatever her part would be to take this asshole down. Too bad shooting him on sight probably wasn't an option.

"Come in, Detective, Aunt Ruth thinks we need cake. Apple caramel."

The Detective gave what was almost a smile. "Those brownies were delicious and I only had one," she said and followed her to the table where Aunt Ruth lifted a cozy-covered teapot, thick slices of cake already on plates. "I can make coffee, but I thought perhaps a mixed berry herbal might be better."

"Thank you and I gather the decision is to stay?"

Lauren exhaled a long breath, her former reluctance banished. There was no turning back. "Like I told you earlier, the only secret I was keeping was why I'd left. I'm not going into details about other parts of my life because they aren't relevant. Let's just say I'm familiar with drug raids and sting operations. They were pretty much routine in whatever neighborhood I was in. How are we going to do this?"

"I have more information now. The man is Calvin Dumond, a cousin of the Baxters. Desean Baxter sent him from New Orleans to avoid an investigation. He's been with a gang in Miami for a few years and a Miami police team will be assisting us. We have located him in town and have him under surveillance."

Aunt Ruth poured the tea. "I don't suppose you can simply arrest him? You would have already done so if you could."

"You're correct. He's broken no laws here and there are no outstanding warrants for him."

There was no reason to waste time. "You're going to have to wait for him to come after me."

The Detective didn't flinch. "There is a chance that if he comes to Skipper's and Butch convinces him you aren't on staff, he'll give up the search. We think it's more likely he'll assume the new female bartender is you, and at a minimum, take some kind of action to confirm it. Again, the likely thing is to be in place after you close and make the attempt or pull back if he's wrong. Even if he does that, we can pick him up on a trespass charge – no doubt also possession of an illegal weapon – and question him. We have a former DEA agent who resembles you. We have more details to work out, but in addition to full audio and camera surveillance, from the time you come on shift, we'll rotate officers undercover in the bar as an added measure. We'll also make a plan in the event he follows you instead, although we don't think that's likely. Skipper's at night is more isolated." She paused for a sip of tea. "It is important for us to take him in to be able to tie him to Tyrone Baxter. But your safety is the priority."

Lauren didn't have to ask what that meant. "What do we do next?"

"I need to return to the station. Stephanie Bryce, the woman who will pose as you, should be there now and the team from Miami will arrive in the morning. If possible, please try to get some sleep and we'll bring you in to go over everything until you're as comfortable with it as you can be."

Lauren strengthened her voice. "I understand. I'm not sure about the sleep part though." She managed a weak smile. "You will keep Butch from trying to be a hero and getting himself hurt, right?"

"Chief Taylor will talk to him," the Detective said and left with a reminder for them to call if they saw or heard anything unusual.

"You sit while I take care of the gate," Aunt Ruth said quietly, and Lauren felt an odd sense of calm. An entire team working to make this right, the four women adamant in wanting her to stay.

"Come in the kitchen with me," Aunt Ruth said stopping between the table and the kitchen. "I knew you wouldn't want to bother with cooking, and the menu is Swiss steak, potato casserole, and herbed green beans. Maybe I had a premonition comfort food was the way to go tonight."

Lauren moved into her aunt's open arms and rested her head against her chest for a moment before stepping back. "I don't know if I have much of an appetite."

"People have been using food in times of crisis for thousands of years. You clear the table and open a bottle of wine and we'll see if we can tempt your taste buds."

Lauren straightened. "You might be right again." In a little more than twenty-four hours, Calvin Dumond would be in custody. She had to trust what the Detective was telling her and believe this was going to work.

CHAPTER TWENTY-EIGHT

Chief Taylor had called a halt to work at ten o'clock after another coordination call from Captain Sanchez and assigning roles for everyone for their primary plan. Stephanie Bryce was impressive and Bev appreciated the Chief keeping his, "I told you so," between the two of them. Their discussion was fueled by pizza, two boxes of Girl Scout cookies, and more coffee than anyone wanted to count. Alvarez had almost masked her disappointment in not being allowed to be on the take-down team and Bev had sympathized with her impatience of being a rookie. The Chief conceded she and Stephanie would arrive at eleven o'clock, Stephanie in jeans and a long-sleeve tee shirt. She would have the wigs and police vest in a gym bag and would have given Lauren a loose-fitting smock to wear to work. The women would change shirts and don wigs after Lauren did last call and cashed everyone out. Alvarez would help her seemingly drunken girlfriend into her car as the last customers leaving and drive Lauren to the station. Bev and Kevin would have been dropped off at the rear to stay in the office until time to take their positions at the back door.

The Miami trio was to be Sergeant Hayes, another officer, and a technician coming in a van with an *AC Repair, 24-Hour Emergency Service* sign. They would arrive in the morning to install unobtrusive cameras outside Skipper's to cover the front entrance, back entrance and side parking lot. There had been a back-and-forth conversation about using the lot of the industrial area a two-minute walk to the south. The locksmith shop and sign and printing company both closed at five o'clock in the afternoon, had no security cameras, and only one exterior light. If Dumond had scouted the area, he could have realized he could park behind the shops and easily make his way to the back entrance of Skipper's where the dumpster was situated. That way no car would be seen at Skipper's, and he could attack Lauren as soon as she locked the rear door. Consensus was to have the back-up team in

Beau's older F-250 King Cab positioned to be shielded between a crane and bulldozer at an adjacent construction site to the north.

"Everyone needs to sleep," the Chief had said. "There's a good chance we'll be up for nearly twenty-fours between our start in the morning and taking down this son-of-a-bitch."

Kyle arrived home before Bev and had a glass of red wine waiting. "Thought one would help us unwind."

"Just another reason why I love you," she'd said tiredly. She'd slept surprisingly well, and Kyle made bacon, scrambled eggs, and English muffins for a quick breakfast assuming Bev would have little time for lunch.

Bev wanted to arrive at the station before the Miami team and she wasn't surprised Les, Kevin, Beau, and Alvarez came in behind her over the span of fifteen minutes. She guessed Les was probably the one who brought in a caterer size box of coffee and two boxes of donuts. That might take them through the morning.

"Surveillance on Dumond said the car never moved. He walked down the street to Marlin Landing for dinner," Beau said. "No sighting yet this morning."

"If he's a heavy coke user like we've been told, maybe he'll be bored with all the waiting around, take some extra snorts and overdose," Kevin said laconically.

"Now that would be goddamn convenient," Les said and looked toward the open door.

"Okay folks, since none of you had enough sense to sleep in this morning, say hello to our friends from the big city." Chief Taylor led the trio in. Sergeant Hayes was as bulky as he'd looked on the video call. He had to have been a fullback if he played football. He easily dwarfed the slender man introduced as Ziggy Maldonado, who was probably the head technician, and Officer Liam Preece was nondescript enough that he would be able to blend into most crowds without raising attention.

Handshakes and nice-to-meet-you's were exchanged. "I'd like to go do the install," Ziggy said, declining coffee. "Shouldn't take more than two hours. Oh, nobody mentioned it. I do have a tracking device to put on Dumond's car. Easy to do and cuts down on guess work."

Damn, not something they had thought of.

"Appreciate it. Not exactly the kind of equipment we're familiar with," the Chief said, waving for everyone to have a seat. "Beau, you go ahead with him, and we can bring Sergeant Hayes and Officer Preece up to date. Bev, is Stephanie picking up Lauren at ten o'clock?"

"Yes. We have time to do a run-through first."

"Good, go ahead with the briefing. You're the one who's been in this from the start."

Damn, that was his version of public praise. Bev explained the roles, sequencing, and positioning with nods and no interruptions from Hayes or Preece. "We're not sure where you'll want the van."

"Ziggy is the man when it come to this shit," Hayes said. "Once he gets the cameras installed, he'll pick the best site. Having your guy with him helps as he knows where everyone else will be, and we know you're probably stretched for officers. As much as we'd like to take Dumond, it's not our show. We'll be glad to do a rotation in the bar." He spread his big hands on the table. "What we're hoping out of this is first, someone finally nailing the slippery son-of-a-bitch with something that can stick. Then after you're done, we'd like a crack at him to convince him he's not getting covered by Miami and maybe we'll persuade him to provide some info we can use. We're booked into an Air B&B, so we can stay out of the way until you get what you need from him."

Bev was glad it wasn't going to be a grab for glory, although she didn't feel badly for being suspicious of motive.

"Sounds reasonable," the Chief said. "We do have normal patrols to run. The two of you as extras will be good. Kevin, work out the schedule."

Kevin nodded. "Will do, Chief. When we're done here, how about I take our partners around and get them oriented?"

"Good idea. Like I've said, there's a lot of hours left in this. We'll meet again at two o'clock and the Assistant DA will join us." He shifted his gaze. "Bev, tell Kyle thanks for pitching in last night. You need anyone else in with Stephanie and Lauren?"

As if they haven't gone over everything a dozen times? What did he think she didn't remember? "I'm good, Chief," she said instead.

The group broke up, Bev and Les adjourning to their office for a few minutes. "Here I thought the Carl Moore situation was going to be the highlight for a while," he said sweeping his hand to the whiteboard. "Just goes to show you never know what might happen." He gave Bev a pointed look. "You get any sleep last night?"

"I did, actually. More than I expected. I think I'm comfortable with where we are. Even if we're wrong and Dumond has someone else involved, we're covered in every direction." She wondered briefly if Les was feeling left out with no active role.

He gave a slight smile. "I agree. I talked to the Chief and my plan is to go home as usual and rest until midnight. While I suspect you can run on that energy reserve you have when you're fired up, it won't hurt for me to be a little fresher."

"Yeah, well… oh, Stephanie and Lauren are on the way," Bev said to the incoming text. She wasn't sure if Les was being practical or gently chiding her. What were they supposed to do? Take goddamn naps like in kindergarten?

Bev settled the three of them in the training room, noting Lauren seemed comfortable and as if she might have slept.

She accepted coffee and a chocolate donut. "Stephanie and I spoke a bit on the way over. I know this may sound odd, but I'm not feeling as nervous as I thought I would. There are men in from Miami?"

"Yes, the technician is installing the cameras and has the two-way communication systems ready. I've been told the cameras won't be visible unless you know what to look for. We've been over the plan several times and Chief Taylor will speak to Butch. Officer Alvarez will be back in a bit and if other members of the team come in, I'll introduce you."

The woman breathed in and out, her expression hard to read. "So many people involved. Butch and I acting normal may be the tough part."

Bev couldn't argue. She wished the hell, and assumed everyone else did too, they didn't have hours ahead of them to wait. "If you're ready, we'll explain everything and go over it as many times as you'd like. We're not even going to allow you to go to work without eyes on you."

"Yes, Stephanie told me Officer Alvarez will follow me to the bar on her motorcycle."

Alvarez had made the offer as they had been discussing what would have been only a short gap where Lauren would not have been covered. "Right. We aren't taking any chances even though we don't expect Dumond to be out during the day." Maldanado's tracking device should be installed soon on Dumond's car. Bev had to admit the Miami team did come with useful resources.

"Aunt Ruth and the others agreed not to go anywhere today and to keep the gate closed. We know that probably isn't necessary, but it will make me feel better."

"I understand. Where do you want me to start?"

Lauren straightened her shoulders and lifted her mug. "How about I say the way I understand it and y'all can correct me or add if there's anything new?"

"Sure," Bev said, the woman's expression shifted into determination. No matter what Dumond did, they were prepared to bring this to an end.

CHAPTER TWENTY-NINE

Everyone who could, or was willing to do so, took a long lunch to get a little rest. Kyle called Bev to suggest lunch at home in what he acknowledged was a waste of time, but he felt obligated to try. In her round of joining Maldanado in the van, he had laughed at her comment of if he needed a break. "For a geek like me, Red Bull, cheddar and sour cream Ruffles, Reese's peanut butter cups with maybe some matcha tea and I'm good for at least thirty-six hours. I can crash later. Deion and Liam will take turns rotating in here and in the other positions planned. That way we have room for you and whoever else you want to have a chance to see what we do. Oh, by the way, no movement on Dumond's car."

Bev spent an hour, her comfort level growing almost as much as her impatience. The decision was to use the two-way communication system with only Lauren, Stephanie, Bev, Hayes, Alvarez, and Beau. Screens showed Skipper's entrances, side parking lot, the bar section and the short hallway leading to the storeroom, office, and back door. Butch was at the bar with four patrons and another six seated at tables. None of the patrons seemed to think anything was different from normal and Butch seemed to be concealing what Bev knew were his concerns with having to use Lauren as bait.

The two o'clock meeting was short with Chief Taylor thanking the team and reminding them plans could change in a snap of a finger and to be prepared if they had to pivot. Alvarez was the first to be fitted with the tiny invisible earpiece since she would be following Lauren's scooter discretely on her motorcycle and would continue straight once Lauren turned into the parking lot.

Bev was, in fact, in the van with Preece at four-thirty when Maldanado straightened. "Huh, a florist delivery?"

Bev looked at the screen. The colorful van wrap for *Blooms by*

Joy, gave the usual information and the delivery boy who looked to be in his early twenties got out with a small mixed flower bouquet in a white vase. He entered the front door and she and Preece leaned in.

"May I help you?" Lauren's voice was clear.

"Lauren Smith? This is for you."

Lauren drew back, puzzled. "For me? Who is it from?"

The man shrugged and pointed. "There's a card."

"I don't know anyone who would send flowers."

He lifted his hands. "If you're Lauren Smith, it's for you."

"Okay, thanks."

The two men in the middle of the bar and the old man at the end watching television weren't paying attention as Lauren opened the card, dropped it on the bar, anguish flashing across her face.

Bev spoke softly in the microphone. "What do you have?"

Lauren glanced at the men. "Guys, I need to pop into the office for a minute. "Everyone okay?"

They all gave a quick wave. The undercover officer sitting two stools from her looked at her quickly, then away when she shook her head and stepped where she couldn't be overheard. "The card says, *Have a nice day. Your secret admirer.* It's him, isn't it?"

Shit. "Maybe," Bev gestured to Maldanado to roll back to when the van pulled in. "It won't take me long to find out. It's still early."

Lauren's back was to the camera. Her voice had steadied. "This is good though if we know, right? I'm okay now. Just took me by surprise."

"Yeah, I'll be back quick as I can." Bev noted the address on the van. Shit, yes. The florist was on the corner leading to Mariner's Landing, the direction Dumond had walked to last night.

"Smarter than I gave Dumond credit for, if it is him," Preece said. "Want me to get anyone else in?"

"No, but call Hayes. He's up for next shift in the bar."

Bev pulled into one of four parking spots in front of Blooms by Joy. A middle-aged woman, dark brown hair in a chin-length pageboy and round tortoise shell glasses looked up from the counter. "Hello and welcome. I'm Joy Bluhme, different spelling of course."

Bev would have been amused, as no doubt intended, under other circumstances. "Detective Beverly Henderson."

Mrs. Bluhme's green eyes widened at the badge. "Oh goodness, is there some kind of problem?"

"You had an order to be delivered to Lauren Smith at Skipper's Bar?"

The woman stepped to the computer to her right to consult the screen. "Uh yes, for this afternoon. Is there a problem?"

Bev held out her cell phone with the picture of Dumond. "They were ordered by this man?"

"Uh, Mr. Deleon, yes. He came in right before closing yesterday and I assured him we could make delivery this afternoon."

"Did he pay by credit card?"

"No, cash."

"Was there anything unusual about his request?"

The woman smiled. "Certainly not as unusual as some requests I get. The thing was he said the women sometime swapped shifts at the bar, and he wasn't sure Ms. Smith would be there. He didn't want the bouquet left if she wasn't at work. He said to bring it back and try again tomorrow."

"Did you verify for him it was delivered?"

She pointed to the telephone on the left side of the counter. "Actually, I called the hotel a few minutes ago after John, the man delivering today, said Ms. Smith has the bouquet. Mr. Deleon thanked me and seemed quite polite. I really don't understand."

Bev could only imagine what Mrs. Bluhme would be telling her co-workers and friends about this visit. She laid a card on the counter. "Some details we're working on in an investigation. I appreciate the information." She turned to exit, only now noticing the scent of the different flowers in buckets against the right-hand wall and the shelving above them filled with assorted vases.

She called Preece as soon as she was in the car to verify it was Dumond and went to the station.

Chief Taylor agreed with Lauren's point. "Bound to be tonight then. This guy has been hanging around for however many days and you know he wants to get this shit over with." He rubbed the top of his head briskly. "Round everyone up and we'll have sandwiches brought in."

The excruciatingly slow sense to the day had been replaced with an urgency no one articulated, yet almost pulsated within the group, in taking final steps of preparation. Bev didn't know whether Butch and Lauren whispered to each other until normal time for Butch to leave and ten minutes prior to his departure he telephoned Chief Taylor wanting one more guarantee for the protection he couldn't see. The point, after all, was for it to not be noticed. He also extracted a promise of a call no matter what time once everything was over.

Despite intense situations Bev had been in with unexpected violent twists requiring immediate response, this was layered planning to set a trap. She hadn't asked the direct question of Stephanie of how many like this she'd been part of, but it was obviously not her first.

Monitoring the screens in the van showed back-and-forth of customers, most arriving singly – only the pool players staying longer than two hours. Dumond's vehicle had not moved by the time Bev and Kevin slipped unseen into the back. Music from the jukebox was too muffled to tell the song. They settled in the small office, waiting quietly. Sounds of customers leaving marked the nearing of closing time.

Bev wished she could observe the hand-off between Stephanie and Lauren, and how Alvarez managed. She would have to wait to see the video. Preece's calm voice came through the earpiece. "They're clear. Beau and Dieon are set."

Stephanie must have switched off the neon *Open* sign because fifteen minutes later, Preece was more urgent, voice lower. "Approaching on foot. All in black, gaiter facemask, long sleeve shirt untucked. Should be behind the dumpster in a few seconds."

Bev and Kevin stood, poised in front of the desk. Stephanie stepped into the doorway, accepted the purse Bev handed her, with the cross-body strap. It was a good quality wig and the resemblance to Lauren was close enough for someone who had only a photograph to go by. Bev realized that if she saw her across a room, she would have assumed it was Lauren.

Stephanie's eyes were steady, her voice low. "We ready?" She carried a bag of trash in her left hand, her right hand free to reach the compact Glock 43 pistol under her top.

They nodded soundlessly and moved into position.

The back door opened and clanked shut.

Stephanie couldn't have taken more than a few steps when Preece shouted, "Shit, go!"

Kevin and Bev barreled out, yelling, "Police, drop your weapon."

Stephanie was sprawled on the ground close to Dumond's feet, his head bent, pistol pointed at her. He snapped straight up. "Motherfuckers!"

He fired wide twice, both double shots from Bev and Kevin hitting their mark. Bev rushed to Stephanie. "You hurt?"

She rolled awkwardly and gestured to the crumpled body. "Son-of-a-bitch started with a knife. I twisted away as soon as I realized it. Lost my balance and couldn't get to my piece."

Kevin helped lift her up. "No problem."

"She's okay," Bev said to Preece, the first siren closing in. Assuming the Chief was already notified, her call was to Alvarez to have her process Lauren's statement and take her home. Next was a text to Kyle knowing the odds were against him being asleep. *I'm here if you need me*, was the immediate response.

The parking lot was soon nearly full, Donna Sweeny the last to arrive. Lights blazed around the scene, techs taking photographs, bagging the switchblade and Dumond's gun.

Bev and Kevin had turned their weapons over to the Chief who hadn't stayed long. "Bev, bring everyone to the station as soon as you can. Let's see if we can wrap this by sunrise."

The team moved out of the way, waiting for the body to be loaded, Hayes shaking his head. "Figured we had about a seventy-thirty chance he wouldn't let us take him alive. Probably couldn't have turned him anyway, but you never know. Phones might have something for us." He and Beau had taken one technician to Dumond's car which had been parked behind the locksmith shop. Two cell phones were recovered, and the car was towed to impound.

The aroma of fresh coffee greeted them in the training room, Les looking a lot fresher than they did. "Pam remembered the days I used to do this shit. There are oatmeal chocolate chip cookies, biscotti, and homemade granola squares." He gave Bev a silent high-five. "The Chief and I will split taking statements from you, Stephanie, and Kevin. Ladies, first?"

She was still with the Chief when the desk sergeant called in. "Oh hell, thanks. Tell her in a minute." He waggled his finger at Bev. "That pest, Ruthven. Jesus, it's not even five o'clock yet. Sign that goddamn statement and go get rid of her."

Bev didn't bother to try and mention him dealing with the press would be far more appropriate. She went into reception and motioned

Sylvia outside, needing some fresh air.

Slyvia was as fully awake as if it was a reasonable hour of the morning other than she was in jeans, a plain blue top and no make-up. "You look like shit, but that means there *is* a great story here."

"You sleep with a police scanner on in your bedroom?"

She barked a husky laugh. "Oh please, technology is far more advanced, and you know a few hours' sleep is not worth letting the big networks break this. Give. I assume you're a star again."

Bev couldn't deny Sylvia was a good reporter and she played fair. "There really is more than one jurisdiction involved and that means we can't release an uncoordinated statement."

She gave an exaggerated sigh. "Yeah, yeah. The station is like an aggravated beehive with comings and goings. I know from a good source there is a dead body taken in, and I'm not the only one who'll hear about it. You talk to me or whatever version first gets posted online probably within the hour is what will be latched onto."

Bev didn't want to know where Sylvia's information came from. "Okay, no names whatsoever, and I'm sure Chief Taylor will agree to give you what we can when we can, and you will be called a couple of hours before a general press release. It might be late this afternoon or tomorrow morning."

She grinned. "I'll take that."

Bev already decided she would leave out the New Orleans connections for now and focus on having received word of a suspected felon from outside the Keys and a joint operation that unfortunately resulted in the death of the suspect. She didn't falter in her short synopsis, having talked the Chief through again how there had been no time to give Dumond a second warning. Unlike Hayes, she'd expected he would drop his weapon. Perhaps he had actually thought he could take them both, or perhaps it had been because he had chosen the kind of life where shooting first was a basic reflex.

What she hadn't said yet to the Chief was she didn't know who else might have realized Dumond's death might or might not be the end of danger to Lauren. What if Tyrone Baxter did have more resources than they thought? Would failing once dissuade him?

CHAPTER THIRTY

The Miami team had left for their beds and Chief Taylor insisted everyone else go home as the morning shift took over. Contrary to what Bev believed, the filling omelet breakfast Kyle had waiting for her, and a long, hot shower did result in sleep until mid-afternoon. She was mostly awake when her cell phone rang, the Chief's voice breaking through the lingering fog. "Kyle said you might be up."

"I'm awake enough," she said swinging her feet to the floor. "I can be to the station in twenty minutes."

"No reason to rush in. The Miami team is coming at five to wrap up. Had a call from a New Orleans detective who's taking an evening flight. He'll get a car in Miami and wants to meet in the morning."

She was fully awake now, having thought they might make first contact. She straightened to standing. "How much does he know?"

"He and Hayes have a history. Marusco's his name, and he's the one who explained the connection between Baxter and Dumond when he showed up in Miami. Hayes gave him the rundown and our techs said they would have information some time tonight from Dumond's two phones to send to New Orleans and Miami."

"Okay, is Stephanie coming in, too?"

"Not until morning unless we need her. Eager beaver Alvarez is in. Bet she didn't sleep more than a couple of hours."

Bev couldn't remember the last time she heard that phrase. "She did really well in all this."

"Yeah, I know. And she's still a rookie. See you in a bit."

Bev wondered how Lauren was doing, and she bet Alvarez checked in with either her or at least Miss Branden and would have a report. The Chief might seem like he was downplaying Alvarez's role, but he'd been the same way during her rookie years. His awareness of the junior officer's potential wouldn't be openly expressed for a while yet.

Les was waiting in the office, fatigue beginning to show on his face. "You okay for the next stretch?"

"I'm fine. The Chief told you about the New Orleans guy?"

"Yeah. Maldonado is retrieving stuff from Skipper's and they're headed back after Hayes and Preece close out with us. Coffee is fresh or you want Diet Coke?"

Bev crossed to the refrigerator. "Coke for now. I expect none of Pam's treats are left."

"You're right about that. Oh, Alavarez is practically bouncing around. Lord, the energy of the young."

Bev grinned. "She did good."

"Yeah, and who knows, her head might get turned by all the excitement and she'll decide the big city is the place to be."

"Hope not," Bev said and sat at her computer. She was able to clear her email inbox before meeting the others in the training room for their wrap-up meeting. Alvarez did look the freshest of all of them and while she wouldn't use the term *bouncing* as Les had, definite energy radiated from her.

"I know you guys want to get on your way," Chief Taylor said with no preamble. "Fill us in on Marusco."

"I had my football scholarship at LSU," Hayes said. "Tony was a receiver and in Criminal Justice. He went straight onto the force after graduation. I did one tour in the Army, military police, then swapped over. We kept in touch, and I reached out to him first time we busted Dumond. They didn't know to be looking for Lauren."

Bev turned to the Chief, noticing Alvarez sitting straighter. "Lauren doesn't know?"

He inclined his head to Kevin and Alvarez. "Detective Marusco is with New Orleans police and will arrive in Miami tonight to meet with us tomorrow. Officer Alvarez, have you spoken to Ms. Smith since you drove her home?"

Alvarez almost kept the eagerness from her tone. "No sir, I talked to her aunt about an hour ago. Lauren – Ms. Smith – is with her and was asleep. She's not going into work tomorrow either. I'd be happy to…"

He swung his gaze to Bev. "Give the aunt a call when we finish here. We'll meet with Marusco first, but the two women need to be told. Take Officer Alvarez with you. Unless something changes, you can both knock off after."

Bev nodded, suppressing a smile. Alvarez probably didn't realize the Chief just paid her a compliment.

"Last thing. I've been in touch with Captain Sanchez and the Public Information guys are working to hold off until the late-night broadcast. Minimal until we find out what the techs can get from the cell phones and know more about the New Orleans end. Okay folks, say your good-byes and let's all get some goddamn rest." He parted from them with quick handshakes.

Hayes and Preece stayed silent until he was gone. Preece grinned. "Bet he's not even a softie underneath all that. And he's got your back when it counts."

"That's for damn sure," Les said.

They only spent a few minutes with their farewells and Bev noticed Preece pressing a business card into Alvarez's hand. Interesting. Bev deliberately used the officer's first name as they filed out of the room. "Magda, come on into the office for the call to Miss Branden."

"Yes, Detective," she said, her face brightening.

Bev dialed Miss Branden's cell phone, not wanting to use the landline if Lauren was asleep.

"Lauren is awake. I'll get her for you," she said.

Lauren's voice was clear. "May I put you on speaker? Aunt Ruth will need to hear whatever this is."

"Actually, I know you're probably tired, but I'd like to come by and bring Officer Alvarez with me. A detective from New Orleans will be here in the morning."

Her voice was shaded with a note of resignation. "I suppose I shouldn't be surprised, should I? Do you know anything about him?"

"Only his name is Tony Marusco, he went to college with Sergeant Hayes, and from what he said, they're still friends."

"We'll be waiting. I'll explain to Aunt Ruth."

Bev agreed to Alvarez driving and her body language wasn't difficult to interpret. Coming down from what they'd experienced, she needed a little reinforcement of her performance. "We've never had an operation quite like this since I've been with the department. It was excellent teamwork, and you did well."

She glanced over, her shoulders relaxing. "Thank you, ma'am. I know things didn't go exactly as planned."

The sight of Dumond firing his weapon rather than surrender flashed through Bev's mind. "Things rarely do. You might as well learn that lesson now."

CHAPTER THIRTY-ONE

Lauren had never really understood the idea of deja vu until she remotely opened the gate again for Detective Henderson. It was different of course since Magda – Officer Alvarez - was with her. Had it only been hours ago they'd all been together in what she had hoped would end the nightmare she kept trying to escape? A detective on the way from New Orleans meant how many more people knew where she was? Had she really thought this wouldn't happen?

As if reading her mind, Aunt Ruth came to stand behind her before she opened the door. "Everything will be okay," she said quietly. "I know it probably doesn't seem that way now. Go ahead and welcome them in."

"Our apologies for not being able to give you more time to recover," the Detective said after quick hello's.

"We understand. I have coffee on the table and I can make tea or get you something cold to drink if you'd prefer," Aunt Ruth said in what Lauren had come to recognize as her way of dealing with almost any situation.

Magda – Officer Alvarez – stepped to the side to allow everyone else to go toward the table and waited until they were seated to take her place. "That's very kind of you, ma'am."

Lauren inhaled deeply and exhaled in the minute it took to tend to coffee. She might as well ask the questions troubling her. "This detective? Has he said what he wants from me? Will I have to go back with him?"

Detective Henderson pulled the coffee mug close to her. "He spoke with Chief Taylor and the reason we will meet him first is to find that out. We have no way of knowing what their investigation into the killing has gotten them."

"So, it is possible they have other witnesses and they just want to hear what I have to say?"

"In every investigation, you try to gather as much information as you can. Even small things can make a difference. An undercover police officer was murdered, and they aren't going to stop searching until they check every source they know or find out about. The fact is, evidence and information collected might not be allowed into court and you want to give the lawyers more than you think they need. As for making you return to New Orleans, I can't answer that."

Lauren clasped her hands tightly around the mug, keeping eye contact. "Do you think the detective will know how they found Aunt Ruth? I mean, Tyrone was big in the neighborhood, and I guess it was my bad luck he had a cousin in Miami. Do you think he can hire someone else?"

"Detective Marusco will have better insight into that. He's arriving soon and has asked to meet at eight o'clock tomorrow morning. It should take about an hour and Officer Alvarez will pick you up at nine if that's okay."

Lauren looked to the younger woman who smiled tentatively, perhaps not certain as to how serious she was supposed to be. "Yes, thank you. I mean, yes, I'll be ready at nine." She turned her head to Aunt Ruth. "I'm okay on my own for this. They've taken care of me so far."

She stretched her hand out to grasp Lauren's. "I agree and I'll be available if you change your mind." She used her other hand to gesture around the table. "Since we really can't resolve anything tonight, I do have a lovely orange zest cheesecake."

The detective lifted her mug. "We appreciate that, ma'am, but we need to get back to the station. You know to call if you have any concerns."

Lauren caught Magda's friendly eyes meant to be reassuring and she appreciated it. The confident young woman had performed her roles well. The chatty girlfriend who helped manage the swap with Stephanie, the fast trip to the safety of the station, remaining with her until they heard the news about the shooting, and she'd brought her home. She was young though and Lauren suspected she saw this as exciting, assuming the worst was over. She wanted it to be true. She wanted the detective from New Orleans to be someone she could trust. For him to tell her she wasn't needed to testify.

Aunt Ruth pulled her into a hug when they were alone again. Lauren rested her head into her chest. "I was planning to make pork medallions in a mushroom sauce, or I have conch chowder left from lunch if you want something light and the cheesecake is delicious if I do say so myself."

Lauren drew back, affection almost overriding anxiety. "You're amazing, Aunt Ruth. I mean, really, in everything you've done. You can't possibly have imagined anything like this was going to happen."

She took Lauren's hands, her voice gentle. "No, I didn't, and I'm not going to pretend I wish it wasn't happening. That would be as foolish as it would be untrue. What's important though is for you to realize, and I know I am repeating myself, you are not at fault here. I'm shocked, too, they were able to find you, but however that came about, it did. I don't know what this new detective is going to say or want from you, and whatever that is won't change anything. I am here for you and will be. We will get through this."

Lauren blinked back threatening tears and managed to smile. "I don't think I will ever be able to explain how grateful I am for you, well, for everyone and we'll see what tomorrow brings. For right now, I'm still tired and I bet you are too. Let's do the easy thing and have chowder and cheesecake. Maybe we can sit on the terrace after with a glass of wine."

Aunt Ruth released her hands and put an arm around Lauren's shoulders, guiding her toward the kitchen. "Excellent choice and maybe everything will be resolved tomorrow."

Lauren nodded and forced away the dark thought she might have mentioned to Detective Henderson had they been talking privately. How could they be sure of this detective from New Orleans? What if he was on Tyrone's payroll?

CHAPTER THIRTY-TWO

Les told Bev he would handle what sounded like an inside-job robbery at a convenience store; he didn't need to be in the meeting with Tony Marusco who had arrived three minutes before eight o'clock, a wide smile and firm grip. She put him at mid-thirty, six feet, raven black short hair with a slight curl and eyes mahogany brown. A cleft in his strong chin and muscled if his shoulders and neck were proportioned to the rest of him. The navy-blue sports coat, ice blue Oxford shirt, and khaki pants were of Brooks Brothers quality. No tie and the brown briefcase he carried was leather.

"Tony Marusco, pleasure to meet you," was said with enough accent to suggest New Orleans. "Deion Hayes speaks highly of y'all."

"He and the others were a big help," Bev said, leading him past the front desk. "Coffee first?"

"Oh sure. Black and as strong as you have it."

"We have a carafe in the training room. It's still set up for operations. We didn't know if you needed to spread out."

"Mostly the file. Chief Taylor said Ms. Smith was coming in at nine?"

"Yes, Officer Alvarez is bringing her." Bev waved him into the room, the Chief at the head of the table.

"We don't stand on ceremony around here," he said, a quick handshake and indicated the chair to his left. His familiar semi-scowl meant he intended to judge Marusco for himself rather than take Hayes's word.

"Makes things easier, doesn't it?" Marusco swung his briefcase onto the table. "As I explained in our call, we didn't know anything about Ms. Smith. The body of the undercover agent was dumped in the river and we hadn't pinpointed the murder scene. The area Tyrone

Baxter operates in covers more than one neighborhood – none of which provide any information. The one reliable snitch swears he's heard nothing, and it might even be true this time."

"The guy Baxter knew the officer was undercover?"

Marusco took a folder from the briefcase. He didn't open it. "We're not sure. Sergeant Lebeau had been on two other assignments and was with another precinct. His cover was as a disaffected soldier from across town. They had enough inside background to make him believable. There are different ways for a cover to be blown. We could only keep it from the media for a few days before they broke the story."

Bev watched a muscle in the side of his neck tighten. "How well did you know him?"

"We were rookies together, never partners. Went separate ways, saw each other occasionally. He was one of the good guys. Ms. Smith being able to give where and when he was killed has already helped the tech guys identify streets to try and find CCTV coverage. There are only so many ways to get to the river." He took a sip of coffee and looked from the Chief to Bev. "I talked to Deion for a while last night. He didn't interact much with Ms. Smith. How credible is she?"

"Don't know if we have the same definition," the Chief said flatly. "She makes her way from New Orleans to here, impresses a couple of people I trust, has this asshole sent to kill her and holds up her part of the operation."

Marusco gave a brief smile. "Point taken. What was her reaction to hearing I was on the way?"

"She's nervous," Bev said immediately. "She doesn't know what you want. Her being found is of obvious concern."

He tapped the folder. "We ran that down late last night." He lifted his mug to the Chief. "Thanks for having your techs send us the info from Dumond's cell. We were able to track one call to a private detective who has a few questionable clients." He shrugged. "He's known to us and let's just say some extra persuasion was used in talking to him. Ms. Smith was clever enough where she could not be easily traced. The guy found her mother's death certificate which led to birth certificate which led to parents' names, maiden name, and place of birth. It was a small town. Obituary for parents led to sister's name. More probing led to Florida in general, then to here."

One of Dumond's burners phones had been for calls to New Orleans, the other for Miami.

"How safe is she?"

Marusco spread his hands. "Hard to say. Baxter is a fucking psycho. His brother Desaun wasn't a good guy, but if you're going to have the kind of shit we have in the real world, he was good comparatively. No unnecessary violence, and he sure as hell didn't initiate what got him killed. He kept Tyrone under control and would never have allowed him to take charge. My point is, with Dumond gone, Baxter doesn't have anyone else anywhere near here. He's probably in a rage having not heard from him and he's probably in touch today with Dumond's boss. From what Deion told me, they – as in Dumond's higher ups - didn't know anything about what he was planning. They are going to want to know where he is and what we'd like to do is let word leak in Miami. Don't need to give them details, just he was out of their territory mixed up in some shit on his own and isn't coming back. When Baxter reaches them, they'll tell them it's not their business. The intent is to rachet up the pressure on Baxter and maybe he makes a mistake."

The Chief drummed his fingers on the table. "Returning to the question of Ms. Smith's safety."

"Baxter can hire a pro, no problem. Someone a hell of a lot smarter than Dumond. He – not to be sexist, maybe she – won't be asking around town about her."

They were silent for a moment. The Chief gave Bev a look she didn't like. "We don't have the resources to keep protecting her."

Shit. Bev tried not to glare at Marusco. "Okay, so what's your plan?"

"I need to get her on tape. This isn't a federal case, but we do have some safe places we've used in the past. If what she has is enough, we can move quickly against Baxter. We can't cut corners, but Baxter killed a cop. We have a prosecutor who will fast track it as much as possible."

"At best, still could take months."

Marusco didn't react to her tone. "You both know how it works. Look, the prosecutor is on standby and as soon as I finish with Ms. Smith, I'll talk to him."

The Chief frowned. "I'm not seeing good choices here."

Bev thought about what they would do if one of their officers had been killed. Wouldn't they lean on any possible lead? "Let's see how Lauren reacts. Even if Baxter does hire someone, we should have at least a couple of days, right?"

Marusco nodded. "Yeah. Let's say he finds out about Dumond today. Like I said, doubt he has anyone who operates outside the city and he's going to be careful this time. He'll need a contact – could take at least two days. He's been through the process enough. He knows we can't move fast." An odd look flashed across his face.

Bev didn't think the Chief saw it. "Yes?"

He waved hand away. "Nothing. Okay, a quick break then to get ready for Ms. Smith?"

Bev wouldn't press yet about what he might be withholding. She wanted to take coffee and water into the interview room before Lauren arrived. Better to get right to the task at hand. One of the points Kyle had raised during discussions was Lauren had not actually witnessed the shooting. While her recollection was significant, there were two other men involved. If no definitive forensics evidence was found,

Baxter would simply claim he didn't fire the shots. It was common for underlings to take the rap for a boss. Maybe what the prosecutor wanted Marusco to confirm was Lauren had clearly seen Baxter with a gun. She brushed the thoughts away. They should know soon enough.

Lauren was prompt and Bev sensed a change to her. In the introduction to Marusco, she stood confidently, the previous conflict she'd exhibited gone. Perhaps with everything that happened, she realized she couldn't put New Orleans behind her. As soon as they were settled in the interview room, she made her position clear.

She inclined her head to Bev. "Detective, I assume Detective Henderson and whoever have explained everything. Maybe I was foolish to think I could stay hidden, but that doesn't matter now, does it? I was born and grew up in different parts of the City – not the parts they brag about to tourists. My mother was an addict and everything that comes with that. I managed to stay out of that life and made my own way. I didn't really know Desaun, but there are always Desauns and unfortunately Tyrones. Getting caught up in it happens all the time. I was just hoping it would never be me. Is your plan to take me back?"

Bev had expected most of what Lauren said and she gave Marusco credit for being straightforward.

"I understand, and you're right. A hell of a lot of people get sucked into bad shit they don't deserve. What I need first is to know exactly what you saw and heard."

The recording started as Lauren recounted the night in the same vivid detail she shared before. She spoke clearly without faltering and Marusco asked no questions initially. "You're positive one of the two men you couldn't see was Tommy Blue?"

"Yes, and I didn't recognize the other one's voice."

"You did see Tyrone Baxter?"

"Yes, the light in the car came on when he got out and he was holding a pistol in his right hand."

"But you couldn't see where the assault took place?"

Lauren exhaled a long breath. "Correct. I heard everything but did not see the shooting. The dumpster was what hid me, and I was able to slip back in as soon as I saw Tyrone clear the car. I thought they would be distracted enough. I heard two shots because I was barely through the door. I was a few steps in from the door when I heard the third shot."

Three men at the scene, plus probably a driver in the car. Despite hearing the one man say Baxter intended to take care of the guy himself and seeing Baxter with a gun, Bev could understand the issue. This was the shit cops hated when it came to what would hold up in court. Any good attorney – and Baxter would no doubt have one – would argue Baxter didn't pull the trigger. One of the others being willing to take the fall with the death penalty on the line might could be exploited if they could be taken into custody. Lauren's account should be adequate for that.

Marusco stopped the recording and looked quizzically at Lauren. "You took what Tommy Blue said to you and giving you money as a warning?"

Her look to him was skeptical. "And you wouldn't have? Why else was Dumond sent here?"

He gave a sharp nod and tapped the folder he hadn't opened. "Do you need a break, Ms. Smith?"

Lauren's voice hardened. "No, but if we need a break for you to talk to your prosecutor, so you can give me a straight answer about what happens to me next, let's take one."

Bev was struggling to stay quiet. She knew any question she asked was likely to be viewed as trying to tell him how to run his investigation. That wouldn't bother her, but pissing him off might make him take a tougher line with Lauren. "You're welcome to use the training room to call."

He tapped the folder again and looked at Bev, then at Lauren. "Not necessary as he and I already discussed at length the options depending on your statement. Tyrone Baxter made a mistake coming after you, but he only spoke with Dumond. Tech can track the number of calls made, locations and their length to tie him directly, but there are no incriminating texts. Tommy Blue, his real name is Thomas Prejean, and William Horne, probably the man whose voice you didn't recognize, were found three days ago. Could have been any number of reasons for them to be killed, but once we heard about you, it narrowed the possibilities. The fact is, Baxter's cleaning up loose ends. Your testimony is strong circumstantial evidence, but it's tricky. As I said to Detective Henderson and Chief Taylor before, Baxter is a psycho and targeting you is what we might ultimately be able to pin on him."

Shit. So much for turning one of the accomplices.

Lauren paled, closed her eyes momentarily, and Bev could only imagine how she was feeling. She snapped her eyes open, this look more fierce than Bev had seen since they met. She raised her hand to indicate Bev. "I was willing to be bait – and let's don't act like it is anything else – because I had to get the danger away from Aunt Ruth and the others and I had all these people who I trusted to keep me safe. How the fuck are you going to?"

Bev gave Marusco additional points for not taking offense. "Only one other person outside my family will know where you are. I have an uncle, a retired cop, on the outer edge of Mandeville. There are fifteen acres – three properties side-by-side. He's in the middle with his two sons on either side. One is a firefighter and the other owns a karate studio and they're all veterans. You'll have to stay on the property, but my uncle has a horse, chickens, goats, and a couple of pigs. My cousin Nick has a nice pond, and Cousin Fransico is a hell of a cook with a big garden. We keep telling him he should open a restaurant someday. Oh, my uncle is a widower, and the guest suite was set up for his mother-in-law so in a separate section of the house. She didn't need it for long. You deserve to know we don't know exactly how we're going to proceed, but the set-up is as safe as we can make it. Baxter will find out soon about Dumond and while he might give up, my bet is he'll hire a pro this time. You run again and what will that really do for you?"

Bev watched Lauren closely, thinking about what she now understood as the kind of childhood she'd endured. She'd made a life the best she could to have even that torn away by things out of her control. It was obvious she knew the stark truth of Marusco's assessment.

Lauren's half smile was sardonic. "I've always wondered what it would be like to live around animals, and I've always wanted to learn to garden. This could be educational."

Marusco's telephone indicated an incoming message. He frowned in irritation, snatched it up and cut his eyes to Bev. "Guess I do need the training room. This shouldn't take long."

Lauren shifted in her chair to face Bev. "It's okay, Detective. You and the others have done what you could. The truth is I do have a chance to make something different of myself here and the only way to find out is to get this shit over with. Detective Marusco seems to be trustworthy."

"I did some checking on him last night." Bev said. "Not that I have any sources in New Orleans, but what I found supports him being solid and Sergeant Hayes trusts him."

They both looked up when Marusco re-entered the room, leaving the door open. His expression was hard to read. "Ms. Smith, Tyrone Baxter was killed in a drive-by this morning. That should end any threat to you, and I have your statement for our file."

Lauren pushed back from the table. "You mean I can leave? I can go home?"

He turned toward Bev. "Unless Detective Henderson needs you for anything else."

That was sure as hell unexpected. Bev stood and shook her head. "No. I'll get Officer Alvarez to take you back, Lauren."

Marusco stepped to the table to shake Lauren's hand. "Thank you and I wish you the best." He opened his briefcase and looked up at Bev. "If Chief Taylor is available, I can close this out and head to Miami."

"He is," Bev said. "I'll meet you in his office after I get Lauren on her way."

Alvarez was at her desk and didn't ask questions for a change. Bev saw Marusco going into the men's room and hurried to knock on the Chief's door, half-open as usual. He was on the telephone and waved her in. "Yeah, thanks. Best goddamn outcome I can think of."

"Marusco's boss by any chance?"

"Yep. Where's Marusco?"

"Packing up his stuff. Alvarez is taking Lauren home. She was ready to go with him though. His plan sounded decent at least."

Marursco came in with the coffee carafe from the interview room and two mugs. "Any chance you keep a bottle stashed for medicinal or other purposes?"

The Chief opened the bottom left drawer of his desk. "Bev?"

Jesus, it wasn't eleven o'clock yet. "I'm good, thanks." She perched on the arm of the chair in front of the Chief's desk as he motioned for Marusco to sit in the other chair.

"Your boss called a few minutes ago. Said you'd give us the details."

"Not many to give," he said. "Drive-by when he was coming out of a barber shop. Got his driver and one bodyguard, too. Car not identified yet and, of course, nobody knows anything. Speculation is Baxter taking out two of his own guys – especially Tommy Blue – was over-the-top crazy. Either one of the rival gangs figured he'd become vulnerable, or someone inside might be jockeying for position. That will all shake out soon. *It may be in someone's interest to talk about who pulled the trigger.* That will close part of the investigation and restore the usual balance."

"You can't close it now?"

Marusco shook his head. "We're still trying to track down how Lebeau was made."

"You think you have a bent cop?"

He grimaced. "Hope not. Can't count it out yet. That's why information about Smith was going to be so restricted. Glad we don't have to worry about it now. She seems gutsy and I hope things work out for her." He drained his mug and stood. "Appreciate the cooperation. Deion has plans for tonight so I'll get on the road if we're okay here. Let me know if y'all come to NOLA. We'll do the locals' places."

"That will be Bev and Kyle," the Chief said as they shook hands. He motioned for Bev to close the door. "How you feeling with this?"

"Relieved," she said without hesitation. "No telling how long the case could have dragged on."

"Yeah. It's been a tough few days. Everyone involved needs to knock off early. We should be quiet for a while."

"Thanks, Chief. I want to go write all this up first."

He replaced the bottle in the drawer. "Suit yourself."

Les was at his desk and held up a folder. "No big mystery on the robbery. CCTV disabled, cash and some items gone, closed sign on the door when the day guy arrived. Owner said night guy was a dipshit, was probably going to fire him anyway. We have his details. Not in his apartment and car is gone. His roommate wasn't in. Went by where he works and he said the suspect has family over near Tampa. Be on the lookout is in. How'd it go with Marusco?"

Bev grabbed a Diet Coke and explained.

"Damn, didn't see that coming. Solves our problem anyway and saves a hell of a lot of taxpayer money."

She walked to the whiteboard where notes about Moore had been erased. She didn't expect Les to add anything about the robbery at this point. Their cold case was it, although Les had included finding the truck. More questions marks assuming forensics couldn't find anything useful.

Les spun his chair. "Funny, having a connection to Mrs. Newton through Lauren and them all living in the apartments. You willing to admit yet we're stuck?"

She exhaled a long breath. If Rosalinde Newton was guilty, did she really think the woman plotted her husband's death? Bev couldn't see that based on everything they'd learned. Wasn't it more likely a moment of reaction against years of abuse? As Les had pointed out, there were no grounds to bring her in for official questioning. If it was the brother Reggie, he was dead and there was no proof unless he'd told his sister. She couldn't see that either when the story of Newton deserting his wife was easy to believe. Maybe she was just over-tired and by tomorrow she'd be ready to go at it again. She shrugged and moved to her desk. "The Chief said we should all go home. I'll have this report done in about an hour and I think I'll take his advice."

Les smiled, not pressing for an answer about Newton. "Sounds like a good idea."

CHAPTER THIRTY-THREE

Ruth knew she wasn't hiding her sorrow tinged with outrage at the unfairness of it. "We're here for you. We'll fight this together, whatever it takes. You're only a year younger than me."

Rosalinde, whose weight loss and paleness could no longer be dismissed, shook her head. "No, Ruth. The doctor wanted me to consult with one more specialist and the news is not positive. I'm not going to say I was ignoring anything. I genuinely thought it was all stress brought on because of them finding Ed. The kind of treatment I would have to go through and little likelihood it would matter for more than a few months at most is not something I want to do. That's why I asked you to be here this afternoon. I need your help."

"Tell me what, and don't think Renata and Rochelle will accept this either."

Rosalinde leaned forward in the armchair. "That's exactly what I need all of you to do. I want everyone to come here for dessert tonight. I picked up a triple chocolate cheesecake earlier and I will explain how this is going to work. My other errand was to meet with hospice and everything is arranged. To be honest, I'm quite tired and need to rest, so please ask Renata and Rochelle to come at eight o'clock. Lauren works tonight, doesn't she? I'm not trying to leave her out, but it will be better for the four of us to talk first. She's had a great deal to cope with and there's no reason to involve her tonight."

Ruth could see the fatigue in Rosalinde's eyes and the truth was, she needed some time to absorb what seemed to be fatalism on the part of her friend. Yes, she knew pancreatic cancer was aggressive, but damn it, there were exceptions – new treatments being developed. "Of course I will," she said, getting control of her voice. "They'll be curious though as to why."

"Just tell them I have something serious to discuss and I'll explain."

Rosalinde swayed a bit when she stood and held her hand out to allow Ruth to steady her. "I'm okay. Come give me a hug and I'll see you tonight."

Ruth managed to keep a smile on her face until she was several steps away from the apartment. Dear God, why? In the two weeks since the admittedly frightening drama surrounding Lauren, their lives had returned to normal, the bond with the younger woman strengthened. In looking back to the celebratory dinner they'd enjoyed, Rosalinde had barely eaten and left before dessert. Ruth had thought perhaps the violence permeating the few days had simply raised stressful memories for her, and she hadn't wanted to express those feelings.

Hospice. She'd been through those weeks of helping Rebecca Schoopman when Arnold's own battle with failing health had taken him. Rebecca had passed quietly in the night, however, at age ninety-three. No prolonged illness, her mental abilities intact, and they'd shared a lovely bayside lunch together the day before. Ruth made it to the kitchen and fixed a mug of lemon-ginger tea, holding the tears until she sat at the table. She dabbed the first ones and realized letting them flow now, here would be better than breaking down later. Whether she agreed with her or not – and she wasn't there yet – Rosalinde would need her – all of them really – to accept her decision. Her tears could be kept private, or more likely, Renata and Rochelle would have the same reaction and they would bolster each other in order to give their friend the support she was asking for.

Renata's response when Ruth called didn't surprise her. "She's ill, isn't she? Seriously ill. Do you know how bad?"

"She wants to explain personally."

"I understand. What did Rochelle say?"

"I'll get her next." Ruth ventured an idea. "Listen, if she guesses, too, do y'all want to come here for dinner and we can discuss the situation?"

"That's a good idea. If this is going where I think it is, we can at least talk beforehand about how we can help."

Rochelle didn't answer her landline and she told Ruth she would call her back in a few minutes when she reached her on her cell phone. "I'm up in South Miami," she said. "An old friend is in town for the day and I'm having early dinner with her before she leaves. I'll be back before eight. Rosalinde is finally getting her appetite back and is having a sweet tooth attack?"

"I hadn't thought about it like that," Ruth said of the ironic question and carried the empty mug to the kitchen. She suspected Renata wouldn't have much of an appetite either and taking the time to do a homemade chicken vegetable soup and rolls from scratch would occupy her hands if not her mind. She hoped this wasn't one of the afternoons for Lauren to stop in for a quick chat over tea or coffee after leaving Adventure Below before going to Skipper's. She ordinarily looked forward to hearing Lauren talk about particularly interesting customers who were in, or on the days when she had a chance to dive, how fascinating it was to be underwater. She wasn't sure – no, she was positive – she couldn't put on a happy face at the moment. She was glad for Renata's perceptiveness and the chance to talk this through before seeing Rosalinde again.

Later, after she pulled the rolls from the oven and the soup was set on low to keep it warm, Ruth felt the need for a long shower using lavender gel, allowing the steam to relax the tightness in her shoulders. She dressed quickly after and was crossing to go into the kitchen at the sound of Renata's knock and her opening the door without waiting this time. She was carrying a bottle of Sauvignon Blanc.

She strode into the kitchen where two wine glasses were on the island. "How bad is it?"

Ruth lifted the lid from the pot, her head turned to Renata. "Hospice is coming tomorrow to the apartment to see what equipment they'll bring."

"Shit." Renata rarely swore – well, none of them did really. "This is so damn wrong. I don't know if we can possibly change her mind. What stage is she?" She twisted the top from the wine, filled both glasses and placed the bottle in the refrigerator.

Ruth stirred the soup. "Pancreatic. She said the proposed treatment isn't likely to give her much longer and she doesn't want to go through with what they described." She moved the pot off the burner. "Take the wine to the table. Rolls and butter are already on it."

They sat down at their places and touched glasses. "It took me a couple of hours to stop kicking myself for not insisting she go to a doctor," Renata said, placing a roll on her bread plate. Steam rose from the soup. "The signs were there and I almost said something to her."

Renata's years as a pharmacist meant she'd seen a lot of people in various stages of illness, and she was acquainted with a few of the local hospice staff. "I know, but we also know she doesn't want us blaming ourselves."

Renata sighed. "You're right. I was a total mess for a long time in feeling so much guilt over Carlos's heart attack, about not scheduling appointments for him to force him to take some of the tests that might have shown signs he would have paid attention to. Making the same mistake twice won't help anyone. She plans to stay here?"

Ruth picked up her spoon. "She didn't want to get into details until she talks to all of us together. At least you and I are able to work through it before we go over. Rochelle is in for a shock. Oh, she's up in Miami with a friend. Quite frankly, I'm glad she didn't want to ask a bunch of questions. I was still shaky when I called her."

"I got that. Our focus now has to be on doing everything we can for Rosalinde." She inhaled and managed a smile. "This smells delicious. I imagine you made extra, planning to give some to Rosalinde."

"Soups tend to be good for this, but if all she wants for every meal is dessert, I will bake up a storm."

"And I'll buy the ice cream."

They ate in companionable silence. Nothing else to say. One more glass of wine while cleaning the kitchen. They walked silently to Rosalinde's who opened the door at their approach. She was dressed in one of her favorite outfits, a blue Batik caftan, bringing out the slight hint of blue in her gray eyes. Rochelle was at the table, putting the cozy-clad teapot next to the white porcelain coffee carafe. Large slices of cheesecake and whipped cream were on the pale rose colored crystal dessert plates and white napkins embroidered with pink roses completed the setting.

She smiled gently at their faces. "I know you well enough, Ruth, that you didn't say anything. You guessed, didn't you, Renata?"

A brief nod and they slipped inside, Rochelle's smile fading. "Why am I getting the feeling I'm the only one who doesn't know what's going on?"

Rosalinde gestured to the chairs. "Not by design, dear. Please, everyone sit and get your coffee or tea."

In the ten minutes she spoke, there was no question of trying to change her mind. Rochelle looked first to Ruth and Renata, then at Rosalinde. "Of all you've said, the only thing I will not agree to is your plan to bring in sitters if you reach the stage where you need twenty-four-hour care. We're here for you and we can manage our schedules."

"Absolutely," Ruth said to Renata's vigorous nod. "The hospice nurse will come every few days to check in and we can handle giving you pain medication or oxygen."

"I don't want to make this more difficult for any of you than it has to be," Rosalinde said. "The doctors couldn't give me an answer other than this could be days or months."

"And we'll manage," Rochelle said, reaching out her hands, left and right. "Think about what we've each dealt with in our lives. Coming through our separate darkness is something we have in common and it's a big part of why living here means what it does. The *us* of our togetherness is why we can do this."

They joined hands, squeezing tightly for a moment until Rosalinde withdrew hers. "All right, under one condition. No tears, no prayers for miracles and right now, we are going to have this lovely dessert." She held up her cup of tea. "A toast, too, for the time we have been given. Let's make the most of whatever remains."

CHAPTER THIRTY-FOUR

Bev sat at the round table on the terrace with a glass of wine, the bottle in the chilled acrylic holder. Afternoon rain had brought the temperature down into the seventies and she'd changed into shorts, a tee shirt decorated with turtle hatchlings, and sandals. Kyle was putting a marinade on the chicken. A fresh manila envelope held a copy of the letter. The original sealed envelope with Bev's name on it and the letter delivered by Ruth Branden had been entered into evidence.

"We're on our way to make arrangements for Rosalinde," she'd said in the reception area. "I've had this for about a week. She wanted to give it to me while she was still lucid. She was on maximum morphine the last four days. It was peaceful and we were there for her." Her smile was bittersweet. "Unless necessary, I don't want to know what she had to say to you."

Bev appreciated the woman's directness. "I understand, and my condolences." She'd wrapped up the report, left a note for the Chief and agreed with Les it was enough for one day.

She slipped the letter out and read it again. It was handwritten, in the kind of cursive from those who were taught penmanship in school.

Dear Detective Henderson.

I appreciate everything you did for Lauren and us. In turn, I want to tell you the truth about Ed and I don't want you blaming Reggie. His only fault was in trying to protect me. I hid the worst from him for reasons I later knew were foolish. If I had told him and accepted his help, perhaps everything would have been different.

I didn't intend to kill Ed. No matter what, I'd never thought about doing that. I had finished making him his favorite pie. I don't know if you recall I told you that would have been our ninth anniversary. I hoped we could have a nice dinner. He came home too early in the evening, not quite drunk, but in a way that meant trouble. He wanted the grocery money to go back out. I made the mistake of trying to explain it was all we had until he got paid. He slapped me harder than usual. I fell to my knees and the gold crucifix I always wore came out from beneath my dress. He grabbed it, snatched it off and said it had to be worth something. The necklace wasn't about religion, it had been my grandmother's. I didn't know I could feel like I did, like I didn't care he was bigger and would slap me again. I got to my feet and the marble rolling pin was on the kitchen counter. He was stuffing the necklace in his pocket, laughing at me. I used both hands and swung up as hard as I could. He fell and I swung again. I was trying to get the necklace and realized he was dead. I didn't know what to do and called Reggie. He told me he was on the way and would take care of it.

I ran into the den and sat shaking. Reggie came and told me to stay where I was. He came out with Ed's keys and moved Ed's truck behind the house. I don't know how long it was, but I could hear him moving around in the kitchen. I was ready to call the police when he came back in. He told me not to do that. He had a plan and I was to trust him. That was when I went to my bed and curled up, trying to blot it out. It must have been hours Reggie was gone. I cried all I could and for three days Reggie stayed with me. He made me drink a little water. I couldn't eat. He kept telling me the story to say. No one would be surprised at Ed leaving and no one would ever find him. He had called work for me and said I had the flu. He said he would go buy me a new chain for the crucifix if I would get up, take a shower, and get dressed. I did and then it was like I suddenly knew he was right. No one would miss Ed, no one would ask about him. I did feel guilty, especially about messing things up for Reggie. I couldn't tell the truth then because he would be in trouble. The story got easier to tell and the nightmares stopped.

That day you came to see me I thought later about telling you the truth. Reggie was gone. Then I thought I would wait for a while to see what happened. You know the rest from there. Ruth, Renata, and

Rochelle were all angry about my cancer, how it wasn't fair. Maybe it has been. I don't know if I could have stayed quiet about Ed. If you can, please don't tell them unless Ruth asks. I want them to remember me as they do. By the time you read this, I will have met whatever judgement awaits me.

Rosalinde Marie Mosely Newton

Bev heard Kyle's steps behind her. He carried his glass, refilled it and sat next to her. "Okay, chicken is marinating. What was it you want me to read?"

She passed the letter to him and looked outward at a pair of queen monarch butterflies moving acrobatically among the butterfly bushes against the fence.

"Okay," he said within a few minutes. "No wonder you weren't exactly cheery when I got home. Case can be closed, so what's bothering you?"

She shifted her chair to face him, tucking a strand of hair behind her ear. "It fits one of our theories. I haven't seen a deathbed confession before."

"And…?"

"The fact is, Les and the Chief both basically told me we should have closed the case and let it go. The situation with Lauren obviously took priority and then, I don't know. I guess I put things in perspective and began to think maybe they were right. We didn't have cause to bring her in for questioning, did we?"

Kyle's blue eyes were sympathetic. "You want a legal opinion?"

"Yes."

"Based on what you've explained about the case, you did not have cause for more questioning and any competent attorney would have advised her of that." He held up his hand. "Is your real question if you had asked to question her, would it have been enough to cause her to confess?"

God, he knew her so well. "Yeah, I guess so."

He poured more wine for her and slid the letter back into the envelope. "Look, let's say she did. The thing is, a good attorney could argue a number of things in her defense. Add that to the fact she led what sounds like a model life after, maybe - only maybe - there would be a conviction of manslaughter. Would any judge have sentenced her harshly? Not likely." He pushed the envelope toward the center of the table. "You did what you do so well. You tracked down what evidence there was, and you narrowed it to two probable theories, one of which was correct. It's not as if some dangerous criminal has been let loose."

She gave him a half smile. "Once again, this is one of the many reasons why I love you."

He leaned in and kissed her lightly on the lips. "Something I always enjoy hearing. Now I suggest we have dinner. Let's come out later and have another drink under the stars."

Bev leaned in for a longer kiss. "What an excellent idea."

CHAPTER THIRTY-FIVE

Lauren set the toaster oven timer for the chorizo, roasted pepper, and Monterey Jack cheese tartlets she was taking to Happy Hour on the beach. Recipe cards were at the grocery store on a display rack matching recipes to ingredients in stock. The bite-size appetizer was one more easy item to add to her expanding repertoire of dishes she was comfortable with making. No, no comfortable with. Dishes she enjoyed making. She wiped the slate blue Formica countertop, still a little conflicted about moving into Rosalinde's apartment. She'd left a note for her and Aunt Ruth urging them to make the swap.

Dear Lauren. What a delight it has been to have you here. I know you are fixing your place up, but if you are all right with moving into mine, I would love for you to. It has been a haven for me and I hope it will be for you. I've left instructions about the plants.

While she had commented on sharing Rosalinde's taste in her décor, she thought her friends might have things they wanted. Aunt Ruth assured her they each had private time with Rosalinde and been given the mementos special to them.

Lauren was touched. Although she had offered to share the sitting duties, the other women insisted since she worked two jobs, they could handle the shifts among them. They did promise they would ask for Lauren's help if needed. Within less than three weeks from when Rosalinde revealed the sad news, she was gone – her last few days mostly asleep. Aunt Ruth had brewed a cup of tea in the afternoon and went in to see if Rosalinde was awake to join her. Her breathing had already become shallow, and it was a moment before Aunt Ruth understood it was over.

The ceremony had been simple. Just a few individuals from the library where Rosalinde had volunteered came to the Retreat for the ashes to be scattered in the bay. They gathered after on Rochelle's terrace to exchange fond stories. Lauren had quietly listened, not because she felt excluded, but because the affection flowing among the women was like luxuriating in a scented, warm bath.

In the same way her living arrangements were better than anything she'd had before, Adventures Below gave her the incredible world of scuba and she was now able to routinely dive once a week or so. Her initial uncertainty vanished and every trip to the reefs was exciting. Next week, she would complete her advanced course and be taken to the *USS Spiegel Grove* to finally experience the huge ship that had been sunk to become an artificial reef. A couple from France had been on the morning dive and claimed it was the best wreck they knew. They purchased the book they carried about it in the shop plus tee shirts as souvenirs.

Lauren had been startled when Butch worriedly asked if she wanted to continue her nights at Skipper's. Aside from feeling more gratitude to Butch than she would express, being friends with the rest of the staff, and having learned all the regulars, working in a neighborhood bar was a good fit for her – another place where she could belong. He had uncharacteristically bought a round for the house to celebrate the fact she was staying. Granted there were only six customers, but it was a heartfelt gesture.

The oven chimed and she opened the door to see the cheese was bubbling. She removed the hot tray and placed it on top of a folded kitchen towel on the stove and would cover them with foil to take outside. Would she stay in Verde Key, and if so, would she continue to live at the Retreat? Those were not questions she needed to answer yet. Even though Aunt Ruth was her only relative, the sense was of extended family and was something she'd never had. It was more than enough for now.

The End